PRAISE FOR SUZY K QUINN

'Frank, disarming and hilarious, it's the best women's fiction I have read since the last Marian Keyes and it made me spit more coffee out than *Bridget Jones' Diary* ever did. I can't wait to read books 2 and 3'
Rachel Read It

'This book made me laugh so much it became dangerous for a mother-of-four to continue'
Books In My Hallway

'Suzy K Quinn is the literary equivalent of hot chocolate.'
Liza Foreman, New York Times journalist

'I read Suzy K Quinn in one sitting, with a break for sleep. This does not usually happen. A terrific read.'
Fay Weldon

'One word: gripping.'
Joanne Harris

GRATITUDE FROM SUZY

I still can't believe so many people read my books.
Each and every day, I am grateful to you.
Thank you so much.
If you want to talk to me online, I'm here:

Facebook.com/suzykquinn (You can friend request
me. I like friends.)

TikTok: @suzykquinn
Instagram: @suzykquinn
Twitter: @suzykquinn
Website: suzykquinn.com
Email: contact@suzykquinn.com

Happy reading,
Suzy xxx

For all the heroes, big and small.

ONE

Michael Lamb

Boys from disadvantaged backgrounds are exposed to a culture of toxic masculinity. This negatively affects their relationships with females.

I've always hated school playgrounds. They are noisy, terrifying places where lunchbox items, such as unwanted sandwiches or empty Ribena cartons, can fly at you from all angles. Sometimes, even whole lunchboxes come your way.

As I crossed the Great Oakley Primary School playground this morning, my hands were already positioned to protect my face. Everywhere was chaos. To my left, two boys engaged in an angry ballet spin, apparently trying to tear each other's shirts off. To my right, a group of children attempted a dangerous cheerleading pyramid, shrieking as they tumbled onto the hard tarmac.

Chaos.

Everywhere.

I hoped to make it inside the school un-assailed, and I did avoid projectiles. But as I buzzed to enter the building, a burly boy who couldn't have been older than ten shouted: 'Those bike clips are lame, mate. Totally lame.'

I'm an average height, middle-aged white man with greying-blond hair. I buy my clothes from charity shops, meaning they must be the same sorts of clothes other people wear. Otherwise, how could they be second-hand? Yet, I seem to invite hostility and aggression from school-aged boys. Especially the ones who play football. I have no idea why.

It was even worse when I was a schoolboy myself. I never did understand the primal rage my haircut and briefcase seemed to instil in my fellow classmates.

As peals of hyena-like laughter rang through the air, I repeatedly pressed the buzzer. Eventually, the main door clicked open and I entered the school reception area.

Once inside, I thought it wise to take off my bicycle clips. There seemed no reason to invite more taunting. My ex-girlfriend, Ifeoma, would have called this move 'cowardly'. But I don't have an issue with being a coward. I am, in fact, an ideological coward, as I explained to my tutor, Bethany Balls, when she insisted I do this PhD research.

'What the bloody buggering hell is an ideological coward?' Bethany asked, as she scribbled over my thesis plan with her purple Sharpie.

Bethany Balls does not fit the usual image of a PhD tutor. She is a loud, overweight ex-heroin addict who almost always has piles of steaming junk food on her desk during our academic meetings.

'I believe bravery to be a masculine construct,' I explained, 'used to make men into better soldiers. Bravery does not exist in the animal kingdom. A mouse does not stay to fight a cat because it worries about what the other mice will think.'

'But sometimes, you have to face your fears,' said Bethany, whacking a BBQ sauce sachet on her desk for emphasis. 'What if someone attacked your loved one? You'd have to stay and fight.'

I told Bethany that, in all honesty, I might run away. And I'd had this exact conversation with Ifeoma on the night she left.

'I told Ifeoma that if I saw her getting mugged, I may well flee the scene,' I admitted. 'Which was an honest response. Because no one knows what they would do under stress. I don't know why she became so angry.'

Bethany gave an outraged laugh, showing many gold fillings, and said, 'Sometimes you can be too honest for your own good, Michael. Is this why you're taking a qualitative research module? To understand people a bit better?'

'Probably,' I admitted. 'Ifeoma often suggested I study people, instead of mathematics. Perhaps I am trying to overcome the dreadful pain I've felt since she left.'

Bethany gave me kind eyes and told me it was better to have loved and lost.

'That's not the case,' I said. 'Because I was reasonably happy listening to Radio 4 and doing jigsaws before I met Ifeoma. And now I'm unhappy no matter what I do.'

'These interviews will cheer you up,' said Bethany. 'Talking to someone worse off than yourself always makes you feel better. And I've found you a brilliant kid for your research. A proper tearaway who gets thrown out of class on a daily basis. He's captain of the football team. He even lives in a pub. You want to study masculine culture? This boy is perfect. And he's got a great story to tell about boy-girl friendships.'

'Bethany,' I said. 'You are describing exactly the sort of child who kicked footballs at my briefcase when I was at school. I can't see the two of us getting along. And isn't qualitative interviewing about building rapport?'

'That's a pre-judgement, Michael,' said Bethany, pointing the BBQ sauce sachet in my direction. 'And it's everything we're against in qualitative research. Maybe you and this kid will end up being best friends. Who knows? Keep an open mind. That's what open interviews are all about. Grey areas.'

I've never liked grey areas, but I accepted Bethany's purple pen corrections and also her research candidate. Hence today's visit to Great Oakley School.

Once in the school reception area, I had to wait rather a while on a low, hairy chair that smelt like disinfectant. But eventually, a smiley, dimple-cheeked lady appeared and announced herself as 'Miss Hussain, Callum's teaching assistant.'

Miss Hussain wore a glittery hijab that matched the sparkles on her fingernails. She was far too glamorous for her surroundings, which were many shades of beige and brown, with a few wonky pieces of children's artwork on the walls.

'Let me take you to the Calm Corner,' said Miss Hussain, leading me down one long corridor that led around the school. Eventually, we reached an orange-carpeted room with tables and bookcases.

'This is the place,' Miss Hussain announced, with a kind smile. 'Callum has seen a lot of this room, so it's nice and familiar. You take a seat and I'll get him. You don't have any allergies, do you?'

'To boys from disadvantaged backgrounds?' I asked.

'No,' Miss Hussain laughed. 'To digestive biscuits and cups of tea with milk.'

People often ask if I have allergies, but I reassured Miss Hussain that I had none. Then Miss Hussain left, and I felt extremely nervous. I busied myself setting up my iPad and dictation software and reading my questions, my leg jittering anxiously under the desk.

Eventually, Miss Hussain returned with a scruffy boy who hopped along on crutches. He had patterns shaved into his hair and wore bright orange trainers. Actually, one bright orange trainer. His other leg was in a moonboot.

'This is Callum, Mr Lamb,' Miss Hussain announced, placing a cup of tea in front of me. 'I'm sorry there's no biscuit. Mr Rafferty ate them all.'

Callum looked exactly like the sort of boy I ran away from at school. The kind who skidded his BMX to expertly throw dust onto my clean school uniform.

I thought of Bethany Balls' words about pre-judgement and having an open mind, and decided that some pre-judgements existed for a reason.

Callum should have sat with me at the desk. But instead, he hobbled over to the sensory materials in the corner and started pulling the fibre optics about.

'Is this the boy I'll be interviewing?' I asked, hoping there had been a mistake. Perhaps Miss Hussain was simply en route to the headmaster's office, where this child would be expelled.

'Yes, this is Callum,' said Miss Hussain. 'You wanted a boy who could talk a lot, didn't you?'

'Those weren't quite the words I used,' I said. 'I requested a child who could speak with self-awareness about boy and girl relationships.'

'Yes, exactly,' said Miss Hussain. 'Callum has a wonderful friendship with a girl. He does struggle to sit still, as you can see. But he's come a long way this year. And he's lovely, deep down.'

I took three difficult breaths. My eyes wandered to Callum, who had picked up a fibre optic and was waving it around like a sword. I half expected him to give me racing tips for the greyhounds. Thank goodness Miss Hussain was staying with us for safe-guarding reasons.

'Have his parents signed the consent form?' I asked.

'Parent,' said Miss Hussain. 'Callum is from a single-parent household. You wanted someone whose family … wasn't straightforward. Didn't you?'

'I requested a disadvantaged child,' I said. 'A boy who had suffered some form of deprivation.'

'Deprivation is in the eye of the beholder, Mr Lamb,' said Miss Hussain. 'If you're measuring love, Callum is one of the richest boys I know.'

'Love can't be measured,' I said. 'Does he get free school meals?'

'Yes,' said Miss Hussain. 'And he always brings his tray back to the kitchen. Unlike some of the kids who pay for theirs.' Then she called out: 'Callum. Come and sit down with Mr Lamb. He wants to talk to you.'

Callum clumped over to the desk, fell heavily onto a chair then started kicking a table leg with his moonboot. It was a friendly sort of kicking, like a play fight. But still, it unnerved me.

'Are you a bit worried today, Callum?' Miss Hussain asked.

Callum nodded and stopped kicking.

'I don't think there will be any questions,' said Miss Hussain. 'This is more about telling Mr Lamb a story.'

'No, there are a few questions to get us going,' I said, pulling a sheet from my briefcase. 'Callum must read these himself. To limit my influence on the research.'

'Give Callum the sheet then,' said Miss Hussain, with a slight smile.

I felt flustered as I passed the paper over, and it flew from my hand and spun to the floor.

'It's alright, Mr Lamb,' said Callum. 'I'll get that for you. And don't you worry about me reading these questions. I am an improved reader now. I'm on the blue table. And I might even be on the silver table by the end of term.' He began to read from the sheet: 'Tell-me-about-your-family.'

I went a little red in the face. 'You mustn't answer the questions until you're holding the iPad. The iPad has special software. It records everything.'

'So these questions are just to kick things off?' Callum confirmed, picking up the iPad. 'And after that, I can do proper storytelling?'

Miss Hussain gave Callum a warm smile. 'You'll be able to talk about Angel Rain soon, Callum. I'll set myself up in the corner and let you two get on with things.'

'Alright,' said Callum. 'Are you sitting comfortably, Mr Lamb? Then I will begin.'

TWO

First of all, thank you for choosing me for your study, Mr Lamb. I think it's brilliant you're speaking to boys about girls. And I will try and answer your questions as best I can.

I reckon I'm a good choice for your study because I am an improved child and good at sharing my feelings. I used to be quite badly behaved, to be honest. I chucked chairs around the classroom and drew blue felt tip on my stomach and stood on chairs with my shirt up going, 'WAAAAAH!'

But since I met Angel Rain, I'm good most of the time and don't bang my desk when I'm angry or make phone calls in class. And I can't remember the last time I shouted 'BULLARD!' behind Mrs Bullard's back.

So I hardly ever get sent to the Calm Corner, anymore. Which is this room, by the way. You might not have noticed the sign, because the year ones drew rainbows all over the words, so you can't read them anymore.

This room is supposed to be a chill-out zone with fibre optics for kids like Danny. But it's never really calm because it is also our school library and medical bay, and also the drama studio.

The last time I was here, year fives were practising their Viking play and using the fibre optics as swords. And Mr Rafferty was doing his marking in the corner. He ate a whole chocolate orange in one go, Mr Lamb. Which is a lot more than one portion. And he should have been with his class, really. But I don't blame him for hiding from the year threes. They are a bit of a nightmare.

Anyway, you wanted to know about my family.

My family are quite unusual, Mr Lamb. I don't live with a mum and dad, like most kids. I live in my grandparent's pub with my mum and nana and granddad and grown-up cousin.

When I tell people that I live in a pub, they think my house isn't nice. Because pubs can be rough places. But our pub isn't rough. It's in the countryside and has a restaurant and a really big garden and gets listed in real ale guides.

I like living with my grandparents, because Nana makes a brilliant ten-item breakfast with potato waffles, Cumberland sausage, Lincolnshire sausage, black pudding, white pudding and a fried slice. And Granddad knows everything. Like how much it costs to put the dishwasher on overnight and what time of day the Co-op puts special-offer stickers on the crumpets.

My mum is really pretty, like all mums. She looks just like Barbie.

My cousin John Boy lives with us too sometimes, in a caravan in the garden. He was in the army and used to drive a tank. But then he ran over his officer's foot, so they took his tank license away and sent him to Afghanistan with a gun instead. Then John Boy stood on a landmine and lost his leg. So now he works in our pub.

So that's my family. Well, the ones I see a lot anyway. What's the next question?

THREE

Callum Duffy interview transcript: *Tuesday 25th September, 11.11 am*

Do-you-have-friends-who-are-girls?

Of course I have friends who are girls, Mr Lamb. My mum is a girl. And my nana. And then there's Angel Rain, of course, who I'm here to talk about.

No offence, but you should cross out questions if I've already answered something. Because otherwise, it doesn't sound like you're listening.

Angel Rain is the best girl in the whole world, Mr Lamb. She's the reason I like books now. And maybe I'll even pass exams and be a vet when I'm older. And you'll hear all about her soon, because Miss Hussain says you want to hear a story about us being friends.

None of the rest of these questions make sense to me, Mr Lamb. I don't know what toxic manulinity means. Or gender. Transgender is boys wanting to dress up as girls, which I am okay with. But I don't know what gender means on its own.

Miss Hussain said you wanted a story about me and Angel Rain being friends. So why don't I just tell you that? I think it'll be loads easier than these questions.

I'll start at the beginning. Which is when our class got tadpoles and Mrs Bullard poisoned them in the art sink.

Now, I know what you're thinking, Mr Lamb. What have tadpoles got to do with me and a girl being friends? Which I know is what you're here to talk about. But sometimes, you have to learn things you don't want, so you can learn things you do want. That's what Granddad says. So bear with me. Everything will make sense soon. But I need to start at the beginning.

A few terms ago, our class got tadpoles.

We should have gone on a class trip to the big pond at the top of the village and fished for frogspawn ourselves. But Mrs Bullard said she couldn't handle me and Dexter and twenty-eight other kids by the water. So she sent Miss Hussain to the pond with a pair of tights on a pole and a carrier bag.

Miss Hussain is a teaching assistant, Mr Lamb. Not a teacher. Which is well unfair, because Miss Hussain is loads nicer than Mrs Bullard and she works harder, but she doesn't get paid as much. And you can tell Mrs Bullard I said that.

Miss Hussain is an indoor person, so she was not happy about fishing out the frogspawn. She's well into her Louis Vuitton hijabs and sparkly fingernails and all of that. But she got the frogspawn for us because she is nice and loves children.

We should have put the frogspawn in a proper tank. But

when we got the tank out of the art cupboard, it had a big crack down the side. So Mrs Bullard filled up the art sink with water and put the frogspawn in there.

After a few days, the frogspawn turned into tadpoles. And I felt so bad for those tadpoles, Mr Lamb. Because it was not a nice living environment in that sink. Especially when Dexter washed his paintbrush in the water. I am quite an emotional person and it upset me, to see those tadpoles in bad conditions.

I like animals a lot. If there was a test at school for looking after animals, I would get a gold star. And that's not me showing off. It's just the truth.

Our cat, Sambuca, loves me because I'm the only one who understands him. Everyone else shouts at Sambuca when he has mental fits and scratches people. But I try to build him up, you know? Even though sometimes he can be quite violent.

I asked Mrs Bullard about getting a new tank for the tadpoles, but she said no. Because the school didn't have enough money. And even though the PTA were doing a Great British Bake Off fundraiser in a few weeks, there were other things the school needed first. Like four new carpet tiles to replace the ones Dexter ruined with his homemade slime.

Mrs Bullard is the wicked witch of this story, Mr Lamb. She has evil blue eyes and a skeleton face and claw hands. And grey hair that looks like Lego. She could also be a troll, because of her breath. And I don't know how she ended up as a teacher, because she hates children.

When I told Nana about the tadpoles, she said, 'Well, Callum. There are two types of people in the world. The ones who let bad things happen. And the ones who do something about it. Which one are you?'

I am definitely a person who does things, Mr Lamb, because I can't sit still. So the next day, I made a poster about sad tadpoles using lots of black and brown felt-tip, and I went on and on at Mrs Bullard about animal cruelty.

I said if the school could afford a Nespresso coffee machine for the staff room, then they could afford a fish tank.

Mrs Bullard said no one ever used the Nespresso machine because the capsules cost too much. And she didn't think you could be cruel to fish, because they didn't feel pain. Which upset me.

'What if I buy a fish tank with my pocket money?' I asked.

Mrs Bullard said that fish tanks were very expensive.

'Well, I'll borrow a fish tank, then,' I said. 'I bet my nana has a spare one. She has everything.'

Which is true.

Last term, I needed a policeman's helmet for the school play. And Nana had a real one, which she'd stolen from a policeman on a CND march in the 1980s. Only the police helmet was massive, so we had to use a toy one instead. And Nana had one of those too. And last Halloween, Nana dug out three real cauldrons from our garden shed.

Mrs Bullard said it would need to be a very high-quality fish tank. Because she wasn't ruining any more carpet tiles with cracks and leaks.

I said that would be fine, because Nana only ever buys good quality. It's Granddad who buys cheap.

When I got home from school that day, Nana was chucking barrels into the beer cellar. My nana is a glamorous gran with blonde hair and glittery dresses, but she is also very big and strong and can lift beer barrels and drunk people.

Nana says she is mostly muscle with a little bit of fat around the edges and a mighty bosom. But to be honest, she is a bit overweight. And she really shouldn't drink so much Guinness or eat so many chocolate mini rolls because she is diabetic.

Anyway.

I asked Nana if she had a fish tank I could borrow. And she said, 'What size do you want, Callum? Small, medium or large?'

I said, large, please. But when we looked in the loft, all Nana's fish tanks were gone.

Nana was really angry, because Granddad had done another clear-out without asking her. So she went downstairs, and Granddad said yes, he had gotten rid of the tanks. And also Nana's leather jackets from the 1970s.

Nana got even angrier about that. She said, 'I was saving those jackets for Callum.'

But Granddad was right. Pointy collars are not well-liked by kids my age.

While Nana and Granddad were arguing, I had a thought.

Mr Holland, our caretaker, keeps tropical fish in his caretaker shed. That is top secret, Mr Lamb. Because Mr Holland's aquarium heater uses loads of school electricity, so you can't tell Mr Blowers, the headmaster.

Mr Holland loves his fish. He says they keep him company, because the teachers only talk about government things and don't share their biscuits. So I thought, maybe Mr Holland had a spare fish tank. It was worth a try.

The next day, I got to school really early and found Mr Holland in his caretaker shed. I told him all about the tadpoles and how they were having a hard time. Mr Holland said I was a good boy for caring about animals, and he'd never liked Mrs Bullard much because she borrowed his tape measure once and never gave it back.

'It's your lucky day, Callum,' said Mr Holland. 'My bully fish died a few weeks ago. So I have a tank going spare.'

'What's a bully fish?' I asked.

Mr Holland said a bully fish picked on other fish and needed to be put in a different tank. And any fish could become a bully fish if it felt stressed, and there was a lesson there for human beings. Then Mr Holland pulled out this massive tank, wiped it with his caretaker cloth and said, 'Will this do you?'

'It's brilliant,' I said. 'The tadpoles will love it. Thank you so much.'

Along with the tank, Mr Holland gave me some fish food and some special stuff to make tap water nice. So Mr Holland is the first hero of this story, because without him, innocent tadpoles would have died.

It was a bit of a struggle getting the tank back to class because it was quite heavy.

Mr Holland said sorry for not helping me, but he'd hurt his back on the skate ramp playing with his grandson. So I put the tank on my bike saddle and carried it that way.

Mrs Bullard was not happy when I wheeled my bike into class. She said my bike tyres were muddy, even though they weren't. And that the tank was too big and looked like a home for tropical fish. But Miss Hussain said, 'You never mentioned size, Mrs Bullard. I think Callum has done very well.'

Mrs Bullard couldn't say anything to that, because it was true.

It was quite difficult filling up the tank with water while the tadpoles were swimming in the sink. But I managed it.

And then Mrs Bullard shouted at me again for using her tea strainer to fish the tadpoles out. But as I told her at the time, I was always going to wash it when I'd finished.

I learned something that day, Mr Lamb.

Water is heavy.

Once the tank was full, I could hardly move it. So the tank was stuck, sort of half in and out of the sink.

I didn't think the tadpoles would be happy like that because they couldn't see very much. And also, Mrs Bullard wouldn't be happy, because she couldn't fill her travel kettle in that sink. So I asked Miss Hussain for help.

Miss Hussain gave me a nice smile and said she'd missed her spin class yesterday so she could do with a workout.

The two of us moved the tank together … one, two, three, heave … like that. Poor Miss Hussain got water all over her new Jigsaw pantsuit and broke one of her pink nails. But she said it was worth it because looking after God's creatures was important, even if it wasn't part of Mrs Bullard's lesson plan.

Together, we got the tank onto the draining board, and then Miss Hussain said we'd better leave it there. Because we didn't want to lose any more water.

It was a good feeling, to see the tadpoles in a nice clean tank. They looked much happier. You could see it on their little faces.

I gave the tadpoles a nice pinch of fish food to start them off in their new home. But Mr Holland said it was best not to overfeed them, so I only gave them one cheesy Wotsit at snack time to share.

I am enjoying telling you this story, Mr Lamb. But I've got to go now, because it's nearly lunchtime. And you have to get to lunch quick on Tuesdays or all the toffee yoghurts are gone.

FOUR

Michael Lamb

As Callum hobbled out into the corridor, I allowed myself a brief moment with my head in my hands. So far, the interview had been a total disaster. I'm studying masculine image and gender relationships, not tadpoles.

From the corridor, I could hear shouting and laughing and chair scraping. I pictured Callum and his badly behaved friends, wolfing down toffee yoghurts and other processed foods in the school lunch hall.

I needed a different child. A more sensitive individual, who could be steered towards matters of gender and was less prone to chair kicking.

There was nothing else for it. An emergency call to my PhD tutor, Bethany Balls, was in order. Bethany had told me to call her in an emergency. Her exact words were, 'If it all goes tits up, call me.' But I got the gist of her vernacular.

While I searched for Bethany's number, Miss Hussain appeared at my shoulder.

'Would you like a free school dinner, Mr Lamb?' she asked. 'It's cheese wrap on Tuesdays. That's one of the better ones.'

I admit, I did shriek. I'd forgotten Miss Hussain was in the room. Once I regained my composure, I said, 'I have an important phone call to make. I may not be staying for the afternoon. But in any case, I have a can of tuna in my bag.'

'You're not going to eat in here, all alone, are you?' Miss Hussain asked. 'The staff room is just down the hall. Mr Rafferty might have picked up some Hobnobs from the All Days shop, if you're lucky.'

I do enjoy a Hobnob, but I declined. A staff room, by definition, has staff in it. And I'd just spent the morning with Callum. I needed a break. Or better yet, an escape plan.

The moment Miss Hussain left, I dialled Bethany Balls' number.

'HELLO?' Bethany barked. Unbelievably, Bethany's phone voice was even louder than her face-to-face one. So loud that I had to hold the phone away from my ear.

Most academics are introverted, quiet types who understand the gentle dance of university politics. But Bethany is extremely loud and complains, with poor grammar, about the university's power structure – which I rather think is biting the hand that feeds.

'There has been an error,' I told Bethany. 'My interview candidate is faulty. I need another.'

'What are you talking about, Michael?' Bethany bellowed. 'I have it on good authority that this boy can talk the hind legs off a donkey. The school has bent over backwards to get you a teaching assistant and two days a week in the Calm Corner. Forms have been signed. You can't swap him. Unless ... well, he does talk, doesn't he?'

'He talks,' I said, wincing slightly at Bethany's volume. 'Too much. That's the problem. He talks nonsense.'

'Talking too much is never a problem,' Bethany boomed. 'This is qualitative interviewing, Michael. You'll get hours of rubbish before you get to the good stuff.'

'But what about gender?' I asked. 'This child doesn't know the meaning of the word. He keeps talking about tadpoles.'

'Well, how many kids do you know who understand the word gender?' Bethany demanded.

'I would have understood it at his age,' I said. 'I was interested statistics, even then, and gender is a common variant.'

'Well, why don't you just interview yourself, Michael?' said Bethany.

'Is that possible?' I asked.

Bethany snorted. 'Look, a nine-year-old kid isn't going to come right out and tell you about toxic masculinity in a language you understand. Your job is to listen, then steer him towards talking about his friendships with girls.'

'This just isn't my skill set, Bethany,' I said. 'I'm finding it too challenging.'

'You're taking this qualification to learn a new skill set,' said Bethany. 'You've got mathematics PhDs coming out of your arse. I thought you wanted to learn about people.'

'Yes,' I admitted. 'But there is no need to go overboard.'

'Look, count your blessings,' said Bethany. 'Most students on this course are hoping to get a job at the end of it. You're doing a PhD in statistics just for the fun of it. So throw yourself in at the deep end and enjoy it.'

Bethany was probably right about counting my blessings.

I already have a mathematics PhD. And, unlike my

fellow students, I have no need to find work. Some years ago, I wrote a mathematics series called The X Factor, which now earns a considerable yearly sum. I can easily live off the royalties, which is lucky. Because since Ifeoma left me, teaching university mathematics gives me panic attacks.

Whilst Bethany Balls ranted about poor job prospects for graduates, my thoughts wandered to Ifeoma. The last time I saw her was eight months ago, not long after our breakup. I had not yet understood the need to avoid public places and was making my usual weekly trip to the eco-refill store.

I should have refilled my quinoa jar and left. But a foolish instinct told me to invest in a refillable washing-up liquid container. And since I was purchasing the container, it made sense to fill it with washing-up liquid.

While I was refilling, Ifeoma appeared at the shampoo refill, an ecologically-minded goddess under strip lighting. She wore a colourful headscarf and carried a giant, empty aloe vera shampoo bottle.

My whole body went into a strange spasm.

'Ifeoma!' I blurted out. And she looked up.

Ifeoma seemed pleased to see me at first. But then her beautiful brown eyes widened in shock.

'My goodness, Michael,' she said. 'You don't look well.'

'I am perfectly fine,' I said. Which on one level was true, because I had no specific health issues.

'But you're so thin,' said Ifeoma. 'What happened, Michael?'

I took a step back. Not because I didn't want to be near Ifeoma. But because I wanted to be near her too much.

'I am eating less these days,' I said. 'The Western diet is excessive. Slimmer people live longer.'

There seemed no need to tell Ifeoma that I'd been living off tinned and packet food since she left.

'But your skin,' Ifeoma went on. 'My god Michael, you look grey. Are you going outdoors regularly?'

'I go outdoors at least twice a week,' I said.

'That's not enough,' said Ifeoma. 'You must get more sunshine. Take exercise.'

'Why would you care about my wellbeing?' I asked. 'You left me.'

It was childish, I admit. But seeing Ifeoma again was quite overwhelming.

'Of course I care,' said Ifeoma. 'I always cared. It was you who didn't care. Every time I talked about our future –'

'Marriage is a capitalist ownership ceremony,' I said. 'It was for your benefit –'

'No Michael,' said Ifeoma. 'You were too scared to have children.'

'We were perfectly happy, Ifeoma,' I said. 'There was no reason to change anything.'

'Life is change, Michael,' said Ifeoma. 'I am thirty-six. I wasted two good child-bearing years on you. It might be too late for me now.'

'Ifeoma,' I said. 'We have had this argument a hundred times. There is no reason to have it a hundred and one times.'

'Fine,' said Ifeoma. 'How are things at the university?'

'I've taken a break from the university,' I said.

'Why?' Ifeoma demanded.

'I started having panic attacks,' I said.

Ifeoma's eyes softened. 'Oh, Michael. I'm so sorry.'

'You don't need to be sorry,' I said. 'Although, technically I could blame you for the panic attacks. Because I never had panic attacks until you left me.'

'What are you talking about?' Ifeoma demanded. 'I didn't leave. I walked out in anger because you said you'd never have children with me. And that you might run away if I got mugged. You never called me. Not once.'

'I sent you text messages,' I said.

'Text messages.' Ifeoma practically spat the words. 'About the bathroom items I left behind? That's all I'm worth? Not one call to try and win me back, Michael? Not one!'

'Why would I try to win you back?' I said. 'You made it quite clear what you thought of me the night you left. You called me a coward. Among other things.'

Ifeoma's handsome face softened. 'Michael. Sometimes, when people get upset they say hurtful things. I do love you. You know that, don't you?' She gave me sad eyes. There was longing and regret in them. I could see it.

'I love you too, Ifeoma,' I blurted out. 'Sometimes, it's unbearable.'

Ifeoma screwed the cap on her shampoo and said, 'Michael, if you ever want to fight for me, you know where I am.'

'I have no idea where you are,' I said. 'If you'd left a forwarding address, I wouldn't have had to text pictures of your belongings.'

'I am back at Donald Cooke Court,' said Ifeoma. 'I thought you knew.'

'But you hated that place,' I implored. 'Your old flat was damp.'

'It's all I can afford,' said Ifeoma. 'And the damp is preferable to living with a cold soul.'

Which was very hurtful.

At this point, I decided to end the conversation.

'Goodbye!' I blurted out. And turned away. But not before I saw a flash of hurt on Ifeoma's beautiful face.

'Goodbye Michael,' said Ifeoma, in a soft, sad voice. When I finally turned around, she was gone and my washing-up liquid container was overflowing over my hiking boots. Which is why I no longer have hiking boots.

The irony wasn't lost on me.

I had just purchased a reusable washing-up liquid container, only to deposit at least three bottles' worth onto the floor. It also took a lot of hessian dish clothes and recycled paper towels to clean up the mess. All in all, it was far more wasteful than simply purchasing a plastic bottle of Fairy Liquid from the Co-op.

When I left the eco store, two teenage boys in hoodies waited by the bike rack. I flinched at the sight of them. Whenever I flinch, someone says something confrontational. And sure enough, one of the boys said 'Nice haircut.' Which I knew meant 'bad haircut.'

I felt dizzy and genuinely feared I might fall over, so I decided to leave my bike on the rack and collect it later. It wasn't worth the confrontation.

It was a long walk with my cloth shopping bags, and by the time I got home, my palms were red and raw. Then I had to walk back in the pouring rain to retrieve my bicycle. Which by this point was missing a tyre.

Since then, I haven't been back to the eco store. I buy my quinoa in plastic from the local Co-op and pay three times as much. But cost isn't an issue for me these days.

What's the point of earning a fortune from mathematics books if I can't buy over-priced quinoa from a shop of my choice?

As thoughts of quinoa drifted away, I realised Bethany was still talking. She'd stopped complaining about job prospects and was now talking about a fitness class she was due to attend in five minutes. It was called 'Fight Klub with a K', she said, and involved hitting boxing bags to thumping drum and bass music.

As mentioned, Bethany Balls does not fit the traditional picture of an academic head of department.

'So I've got to go lace up my boxing gloves, Michael,' Bethany concluded. 'See you later.' And she hung up the phone.

With a heavy heart, I picked up the iPad and opened a fresh document for the afternoon's recording.

FIVE

Callum Duffy interview transcript: *Tuesday 25th September, 2.34pm*

It smells quite funny in here, Mr Lamb. No offence. Did you have tuna for lunch? I didn't see you in the dinner hall. You missed out there. They always give visitors a free dinner, which includes a dessert and a drink – either Ribena or orange squash. But it's not real Ribena. It's own brand.

I hope you had a nice lunch, Mr Lamb.

We had sausage roll, which was good. Sometimes, you get a crunchy bit in the sausage roll and it puts you right off, but today was alright.

Anyway, where were we?

I was telling you about the tadpoles. But I see you've written down another question here:

'Tell-me-about-Angel-Rain'.

Don't you want to hear how I rescued the tadpoles from school in a daring escape? Alright then. Well, I did rescue the tadpoles, and they're now on the bar in my grandparents' pub. There were ten of them in the beginning and I gave them all names:

Black Widow

Bomber

Geronimo

The Rock

Juggernaut

Baron

Bellatrix

Venom

Killer

And the little guy, Judge Dredd

But anyway. You don't want to hear about my tadpoles, so I'll get right to the bit where me and Angel Rain met in hospital. But first I need to tell you how I got there. And this bit of the story is quite violent.

Do you know the park over the road from Nana and Granddad's pub in Great Oakley, Mr Lamb? That's where the violence happened, which is how I ended up in hospital. It was during the summer holidays, and me and Dexter were doing our pug game in the play area, running around on all fours. Which sounds childish, but it's good fun.

While me and Dexter were chasing each other around the slides, these teenagers came into the play area.

One of the teenagers was called Chris Whippy. I don't know if you've heard of Chris Whippy, Mr Lamb, but he used to go to this school. He was the kid who poked holes in the cloakroom ceiling and blocked the boy's toilets with loo roll. And he got cautioned by police for stealing a massive Ferrero Rocher Easter egg from the Co-op.

The teenagers were too big for the play park, but there

weren't any adults around to tell them to leave. Just kids like me and Dexter, who were old enough to look after ourselves. And it was a bit scary, because Chris Whippy and his friends were playing swearing music from a speaker and trying to chuck the swings over the top of the bar.

Also, Chris Whippy had a baseball bat. He was swinging it around, hitting things like the slide and the roundabout. Clang! Clang! And the two girls on the roundabout looked scared.

So I said to Chris, 'Excuse me. You should be careful because girls are playing here and you might hit them with your bat.'

Chris Whippy didn't like me standing up to him. He got mad eyes, like Doctor Octopus in Spiderman. And he said, 'Why don't I hit YOU with my bat?' And all his teenage mates started laughing.

But I stood my ground.

I was frightened of Chris Whippy, Mr Lamb. You'd have to be stupid not to be scared of a mad kid with a baseball bat. I wanted to run away. I did. But that would've been wrong.

So I said, 'I know why you're called Chris Whippy. Because you're soft, like a Mr Whippy ice cream.'

Maybe I should have made a run for it then, but I didn't. And Chris Whippy got even madder eyes and swung his bat around and hit my head with it.

I didn't know what happened at first. I just knew I was on the ground, watching Dexter legging it out of the play park. Which is typical Dexter, for all his big talk. And that's why he gets picked on more than me.

When I got up, Chris Whippy said: 'Don't tell anyone I hit you. Or I'll have your family killed. I know gangsters from London.'

Then he and his mates left quickly. Probably because they knew they'd gone too far.

I went to sit on the roundabout, feeling all sick and dizzy and weird. Then one of the girls on the roundabout said, 'Oh! You're bleeding. I'll take you to hospital.'

And she started spinning the roundabout really fast and going, 'Nee nah, nee nah, you're in my ambulance.' So I had to get off before I threw up.

That's when Dexter came back.

I said: 'Where'd you shoot off to?'

'I went to get help,' said Dexter.

'Where's the help then?' I asked.

'I changed my mind and watched from the bushes,' said Dexter. 'In case you needed a witness for the police.'

'We can't tell the police,' I said. 'Chris Whippy will have my family killed.'

'You'd better clean up all that blood then,' said Dexter. 'Or your mum will know what happened.'

Dexter helped me wash off some of the blood in the park toilets. But my head wouldn't stop bleeding, so Dexter helped me home and told me to put superglue in the cut. Because that's how doctors fixed his cousin when he fell off the kitchen counter.

The glue sounded like a good idea. Except Mum caught me in the bathroom with the tube of Loctite before I could stick myself back together.

Mum was upset when she saw the blood. She thought I'd been hit by a car and screamed at me for crossing the road without looking both ways.

'I wasn't hit by a car,' I said. 'There was a bit of bother in the play park.'

I didn't tell her about Chris Whippy, because I thought

it would be dangerous. So I said I'd been rude to some teenage boys and had fallen over running away.

Mum believed me, because I'm just the sort of kid who shouts names at big kids and runs off. Then she drove me to hospital really fast, not even slowing down at amber lights. And that is where I met Angel Rain.

Have you ever been to children's accident and emergency, Mr Lamb? It's not very nice. There are loads of worried parents and crying babies, and the toys are quite old.

Me and Mum had to wait for hours and hours. I should have been a top priority because I was a head injury. But there were more serious head injuries that day because there'd been a toddler bouncy castle party in town. So I was a long way down the list.

It was well dull in accident and emergency. After I'd done all the jigsaws and clacked the bead toy about a hundred times, I was dying of boredom.

I looked around to see if there was anyone I could play with. The other kids were all either really sick or babies. But then this girl came in. She looked about my age and not especially ill. No blood, anyway.

There weren't many seats left in the waiting room, so the girl ended up sitting on her own near the play stuff, a little way from her parents. Only she didn't play with anything. She just read a book. A massive book.

Sometimes, the girl sighed a bit, like the book was sad. She looked just like Moana, only with a fringe and golden eyes instead of brown ones. And she had on a frog t-shirt and a skirt that looked like a curtain. And white socks with shiny red shoes. Proper smart, you know?

The girl looked a bit upmarket for me. But I thought the frog t-shirt might be a way in. So I went over, all confident, and hit her with a killer line: 'You like frogs, yeah? I've got tadpoles.'

Now I don't want to be a smarty pants, Mr Lamb. But if I hadn't told you about my tadpoles, that would have made no sense, would it?

Anyway.

The girl put her book down and said, 'Yes, I do like frogs. They are my favourite animal. Are you sure you have real tadpoles? Tadpoles usually turn into frogs by the summertime.'

'Yeah,' I said. 'They haven't turned into frogs yet because my teacher, evil Bullard, poisoned them in the art sink and stunted their growth. But I'm keeping my fingers crossed that they'll become frogs by the end of summer.'

'Maybe your tadpoles will hibernate,' said the girl. 'Sometimes tadpoles do that. And they'll become frogs next year.'

'Yeah, maybe,' I said. 'Do you want to play a game with me? Like Zombie Army? It would be really good to do in here, because this place looks like the headquarters of an evil villain, with all the sliding doors of doom and that.'

The girl said, 'I'd like to, but ...' Then she looked at her parents and said, 'I should read this. It's for school. I'm very behind.'

'You can't do school work on a Sunday,' I said. 'It's against the law.'

The girl looked worried then, and said, 'Is it? I should tell my dad. I don't think he knows.'

'Not really,' I said. 'I'm only joking.'

The girl gave me a funny smile then, with all these gaps in her teeth. One of her front teeth stuck out a bit and looked really nice.

'What's your name?' I asked.

'Angel Rain Grace Christina Pegg,' she said. 'Angel Rain is my first name. And Grace Christina are my middle names.'

'Do you really have all those names?' I asked. 'Or are you getting me back for that joke I made?'

Angel Rain said, 'No, I do have all those names. Angel Rain is from a prayer. Because I was born with a heart defect and the doctors thought I would die.'

'Is that why you're in hospital?' I asked. 'Because of your heart?'

'Yes,' said Angel Rain. 'I have a donor heart now. But I've only had it a one year. And I had breathing trouble earlier, so my parents are worried.'

'What's a donor heart?' I asked. 'It sounds like a weird kebab.'

Angel Rain said a donor heart was a new heart from someone who had died.

Then I felt really bad about the kebab comment.

'So you have someone else's heart in your body?' I asked.

'Yes,' said Angel Rain.

'Wow,' I said. 'You're like some kind of superhero.'

'I don't think superheroes spend so much time in hospital,' said Angel Rain. 'What's your name?'

'Callum Duffy,' I said. 'The one and only Callum Duffy.'

We smiled at each other then, and it was nice.

Don't worry, Mr Lamb. That's only the home bell. I know it's loud, isn't it? Much louder than the lunch bell. It can give you a bit of a shock.

Well, I suppose I'll be going home then. But I'll be seeing you a lot from now on, won't I? Twice a week, Miss Hussain said. All the kids in my class think I'm really lucky.

By the way, there's an emotional bit coming up. Just to warn you.

Take care of yourself. And maybe get yourself some decent trainers, if you're going to be hanging around here a lot. Because the kids will pick on you for wearing those Velcro trekking shoe things. And your feet must be freezing in this weather.

SIX

Michael Lamb

After the interview, I cycled home reflecting on the day's progress.

I had to admit, Callum defied first impressions. He seemed more sensitive than his shaved haircut suggested, and it was thoughtful of him to offer footwear advice. However, I have learnt very little about toxic masculinity and how boys from disadvantaged backgrounds behave poorly towards girls and women. If anything, Callum seems quite the gentleman.

But surely this cannot be the case.

As I turned onto my street, I considered how I could steer Callum towards discussions of gender. And specifically, gender issues. Surely, Callum, as a disadvantaged boy, must have many of them? I certainly hoped so. It is, after all, what my whole thesis is based around.

My house is in an interesting part of town. The area was

developed in the early 1900s as part of a social experiment.
Detached Victorian mansions were built between rows of
terraced houses, in the hope that working-class and middle-
class people would live harmoniously and learn from one
another.

The experiment has not worked in my case, because I
am anti-social. I sit in my large, detached mansion with my
bank full of money, never interacting with my terraced-
house neighbours. Unless it is a brief conversation about
recycling collection dates.

Since Ifeoma left, I am more of a hermit than ever. And
I must say, it was a relief to get back to my house today, away
from all the noise and chaos of children.

Why do people have such an issue with socks and open-
toed shoes? They're a very comfortable combination and
serve for both indoor and outdoor wear.

True, it's getting a little cold for stocking feet. But these
days, I seldom notice things like cold feet. Or cold in
general.

My house, for example, is rather cold. But I don't feel
the need to put the heating on, except on very cold days
when the pipes might freeze.

Additionally, a heated house reminds me of Ifeoma.
And I do not like to be reminded.

I reached my front porch, considering a new set of
interview questions. But as I turned the door knob, a
memory of Ifeoma leapt to the surface.

When Ifeoma moved in with me, she hung an
impractical wooden heart on the door handle and said, 'You
have my heart now, Michael. Please take good care of it.'

I always found the wooden heart to be highly irritating,
impeding the door-handle-turning process and making a
noisy clunking sound whenever I entered the house.

When Ifeoma left me on Boxing Day, she took the wooden heart. We'd had yet another argument about my cowardliness, culminating in Ifeoma telling me I was a robot with no feelings.

Ifeoma looked more furious than I'd ever seen her. And I'd seen her pretty furious. For example, when I gave her a hat and gloves for Christmas instead of an engagement ring.

Ifeoma's parting words were, 'You run away from difficulty, Michael. Which, ironically, causes a lot of difficulty.'

Later that night, Ifeoma messaged, asking me to put her things on the porch.

Her message said, 'Michael. I do not wish to see you. Please leave my things outside.'

I didn't have any boxes, so I put Ifeoma's possessions in bin bags and placed them on the porch. Which on reflection, may have come across as uncaring.

The next day, Ifeoma's things had gone and I realised we'd broken up.

Months of heartache and depression followed. It was a great emotional trauma. Probably the greatest of my life. But I have found ways to deal with it. For example, by not going out unless I have to. And when I do go out, I'm especially careful on the roads in case I have an accident and end up in the hospital, where Ifeoma works as a nurse.

I've heard, through the Green Party grapevine, that Ifeoma is seeing a new man these days. A manly stockbroker who wears rugby shirts and drives an oversized car with a grill like an angry face. I seem to offend men like that on sight. I'm not sure why, because I am inoffensive on all levels.

I don't remember entering my house or climbing the stairs

to the office. But once I was in the office room, I gave my toes an inquisitive wiggle. Yes, they were cold. But did it matter? Did it warrant the effort of shopping for new hiking boots at the Walk This Way store, and possibly bumping into Ifeoma? True, Ifeoma isn't an outdoor store person. But one never knows where an ex-girlfriend could turn up. It just isn't worth the risk.

In my cold, slightly damp, office, I considered today's disastrous interview.

Callum and I had barely touched on gender issues, even after several hours of dialogue. How long would it take to understand Callum's attitudes towards women? At this rate, it could be months. I certainly did not want to spend months at that school.

School days were not the best days of my life. In fact, they were probably the worst. The name calling. The simmering threat of violence. And the constant bullying about my briefcase.

Briefcases seem to unlock some kind of primal rage in school-aged children. I remember a large, angry boy named Thomas Carter snatching my Alpine Swiss from me on a rainy Thursday afternoon and emptying the contents over the playground floor.

My fledgling science fiction novel, Peace on Mars, fell into a muddy puddle and was ruined. I'll never forget the mud stains on the birds of peace deployment stations and the dove feather bombs.

After such a violent act, my mother decided enough was enough. She moved me to Homewell House – a private school with richer, supposedly nicer, children. Only they weren't nicer. There were macho boys there too. And they sought me out for immediate shoving and name-calling. Then on the way home, the boys from my old school teased me about my 'posh' purple blazer and threw left-over food at my back.

It was the worst of both worlds.

I sat for a long time in my office, attempting to analyse Callum's interview. But what was there to analyse? Callum had revealed very little about toxic masculinity or his understanding of gender. I needed to probe further.

After a wasted hour writing and deleting the same sentence, I went downstairs and heated a tin of Campbell's tomato soup for supper. I added some Bachelor's instant noodles to the dish, and then sat alone on the hard, wooden chair in my lounge, eating and contemplating.

Once upon a time, I had a sofa. But when I stopped turning the heating on last winter, the sofa went mouldy and had to be disposed of. Ditto, the easy chair, curtains, cushions and rug.

These days, I have a single wooden chair in my living room. Wood can't go mouldy. And I do not need more than one chair, since I live alone and do not welcome guests.

Here is what I contemplated: Callum needs to be steered towards more fruitful interview dialogue. Such as how he doesn't see women as equals. Perhaps he will use the word 'birds' at some point, or suggest that girls don't know how to play football.

Statistical analysis proves that disadvantaged boys grow up to be violent towards women. Tangibly. My job is to back this up with qualitative data.

I will see Callum again on Thursday, as planned, and attempt to get more significant findings to back up my thesis statement. Probably, I will fail. Then I will tell Bethany Balls that Callum cannot be used for my thesis. After that, I will find a new interview candidate. Ideally, an older child with neater hair, who doesn't kick the table quite so often.

SEVEN

Callum Duffy interview transcript: *Thursday 27th September, 1.37pm*

It's good to see you again, Mr Lamb.

I wasn't sure if you'd come back, to be honest. Because you didn't seem all that happy last time. And you didn't get your free school dinner.

I saw you taking your bicycle clips off on the way through the playground. Did you do that because Tyler called them lame? I'd be careful, because kids like Tyler are sharks. They're looking for weakness.

Don't get me wrong – your bicycle clips are lame. But you have to rock your look, don't you? If Tyler thinks you took your bicycle clips off because of him, he'll only pick on you worse. He's a bully. So you have to set boundaries. I've had to stick his head down the toilet loads of times.

Anyway.

Let's get back to the story, shall we?

After me and Angel Rain found out each other's names, we got talking.

I asked lots of questions because I like getting to know people. The first thing I found out was that Angel Rain lived by DeMontford Park, which made her totally out of my league.

But I like a challenge, Mr Lamb. My family are winners. If there are obstacles, we kick them right over and keep going. And if there are other people along the way who fall, we help them up and kick obstacles down for them too. Because we are winners and also helpful.

At first, it was hard to find things in common with Angel Rain. Because her life was quite different to mine. But here is the thing, Mr Lamb. If you ask the right questions, you'll always find something. Which you must know because you do research.

Anyway, I kept asking and here's what I found out.

Angel Rain liked reading and science and maths and did well at school. She was also mad about frogs and had a frog schoolbag, plastic frogs in the bath and a soft frog in her bed called Frogger. Her favourite colour was green, because of frogs. Her favourite food was pizza with an egg on top from the Italian restaurant in town. And her favourite drink was elderflower cordial, which, by the way, is rank and tastes like perfume.

Angel Rain didn't like football or cricket or darts, but she liked watching the Winter Olympics. Also, her favourite book was called Heidi, and she liked it because it was about snow and mountains.

I've never really been into cold weather or the colour green myself. I'm more of a red man, because of The Arsenal. Who, by the way, get a capital 'The', because they went a whole season undefeated. And that is a proper capital letter rule, no matter what Mrs Bullard says.

It took a lot of questions to find something in common with Angel Rain. But after a bit of talking, I found out we both liked stars and space.

Angel Rain was more into the science side of things. Like, she knew all the planet sizes and how stars explode and become red giants.

I'm more into just looking at stars and seeing my favourites come back at different times of year. But we both wanted to go into space in a rocket because we liked the idea of flying really fast, so we talked about that for a while. And Angel Rain said skiing would probably feel a bit like flying and that's why she really wanted to sky one day.

Then Angel Rain asked me what I wanted to be when I grew up.

'A vet,' I said. 'Because I'm good with animals. But you need exams for that and I'm no good at school. So I'll probably just be a millionaire entrepreneur or a crime lord. What do you want to be?'

Angel Rain said she wanted to be a chief actuary. Which was something to do with maths and taking risks, but she wasn't quite sure how it all worked.

'If you don't know what a chief actuary is, why do you want to be one?' I asked

'Dad thinks it's an excellent job for me,' said Angel Rain. 'Because I'm good with numbers. Dad says I should have a goal. To keep me going, because I am sick a lot and often feel scared that I might die. So my goal is to pass a difficult exam and get into grammar school and be a chief actuary. That's why I'm doing school work on a Sunday. Because it will help me to live longer.'

Which seemed fair enough.

While we were talking, I noticed Angel Rain's parents looking over, sort of unhappy. Which I understood because I did have blood all over me. And shaved bits in my hair. And neon-orange Nikes and a football shirt and joggers. From experience, most adults don't like those things.

Come to think of it, Mr Lamb, you gave me the same sort of look when you first met me.

Anyway I gave Angel Rain's parents a little wave. But they both frowned.

They're a funny pair, those two.

Angel Rain's dad looked like an angry elf. He had one of those noses you could see up, a shaved head and frowny eyebrows. He looked suspicious too. Like he thought everyone was planning on nicking his wallet. And he was wearing a flashy, gold watch with a rugby t-shirt, ironed blue jeans and shiny leather shoes. And those things are crimes against fashion when worn together.

Angel Rain's mum was like a tiny, worried Christmas tree, hanging with all this glittery stuff. Liked diamond earrings and bracelets and a sparkly scarf. She had worried eyes that wanted to jump out of her head, and shiny black hair like Angel Rain. And she was sitting all stiff, with a packet of antiseptic wipes on her lap.

I said to Angel Rain, 'Your parents don't look too happy about me talking to you.'

Angel Rain gave me serious eyes and said, 'My dad is quite old-fashioned. He doesn't think girls and boys should be friends, because girls don't learn with boys around.'

'Well, that's not true,' I said. 'Francois in our class knows everything. And loads of girls copy his work and get better marks because of him.'

Angel Rain got the giggles, then. She started laughing, and I started laughing too. We were cracking up

While we were laughing, Angel Rain's dad stood up and asked Angel Rain how her work was coming along.

Angel Rain said, 'I was just taking a little break.'

'Maybe you should come and sit here,' said Angel Rain's dad. 'So you can concentrate.'

Angel Rain crossed her arms, but her dad kept glaring at her. So Angel Rain said, 'It was very nice to meet you, Callum. But I have to go now.'

She stood up and shook my hand, then took her book and went back to sit with her parents.

After a bit, Aunty Julesy arrived to take over, so Mum could go home and get some sleep.

Aunty Julesy is like a classy version of my mum. She doesn't wear half as much make-up, and her hair is natural brown-blonde and curly. And she talks in a smart voice because she's been to university. Aunty Julesy thinks she's fat, but she isn't. She's cuddly and nice-looking.

When Aunty Julesy asked what happened to my head, I said I'd punched a big kid in the face. Which was a lie, and I know that's bad.

I was hoping Angel Rain would hear and be impressed, Mr Lamb. But I was being a total idiot, because when I looked over at Angel Rain, she was gulping at the air like a goldfish.

It was really bad. So frightening.

Sorry. Just give me a minute. This is a bit upsetting so I need to get myself together.

EIGHT

Callum Duffy interview transcript:
Continued ...

I was so scared, Mr Lamb, seeing Angel Rain breathing like that. I didn't know what to do. She was in real trouble.

Angel Rain's Dad was standing over her shouting, 'Breathe! Breathe! Be calm!'

And Angel Rain did look quite calm. But her mum was having hysterics, shrieking and making upset noises.

After a bit, Angel Rain started making this weird 'harg, harg' noise. Her eyes went all big and scared and it was so bad.

Angel Rain's dad jumped up then and rang the buzzer next to the sliding door of doom. Which was the door that separated us commoners from the doctors and nurses. But no one came. Even though he pressed the buzzer about twenty times.

I ran up and banged on the sliding door, shouting, 'Hey!

There's a girl here who needs help!' And Aunty Julesy banged on the door too.

Aunty Julesy told Angel Rain's dad that the doctors and nurses probably ignore the buzzer most of the time. Because kids like me press it for fun. Which I thought was harsh.

But still, no one came.

Then I saw a nurse walking past the waiting room, eating a bag of Maltesers. I ran out shouting, 'Nurse! Nurse! A girl is dying.'

The nurse didn't take me seriously at first, because I was a shaved-head kid in a football shirt. But then Aunty Julesy came out and said I was telling the truth and a girl was in trouble.

The nurse believed Aunty Julesy, because Aunty Julesy is a respectable-looking lady. She has curly hair, and she leaves it natural and doesn't straighten it like Mum does. She still dyes her hair blonde, but in a posh way with highlights, so it looks like it could be real. Which Mum says is a total waste of money, because it costs a hundred pounds and you can hardly see the difference.

The nurse did come into the waiting room after that. She dropped her Maltesers all over the floor when she saw Angel Rain and used her special plastic card to get the sliding door open. Then another nurse came running out, and Angel Rain was carried through the sliding door of doom. Her parents went too, and the door closed behind them.

The waiting room was really quiet then. Except one little kid said, 'Mum, can I have a Malteser?'

I was so worried about Angel Rain.

I kept asking Aunty Julesy, 'Is Angel Rain going to be okay? She won't die, will she?'

Aunty Julesy said she was sure Angel Rain would be okay, but she didn't sound like she was telling the truth.

'Why don't you make her a nice card for when she's feeling better?' said Aunty Julesy. 'Then maybe you'll stop kicking my chair and driving me mad.'

I thought that was a good idea.

The card wasn't my best effort, because the only paper I could find was an All the Fours Taxis flyer. Who do seven-seaters and also airport pickups, if you're interested.

Also, the Vitalite tub of felt tips only had three working colours. But luckily one of those colours was red, so I drew a massive heart and spent ages filling it in. Then I drew two men shooting each other with guns because I'm good at drawing that.

Finally, a doctor called Dr Chang came to the sliding door of doom and called my name.

Aunty Julesy had fallen asleep with her mouth open by then, even though she told everyone she'd stayed up until three in the morning. But that's just between us, Mr Lamb, because I don't tell tales.

Dr Chang was a nice man. He was very tall and very, very awake, even though he had been working for nearly twelve hours. He said his secret was Lucozade Sport, tropical flavour, and then took us into a special bed and pulled a curtain around.

I thought Dr Chang might have some clever doctor's way of healing my cut. But he just wiped all the blood out and glued my head with special doctor superglue, which killed. It was totally brutal. And it was just like Dexter said – I could have done it at home if Mum hadn't stopped me.

I tried to be all manly, but I did cry a bit. And that's okay, because cousin John Boy cries when he watches the Lion King and he's been in the army.

Doctor Chang was really nice. He asked me about school and all sorts while he was holding my head together with glue.

I told him I didn't like school, because I'm the thick kid who gets into trouble.

Dr Chang said he understood how I felt. Because in China, he'd been bottom of his class too, even though he had four hours of extra lessons after school and did homework until midnight. And sometimes he fell asleep in class and got hit with a cane.

Dr Chang said his school had been good practice for working in a hospital.

'Except here, I can never fall asleep,' said Dr Chang. 'Because someone might die.' And he laughed in a mad way and his eye twitched a bit.

After Dr Chang had glued my head together, I gave him the get well soon card for Angel Rain and said, 'Can you give it to the girl who was having breathing trouble? How is she doing, by the way?'

Dr Chang said he wasn't allowed to talk about other patients, which made me feel worried.

'Did she die?' I asked.

'No child has ever died on my watch,' said Dr Chang. 'I have Chang power.'

Which made me feel loads better.

Then we heard Nana shouting, 'Callum! Julesy!'

Aunty Julesy looked embarrassed and said, 'Sorry, Dr Chang. That's my mum.'

Dr Chang was really confused and asked how Nana had gotten through the sliding door of doom.

'That door can only be opened by staff,' he said. 'It's made from bulletproof glass. Does your mother work at the hospital?'

Aunty Julesy laughed and said no way. Because Nana would be rude to patients and forget to wash her hands.

'But you need a key card to get in here,' said Dr Chang.

'Oh, Mum probably just pulled the door open,' said Aunty Julesy. 'She's very strong. She runs a pub. She lifts grown men over her shoulder at kicking-out time.'

Dr Chang wanted to meet Nana then, because he said she must be 'an astonishing athlete'.

He didn't have to wait long, because Nana pulled back the curtain a few seconds later and said, 'There you are! I've been looking everywhere. Who wants a KitKat?'

Dr Chang hadn't eaten since lunchtime, so he took a KitKat, a sausage roll and a bag of Hula Hoops from Nana's picnic bag, and a Capri-Sun drink for later. Then he asked Nana how she'd opened the sliding door of doom.

'One of the hospital porters opened it for me,' said Nana. 'He drinks in my pub. I promised him a bottle of Magners and a big bag of Scampi Fries for his trouble.'

After that, we were allowed to go. Which should have been good, because I was well tired. But I wanted to see Angel Rain before I left and give her my love.

I wasn't allowed, though.

So we just went home.

NINE

Callum Duffy interview transcript:
Continued ...

When we got back from hospital, I just wanted to go to sleep. But Mum wanted to know what happened at the park. She was hearing different stories, she said. And wanted to get things straight.

I was tired and couldn't remember my lies. So I just said, 'I told you already. I think I'll go to sleep now.'

Mum said, 'Dexter's mum is saying something about a baseball bat.'

'You know what Dexter's like,' I said. 'He's always making stuff up.'

But Mum kept asking me questions, and I got really confused. So in the end, Mum got the truth out of me about Chris Whippy.

Then it all kicked off.

Mum, Nana and Aunty Julesy got all got angry and started threatening violence. Which is normal for the women in my family, Mr Lamb. The men in my family are a lot calmer. Granddad is quite peaceful really, with his gardening and his wholemeal bread. And John Boy used to be a soldier, so he prefers calming down bad situations. He's seen enough violence in his life.

Anyway, Nana was going on and on about Chris Whippy, saying she was going to find him and give him a piece of her mind.

'No, Nana,' I said. 'Chris Whippy is a dangerous criminal. He stole a Ferrero Rocher Easter egg from the Co-op.'

Granddad was shocked by that.

'That's brazen theft,' he said. 'Why couldn't the boy content himself with a child-sized Smarties egg or Cadbury's Buttons? A Ferrero Rocher egg is just plain greedy.'

Nana said she'd ask Chris Whippy that question while she was thumping him.

I got upset then and said, 'No, Nana. Please don't. Chris Whippy knows gangsters in London.'

Nana laughed and said: 'So do I, Callum. And what's more, they owe me favours.'

Then she went off to the park.

Mum told me not to worry, because Nana handled angry, drunk men all the time and everyone in the village was scared of her. But I did worry because I love my Nana very much.

Half an hour later, Nana came back. And guess what she had, Mr Lamb? Chris Whippy's baseball bat. She put it behind the bar with the other last-orders weapons and told me that Chris Whippy wouldn't be bothering me again.

I couldn't believe it.

'Did he give you any trouble?' I asked Nana,

'No, Callum,' said Nana. 'He made the very sensible choice to walk away on two working legs.'

I felt a lot better after that.

It's true what they say, Mr Lamb. It's always best to tell an adult. No matter how scared you are.

Nana said I deserved a takeaway curry that night because I'd been really brave and told the truth. And while we were having our curry, I told everyone about Angel Rain. I said she liked science and space and her favourite colour was green. And she also liked silver because it was the colour of stars. And she hardly ever watched TV, because she liked reading better. And her favourite animals were frogs, which is great because I have tadpoles now. And when they turn into frogs I can show them to her.

Granddad said my tadpoles wouldn't turn into frogs, because it was too late in the year. And most likely they would die soon. But he also said that Angel Rain sounded like a very nice young lady and he sincerely hoped she felt better.

I said I hoped so too. But I honestly didn't think I'd see Angel Rain again, Mr Lamb. Until the brilliant thing happened.

I will tell you about that next time because the bell just rang. And you did much better today, Mr Lamb. You hardly jumped at all.

TEN

Michael Lamb

Before I left the Calm Corner, Callum helped me pack away my iPad and paperwork.

'Do you know something, Mr Lamb?' he said. 'You've been asking all about me, but I haven't asked a thing about you. It's very rude of me. Tell me something about you, Mr Lamb. And your family.'

'There's not much to tell,' I said. 'I am an only child. My parents have moved to New Zealand. I am unmarried and have no children.'

'Have you ever been married?' Callum wanted to know.

'I don't believe in marriage,' I told him. 'It is bad for women's rights.'

'But girls like weddings,' said Callum. 'Don't they?'

'Some do,' I said. 'But weddings aren't good for women.'

'I don't think telling girls what's good for them is good for them,' said Callum. 'But each to their own. Do you live with someone then? If you're not married. Like a boyfriend or girlfriend?'

Something about Callum's earnest brown eyes invited confidence.

'I used to live with a woman,' I said.

'What was she like?' Callum asked.

'Strong,' I said. 'Funny. Disorganised. And very caring.'

'So, why did you two break up?' Callum wanted to know.

'Because she wanted children,' I said. 'I never understood why. She was a paediatric nurse and spent all day with children. Why would she want them at home as well?'

'A paediatric nurse is a children's nurse, isn't it?' Callum wanted to know. 'Does your ex work at the local hospital? What's her name?'

'Ifeoma Kolawole,' I said.

Callum clicked his fingers. 'Nurse Kolawole! I do know her. She was the one who fixed my broken bed when I stayed on the children's ward. I haven't told you about the children's ward yet, but it's coming. We've had some good chats, me and Nurse Kolawole.'

'I should be going,' I said. 'I'm sorry Callum. I can't talk anymore on this subject. We must keep a healthy distance between interviewer and interviewee. I will see you next time.'

As I cycled home, anxious thoughts bubbled in my brain.

Had Callum really met Ifeoma at the hospital? She was a children's ward nurse. If Callum had stayed on the children's ward, well ... it was possible.

I had to be careful. Researchers must adhere to ethical

practice and not use interviews to find out personal details about their ex-partners.

Still, I thought about Ifeoma the whole way home.

Was she still seeing the manly man? Had they moved in together? And most importantly, was she happy?

I wished I could find out.

ELEVEN

Callum Duffy interview transcript: *Tuesday 1st October 1st, 9.04 am*

You're here nice and early today, Mr Lamb. Which is brilliant for me, because it gets me out of assembly.

Assembly is so boring, isn't it?

Before we get started, I want to give you something. Because you don't have a girlfriend and you live by yourself. So ... let me get it.

(Inaudible)

This, Mr Lamb, is a very special mug. You see what it says on it? Hug in a Mug. So when you have a cup of tea from this, you'll feel the love. And I know you're a man from an older generation so you'll probably be like 'I don't need love', sort of thing. But you do. We all do. So this mug will help you out.

No need to thank me.

Anyway, how are you, Mr Lamb? Well, I hope? It's good to do ice breakers with people when you first see them isn't it? You haven't asked me how I am, but don't worry – I'll tell you anyway.

I'm good. Thank you for asking.

I'll get back to the story now.

You remember last time I told you I'd probably never see Angel Rain again? And then I got a nice surprise?

Well, this was the surprise – I got a letter from Angel Rain in the post. Of course, I didn't know it was from her at first.

Nana called me in from the pub garden and said, 'Someone is writing to you, Callum. Probably one of your girlfriends from school.'

But I didn't have any girlfriends at that time, because they were getting jealous of each other. And it was taking me ages to walk them all home.

I thought the letter might be from my dad. Because I couldn't think of anyone else who would write to me. So I was all ready to rip it up. But when I got to the kitchen, I saw the envelope had really neat, girly writing.

I had a feeling. Like, maybe the letter was from Angel Rain. But that didn't make any sense, because Angel Rain didn't know my address and why would she write to me anyway?

Then I turned the envelope over and saw frog and star stickers on the back. And I couldn't stop smiling because I knew.

'This is from Angel Rain,' I said. 'The girl I met in hospital.'

Granddad was impressed that Angel Rain had written to me. He said that letter writing was a lost art and more people should do it. And that the world had been ruined by phones and text messages.

While Granddad was going on, I opened the envelope

really carefully. The letter inside was made of nice, white paper with a furry feel, and the handwriting was amazing. Better than Mrs Bullard's.

At the bottom of the letter was Angel Rain's name: Angel Rain Grace Christina Pegg.

This is what the letter said:

Dear Callum,

I hope you are well.

I am feeling much better.

Thank you for your card. You are very good at colouring. I am very glad you told me you lived in a pub in Great Oakley, because it made it very easy to find your address. Unless there is another pub in Great Oakley, but I don't think there is because I checked three times on Google.

Mum and Dad would like to say thank you for your quick thinking and courage in accident and emergency.

They would like to buy you an ice cream with a topping and a sauce. Can you come to the DeMontford Park cafe this Saturday at 2pm? They have very good ice cream there. It is Italian.

Please RSVP.

Yours sincerely,

Angel Rain Grace Christina Pegg

There were some more star and frog stickers on the letter and one heart sticker. Angel Rain had written her address at the top too, which was:

The Acorns, DeMontford Park Road.

. . .

She'd written the date under that, which was the 2nd of
August.

I was so pleased about that letter. I showed it to my
whole family.

Granddad said that Angel Rain had very good spelling
and punctuation.

'She's a step up from your last girlfriend, Callum,' said
Granddad. 'C U Z isn't a word. It's just atrocious spelling.'

I told Granddad that Angel Rain wasn't my girlfriend.
Just a friend. Then I asked him what RSVP meant.

'It's French,' said Granddad, 'for Respondez S'il Vous
Plait. It means please reply.'

'So I have to write back to her?' I asked.

'Yes Callum,' said Granddad. 'Because it says RSVP.'

I felt a bit nervous about writing back. First of all,
because DeMontford Park is well fancy and I didn't feel
good enough for it.

Nana was like, 'We're fancy enough for DeMontford
Park. I've got a Fitbit.'

And John Boy was like, 'I've got a pair of Gucci loafers.'

But Aunty Julesy said John Boy's Gucci loafers didn't
make him classy. Because he has his steak well done with
ketchup and a can of Stella Artois.

The other reason I felt nervous was because Angel
Rain's handwriting was perfect, and she'd used all those big
words and a question mark. I didn't want to show myself up
as a slow learner.

'Will you write the letter for me?' I asked Granddad.
'And make me look like one of those kids who reads hard
books?'

Granddad said that would be fraud. Then he said: 'If

you want to improve your reading, Callum, I have many childhood treasures just waiting for young hands. Like the *Tip Top Book for Boys* and *A Marvellous Holiday by Rail*.'

'But you know I don't get on with books, Granddad,' I said. 'Help me out. It's just one letter.'

'No Callum,' said Granddad. 'I will not write the letter for you. But I will help you with your reading. It's no wonder you're struggling with those dreadful phonics books you bring home. They don't make any sense. How can Gran be bad and sad and mad all at once? And not all rice is nice. Some of it has salmonella.'

'Mrs Bullard says those books are my level, Granddad,' I said. 'Only the gold, silver and blue tables are allowed books without pictures.'

'I'm not sure Mrs Bullard understands your level, Callum,' said Granddad. 'You've been on picture books for far too long. Why don't you borrow my *Little Neddy* books from the 1950s? They're wonderful stories. None of this *Pip and Pop on Top* nonsense.'

Granddad went on about his *Little Neddy* books then, and all the dangerous things Little Neddy does that wouldn't be allowed these days.

'You'll love *Little Neddy Camps Out*, Callum,' said Granddad. 'Neddy makes a real fire and plays with knives in that one. All without supervision.'

'But *Little Neddy* stories are well confusing,' I said. 'I don't know what a shilling is or an eiderdown or any of those foreign words. And I don't need to be good at reading to write a letter. I need to be good at spelling and handwriting and full stops.'

Granddad went red in the face and said all of those things came from a love of reading.

In the end, I got fed up with arguing and wrote the letter

without Granddad's help. Except, Granddad did help in the end. Nana was right. When I showed Granddad all my mistakes, he got his red pen out.

I wrote the letter out five times and this is what it said:

Dear Angel Rain, the date is the 3rd of August.

That first bit was Granddad's idea. He said you should always write the date at the top of a letter.

Then I wrote:

Thank you for your message from the 2nd of August.

Because Granddad said you should say the date someone else has written too. Then I wrote:

I am very well. I hope you are well. Thank you for your invitation to the park. I will come. All the best, Callum.

Then I drew two smiley faces and two hearts.

I spelt invitation wrong four times, but now I'll always know how to spell it right.

I.N.V.I.T.A.T.I.O.N. Invitation. See?

I thought it was a really good letter and I hoped Angel Rain would think so too.

After I posted the letter, I asked Mum if she could take me to the park on Saturday.

'Why didn't you ask me before you said yes?' said Mum.
'I have a beauty exam this weekend. I can't miss any more of
them.'

I had a bit of a panic then and a small cry, but luckily,
cousin John Boy said he'd drive me. Which was even better
than Mum, because John Boy said he'd get us both a bacon
sandwich from the park cafe.

So on Saturday morning, cousin John Boy drove me to
DeMontford Park in his beaten-up old Land Rover.

People think a Land Rover is a fancy car, but John Boy's
Land Rover isn't fancy at all. Because it's from the 1980s
and all square, like Lego bricks. And it has rust and chips
and bumps.

One of our pub regulars, Tall Paul, gave John Boy the
Land Rover for free, because it cost more in repairs every
year than the car was worth. But John Boy loves repairing
old cars, so it all worked out for the best.

I don't know if you've ever been to DeMontford Park,
Mr Lamb. But it's quite smart. Which did scare me a bit,
because at the time I didn't look or act smart. And our Land
Rover looked really tatty next to all the new four-by-fours. It
was like seeing one of our pub regulars at a Pizza Express.

All the mums in DeMontford Park were old, like thirty
or forty. And some of them were wearing horse-riding
clothes. The dads had suit jackets and shirts tucked into
their jeans. And there were pedigree dogs everywhere – the
ones that cost ten-times more than normal dogs, but get
health problems.

Me and John Boy were a bit out of place in our sports
gear. You could see everyone looking. So we tried to look
confident, giving it swagger.

We got to the park a bit early, and I was well nervous. So
John Boy said we should play spies.

Usually, spies is a fun game, but it's not good when you're nervous, Mr Lamb. Because it makes you quite jumpy.

John Boy shot off like a one-legged rocket, and after a few minutes, I couldn't see him anywhere. So I hid behind the bandstand, holding a pretend gun.

That's when I felt this tap on my shoulder.

I screamed my head off, Mr Lamb. Talk about embarrassing. Especially when I saw who was tapping me.

Guess who it was?

TWELVE

Callum Duffy interview transcript:
Continued ...

I'll give you a clue about who was standing behind me, Mr Lamb.

It was Angel Rain. She looked just right for DeMontford Park in these frilly, white socks and a dress with spatulas and whisks all over it. And a lady's handbag that looked like a watermelon. Her hair was all brushed and wavy and her fringe was dead neat and straight.

It was so nice to see her.

When I finally stopped screaming, I asked Angel Rain how she was feeling. She said she was quite well.

'But I do have a lot of school work to do,' she said. 'I am very behind. Who is that man in the tree?'

I looked to where John Boy was climbing down a big oak tree with his false leg.

'That's my grown-up cousin, John Boy,' I said. 'He

brought me to the park. We're playing spies. Are your mum and dad around? I should say hello.'

Angel Rain said her mum and dad were very sorry, but they couldn't come. Because her dad was writing a speech for an insurance dinner and her mum had too much cleaning to do.

'And also, my twin brothers are being very difficult this morning,' said Angel Rain.

'You have twin brothers?' I asked. 'That's epic.'

'It's okay, sometimes,' said Angel Rain. 'But they can be quite troublesome. Usually, our old pear looks after them, but she is too tired today.'

'What's an old pear?' I asked.

Angel Rain said an old pear was a French girl who looked after children.

'A bit like a nanny,' said Angel Rain. 'Only they are quite young, so you don't have to pay them very much. My old pear is called Elodie. You'll meet her soon, when we have ice cream.'

'Shall we go and look at the marigolds first?' I asked. 'There are some amazing ones by the west gate. They're a really good colour.'

Angel Rain said, 'Are marigolds flowers?'

'Yes,' I said. 'They're really good summer flowers. Insects like them. Which is important, because insects are good for the garden. I know quite a lot about gardening, because Granddad teaches me things, even when I don't want to listen. You should see these marigolds. They're a brilliant colour.'

Angel Rain looked serious and said she had to stay where a parent or carer could see her. And Elodie was watching from the cafe.

'Do you want to have ice cream now, then?' I asked

'All right,' said Angel Rain. 'Since we are both early birds, let's have ice cream early. Tweet tweet!' Then she did her nice, big, gappy smile.

While we were smiling at each other, John Boy came over and said, 'You must be Angel Rain. Good to meet you.' Then he turned to me and said, 'Callum, mate. You could have told me we'd stopped playing spies. I was in that tree for ten minutes. If you think it's hard getting up a tree with one leg, try getting down again when that one leg has gone numb.'

Angel Rain giggled when John Boy said that. And I was glad. Some people are scared of my cousin, because of his false leg and tattoos and that. But Angel Rain wasn't scared of cousin John Boy. She saw his heart straight away.

'So what's the plan?' asked John Boy.

'We're going to get ice cream now,' I said.

'Should I come with you?' asked John Boy. 'Or shall I make myself scarce?'

'You should come and talk to Elodie,' said Angel Rain. 'She wants to practise her English. It will be good for her to have an adult to talk to.'

So off we all went.

When we got to the cafe, Angel Rain pointed to this skinny, pale girl by the window and said, 'That's Elodie.'

Elodie had big, frightened rabbit eyes and held a cup of coffee like her life depended on it. She looked like a white t-shirt that had been through the wash too many times. When Elodie saw Angel Rain with us, she said, 'Angel Rain. Who are these men?'

Angel Rain said, 'This is Callum. The boy who helped me in hospital. We're buying him an ice cream.'

'But what about that man?' said Elodie, pointing at John Boy.

John Boy held out his hand and said, 'All right? I'm John Boy. Callum's cousin, carer and chauffeur. Nice to meet you.'

Elodie stared at cousin John Boy, but she didn't shake his hand. So John Boy pulled out his wallet and asked what ice cream everyone wanted.

'No,' said Elodie, looking even more worried. 'I must buy the ice cream. I must do as Angel Rain's father says. Otherwise, he will be angry.' And she took five pounds out of an old lady purse and said: 'Go and choose your ice cream, children. With one sauce and one topping.'

'You hold onto that fiver,' said John Boy. 'And tell Angel Rain's dad that I'm paying because I'm a gentleman. And if he has a problem with that, he can come and talk to me.'

Elodie gave a little smile then, and she didn't seem so scared of John Boy after that.

John Boy gave me ten quid and told me to buy Angel Rain as many toppings and sauces as she wanted. Then he bought Elodie another black coffee and himself a milky tea, and pretty soon he and Elodie were chatting away. John Boy was even doing a bit of French, saying 'bonjour' and 'merci'.

That's the break bell, Mr Lamb. No need to worry.

I'll be back soon.

Alright?

THIRTEEN

Callum Duffy interview transcript: *Tuesday October 1st, 11.02 am*

What did you do at break time, Mr Lamb? You didn't sit in here on your own, did you? I hope not.

Anyway, I'll get back to the story.

I was telling you about ice cream, wasn't I? Angel Rain took AGES choosing her ice cream. It was so funny. Like it was the biggest decision she'd ever made. And do you know what she ended up with?

Vanilla. With no sauce or topping.

I said to her, you can have vanilla any time. But look, they've got Reese's Peanut Butter Cup flavour and New York Cheesecake here. Why not try something a bit more exciting?

But Angel Rain was happy with her choice. She said she knew what she was getting and didn't want to make a mistake.

I got a mixture of Reese's Peanut Butter Cup, Oreo and

Biscoff all mixed up into one scoop, with butterscotch sauce and popping candy toppings.

Angel Rain laughed and laughed at my order. Then she gave me a big smile and said, 'Callum, you are SO much fun.'

And I got the feeling that just having ice cream with a friend was quite a big deal for Angel Rain.

Once we'd finished our ice creams, I asked Angel Rain if she wanted to play by the nature area at the back of the play park. Because it had a pond and there might be frogs.

'You like frogs, don't you?' I said.

Angel Rain clapped her hands, really excited, and said, 'Yes, yes, I LOVE frogs.'

But Elodie wasn't happy.

'It sounds dangerous, Angel Rain,' said Elodie. 'Your father won't like it.'

Angel Rain crossed her arms and said she was allowed to do anything a normal child could do. And she'd never seen a frog in real life and this could be her chance.

'You've never seen a real frog?' I asked. 'Ever?'

'No,' said Angel Rain. 'I wanted to see the reptile house when we went to the zoo, but Mum didn't like the smell so we had to leave.'

'I suppose you don't get many frogs in town,' I said. 'We see loads in the countryside. Half the time they're squashed flat on the road, but we do see living ones too.'

In the end, Angel Rain was allowed to go to the nature area as long as she stayed in sight of the cafe.

'And do not go near the water, Angel Rain,' said Elodie. 'Or my life won't be worth living.'

When we got to the nature area, Angel Rain was so excited. She couldn't stop talking about frogs.

I said, 'We have to be still and quiet. Otherwise, the

frogs will be scared and won't come out.' And I told Angel Rain about hiding in the grass and looking for frog eyes in the water. But Angel Rain wasn't good at being still, because she said the grass was itchy. So we gave up on seeing frogs and went to the play park instead.

On the way to the play park, I told Angel Rain about my tadpoles.

'You should come to my pub and see them,' I said. 'Hopefully, a few of them will be frogs soon.'

'I don't think your tadpoles will turn into frogs,' said Angel Rain. 'Because it's already summer and they should have metamorphosised by now. You might just have to accept them for what they are.' Then she looked at her frilly socks and said, 'I might not metamorphosise either. It's hard to grow when your heart isn't working so well.'

'Of course you'll grow, Angel Rain,' I said. 'All kids grow. That's the way it works. And you've got a new heart now, haven't you?'

'I have a new heart, but I'll still be on medicine for the rest of my life,' said Angel Rain. 'And we're still not sure if my body is liking this new heart. The doctors are keeping an eye on me.'

'You'll be okay,' I said. 'You're worrying. I do that sometimes.'

Angel Rain nodded, but she was still looking at her socks.

'So when do you want to come and see my tadpoles, then?' I asked.

'I don't think I'll be allowed around your house, Callum,' said Angel Rain. 'Because I have to be very careful about germs.'

'But our pub is really clean,' I said. 'It wins the Little Mop award for the cleanest bar area every year. My cousin

John Boy was in the army, so he likes things to be spic and span. He's got cleaning products to clean cleaning products. Bring your parents and brothers along. Make it a family day out. Our pub is brilliant for families. We have swings in the garden and trees and all sorts. There's less for adults to do. They usually just drink beer, but they never seem to mind it.'

Angel Rain said she'd ask her dad, but he'd probably say no.

'My dad has trust issues,' she said.

'We'll work something out,' I said. 'Maybe I can come to yours instead.'

And Angel Rain said, 'Maybe.'

After that, I asked if Angel Rain fancied going on the slide. But she said she'd better not. Because of her heart.

'The doctors say I can do anything a normal child can do,' she said. 'But my dad doesn't like me going on scary things.'

So we sat on the springy animals in the park and played the genie game instead. The one where you get three wishes for your whole life, but only three. And you can't wish for more wishes, because that's cheating.

I went big with my wishes. I said I wanted be a formula one race car driver, a premiership footballer and to see the real Santa Claus. And that last one is a clever workaround to the three wishes rule, because you can ask Santa Claus for more wishes.

'I've seen the real Santa Claus,' said Angel Rain. 'He came to the hospital when I was there on Christmas Day.'

I was dead impressed.

'Wow,' I said. 'What was he like?'

'Fat,' said Angel Rain. 'And he smelt like Dettol. He didn't stay long. Hospitals aren't very nice places to be at

Christmas. All the doctors and nurses want to be home with their families. The nurses did cheer up in the evening, though, because a doctor gave them Bailey's Irish Cream. And they raced each other down the corridor on hospital gurneys.'

Then Angel Rain told me her three life wishes, which were:

To see a real frog
  To see a shooting star
  To go skiing

'Remember these wishes are for your whole life,' I told her. 'Are you sure you don't want to be a pop star or something? Because then you'll earn lots of money and you can buy frogs and skis and save the other two wishes for something better.'

Angel Rain said she was fine with her wishes the way they were.

'I get it,' I said.' You're using your shooting star to get another wish, right? Like my Santa Claus workaround?'

But Angel Rain said no. She didn't want another wish. She just wanted to see a shooting star, because she never had. And she thought they sounded very magical.

'They're alright,' I said. 'A bit overrated, to be honest.'

'Have you seen one?' Angel Rain asked. 'A real one?'

'Yeah,' I said. 'At the nature reserve. If you go on meteor shower nights, you see loads of shooting stars. I've seen a real frog, too. I've never been skiing, but I'm sure I will one day. These are really easy wishes, Angel Rain. Why don't you go bigger?'

'Those wishes might be easy for you,' said Angel Rain. 'But not for me. If I saw a real frog, I would be the happiest girl in the world.'

'I'll make it happen for you, Angel Rain,' I said. 'My tadpoles will turn into frogs soon. You'll see.'

Then Elodie came out of the cafe and said it was time to go home.

Angel Rain said, 'Callum, I think I know a way we can see each other again. Why don't you come to my house for a meal? My parents don't like playdates. But they do like meals.'

I felt a bit scared by that invitation. Because a meal is quite full on, isn't it? Especially at a fancy DeMontford Park house. So I said, 'Your parents don't have to go to the trouble of doing a meal. We can just have a playdate.'

But Angel Rain said her parents liked to have meals with people when they first met them, because it gave him a lot of time to get to know them.

'All right,' I said. 'A meal, then. What's your mobile number?'

'I don't have a mobile phone,' said Angel Rain. 'I'm too young. Mobile phones are more addictive than cigarettes.'

'Well, I don't know about phones being addictive,' I said. 'But I can't live without mine. How are we going to set up this lunch if you don't have a phone?'

'We can write to each other again,' said Angel Rain. 'I like getting letters. Don't you?'

Well, truthfully, I did like getting letters. That letter from Angel Rain was the best surprise ever. A thousand times better than a text message.

But writing another letter filled me with terror. The first one had been hard enough. How was I going to keep up the handwriting and the spelling and the full stops all over again? It took me ages last time.

'I'll write to you when I get a date from my parents for the meal,' said Angel Rain. 'And then you can write back and tell me if you can come.'

I told Angel Rain she was a total genius, writing letters the way she did.

'Everyone says that,' said Angel Rain. 'But I've never seen a frog in real life, like you have.'

And I decided there and then that I would make Angel Rain's frog wish come true. And if at all possible, I would make her other wishes come true as well. Because all she wanted was to go skiing and see frogs and shooting stars. And that's not a lot to ask for in life.

Angel Rain had to go after that.

And I have to go too, Mr Lamb. Can you see all the kids lined up outside? That's our monthly mile. We have to run around the school in our normal shoes, which kills your feet. All the other kids complain, but I just get on with it, and that's why I always come first. Sometimes, I'm so far ahead that I run the last lap backwards, just to make it interesting.

And FYI – Francois ALWAYS pretends he's done more laps and never does the full mile. And he's been made Head Boy now because he's good at maths and English. Which just goes to show. You don't have to be a decent person to do well at school.

That's messed up when you think about it.

After the monthly mile, it will be lunch time. But I'll come back and see you after that.

Alright?

FOURTEEN

Callum Duffy interview transcript: *Tuesday 1st October, 1.31pm*

The monthly mile was good, Mr Lamb. Thanks for asking. And that is a good ice breaker question, by the way. You're learning. And I won the monthly mile, in case you're wondering. Like I always do. It's not supposed to be a race. But when you put a load of kids together and tell them there's a finish line, it always turns into a race, doesn't it?

Anyway.

After me and Angel Rain met in the park, I went home and waited for her letter.

Over that weekend, four more of my tadpoles died. Baron, Bellatrix, Venom and my second-biggest tadpole, Killer. So I was really sad at breakfast on Monday. I couldn't even finish my potato waffles with smoked salmon, which Nana had made specially.

Then the post came.

Nana shouted upstairs, 'This will cheer you up, Callum. There's a letter from your friend. You go bury those tadpoles and I'll help you read it.'

I don't think I've ever buried tadpoles so fast, Mr Lamb. I stuck them in the garden, said a two-second blessing and ran back into the house to open my letter.

This is what Angel Rain wrote:

Dear Callum,

I had such a nice time with you in the park. I am still smiling when I think about all your ice creams mixed together. You are so funny!

I asked my parents if we could have a meal with you and your parents. They said yes!

We would like to invite you to our house for Saturday brunch on the 11th of August.

I hope you can come.

Yours sincerely,

Angel Rain Grace Christina Pegg

Please RSVP

I was nervous after reading that letter, Mr Lamb. Because I had no idea what a brunch was. And I didn't have parents, only one parent and three-to-four carers. And also, I was worried about writing back and showing myself up as someone who couldn't spell or write properly.

There was no one who could help me write a letter, either.

Granddad had gone to pick up the cider order. Mum is dyslexic and John Boy failed his GCSEs because his handwriting was so bad. And don't even get me started on Nana. She thinks spellings are fascist and won't be told how to write words by 'the man'.

So I was on my own.

This is what I wrote back:

Dear Angel Rain I would like that from Callum.

I thought the best idea was just to keep things simple and go with words I knew. But I still had to write the letter three times because I made mistakes.

I did add my address and Angel Rain's address and the date and that. And a big signature at the bottom to try and make the letter look longer. But it was still pretty short.

After I posted the letter, I downloaded an app called, 'Word of the Day for Kids', to help me out in the future. I've learned loads of words from that app now, and it has helped me. So I left a five-star review because you should always do that to show your thanks.

Luckily, Mum didn't have any exams that Saturday, so she could take me to Angel Rain's house. I am a lucky man, Mr Lamb. Just watch me rolling dice. After twenty or so tries, I always get a double six.

On the Saturday morning before the brunch, I was nervous. First of all, I didn't know what a brunch was. Mum said it was like a second breakfast, but did that mean I should have a first breakfast? Or what?

No one knew.

So I had a bowl of cornflakes and two bits of toast and jam, just in case. Then Nana did me beans, bacon and five

McCain's hash browns because she was worried about me not eating until gone 11am.

After the cooked breakfast, I had to work out what to wear.

I thought about my Arsenal bruised bananas shirt, which is like the one worn by Ian Wright in his 1991 football debut against Leicester. John Boy got me that shirt, and he says it's the best football shirt ever made. But Angel Rain's family didn't seem like people who would appreciate sports clothes.

So I tried on the suit I wore to Aunty Julesy's wedding. It was an awesome white suit with a black shirt, and I looked the business. But kids grow up so fast, Mr Lamb. Don't they? And the suit didn't fit anymore. So in the end, I chose my school shirt, school trousers and school shoes. It was a bit lame, but I was trying to be smart for Angel Rain's family, you know? Make a good impression.

Mum took one look at me and said, 'Why are you wearing your school uniform?'

So I said, 'All right, I'll change if it looks bad.' But Mum said we needed to leave now or we'd be late. Then SHE took ages getting ready and used a hairdryer AND straighteners.

I kept saying, 'Mum, you are well pretty. You don't need to do all that work.' But Mum cannot leave the house without drawing her eyebrows on and clipping in armloads of fake hair, Mr Lamb. That's just how she is.

When we got to DeMontford Park, we had parking trouble. Because Mum can't park between two cars. So we had to drive around for ages, looking for a big enough space.

To be honest, none of my family thinks Mum should have passed her driving test. But Mum's driving test person got his contact lens folded over in his eye on test day and didn't notice she reverse parked half a metre from the curb.

This iPad is doing something again, Mr Lamb. You've got all these notifications going, see? Let me turn them off for you. I'll carry on, shall I?

FIFTEEN

Callum Duffy interview transcript:
Continued ...

Alright, I'll carry on then.

I was bricking it, being on Angel Rain's posh street, Mr Lamb. It was a proper suit and shiny shoes sort of place. And I knew my school uniform didn't cut it.

After me and Mum found a parking spot, we walked up and down DeMontford Park Road looking for Angel Rain's house. Me and Mum had a bit of a row doing that, because Mum had high heel boots and couldn't walk very fast. Then we saw Angel Rain and her parents waiting outside one of the houses.

I hoped they hadn't heard me and Mum arguing. But they probably had, because they looked a bit stiff and awkward like they were standing for a photo.

Angel Rain's house wasn't as big as some of the other houses on DeMontford Park Road. But it was very tall and new, like someone had scrubbed the bricks clean. And there was a double driveway with three shiny cars on it – a BMW SUV, a BMW sedan and a Mini Clubman Sport.

Even though the house wasn't that big, there were pillars by the front door. And also two stone statues that looked like permed dogs. And a security camera.

Angel Rain had on this sailor dress, which I thought looked really nice.

'Callum,' said Angel Rain, and she crossed her arms. 'You are twelve minutes late.'

Then I heard a whirring sound. And this drone came flying towards Angel Rain's house.

'What the hell is that?' said Mum.

'That's Dad's drone,' said Angel Rain. 'He was using it to look for you.'

Angel Rain's dad made the drone land at his feet with a remote control. He was still dead grumpy looking. Like a short, angry barrel in a rugby shirt, with elf ears and a bald head.

Angel Rain's mum said, 'Gus was worried you had got lost.' And she had a nice Spanish voice, like a Bond girl. She was as pretty as a Bond girl too, with shiny black hair and white teeth. But there were loads of worry lines across her head, like guitar strings.

Angel Rain's dad said, 'Welcome to the Acorns. I'm Gus. This is my wife, Luciana.'

'Sorry we're late,' I said. 'We had a bit of parking trouble.'

I didn't grass Mum up about the hair straighteners.

'It can be hard to park around here,' said Luciana. 'In Spain, there is room for big cars. But here, the spaces are so small.'

You could see Luciana was trying to smile, but not quite managing it. And she had one of those really expensive

handbags on her arm. The ones with stars and flowers and
'Vs' all over it. Which was a bit weird, because she wasn't
going anywhere.

'There're always a few spaces at the top, though,'
said Gus.

'They weren't big enough,' said Mum. 'I need loads of
space to park.'

'Do you have one of the new SUVs, then?' said Gus.
'The Lexus or the Mercedes? I've seen women struggle with
those sometimes.'

'No, I have a Kia,' said Mum.

'What kind of Kia?' Angel Rain's dad asked.

'A small, pink one,' said Mum.

Gus frowned. Then he said, 'Where are Callum's
parents? Are they on their way?'

'I'm his parent,' said Mum.

'You're his parent?' said Gus, and he looked surprised.

'Do I look too young to be a parent, then?' Mum asked.
Because she likes to get straight to the point.

Gus said, 'I ... well, no. There was another lady with
Callum at the hospital. Who was she?'

'My big sister, Julesy,' said Mum. 'She's a single mum
like me, so we both help each other where we can.'

'Both of you are single mothers?' said Gus.

'That's right,' said Mum. 'And don't worry. You're not
the first person to think I'm not Callum's mum. Half the
time, people think I'm his big sister. And the last time I came
into school, the office thought I was the new dinner lady and
asked me to unpack a load of jelly pots. I'd done two box
loads before they cottoned on. And I got a telling off about
my tongue piercing. Anyway. I'm Brandi. Nice to meet you
both.'

Gus said, 'Branday?'

'Brandee,' said Mum. 'Like the drink.'

'Shall we go inside?' said Luciana. 'And Callum. We are so grateful for your help at the hospital. We hope this meal goes some way to showing our thanks.'

'And we can get to know you, too,' said Gus. 'This young man Angel Rain has taken a shine to. It's always good to get to know your children's friends, isn't it?' And he looked at Mum, all serious.

'Depends on the friends,' said Mum. 'Some of Callum's mates do my head in.'

And Luciana laughed, but Gus didn't.

'This is a nice house,' I said. 'Those stone dogs are brilliant.'

'They're lions,' said Gus. 'English lions. Guarding our castle and keeping out unwanted visitors.'

'I wouldn't have thought you'd get many unwanted visitors around here,' said Mum. 'It's a well nice area.'

'Crime is everywhere,' said Gus. 'In my line of work, I see more than most.'

'Are you a policeman, then?' asked Mum. 'I should have guessed by the shoes.'

'No,' said Gus. 'I work in insurance fraud. You see the worst of people in that job. One in two people lie on their insurance policies. One in two.'

I thought I'd better lighten the mood, so I asked Gus what football team he liked. But he said Chelsea, so that fell a bit flat.

Then Gus said, 'We're quite old-fashioned here, Callum. And I do like Angel Rain's friends to call me sir.'

'Sorry, Sir Gus,' I said.

Luciana gave me a kind smile and said, 'Shall we go inside?'

Inside Angel Rain's house, it was really neat and tidy

and smelt like Febreze Cotton Fresh air freshener. The
hallway looked like an advert for weddings. There were
loads of pictures of Gus and Luciana in wedding clothes,
and one big canvas of them cutting a wedding cake.

There were a few pictures of the whole family too –
Gus, Luciana, Angel Rain and the twin boys. They were
proper portraits, like the ones we have done at school. So the
family all had tight smiles and didn't look very comfortable.
You could tell the two boys were trying to make a run for it,
but Gus had his hand tight on their shoulders.

The second we stepped inside the house, Gus said,
'Shoes off! Luciana likes shoes off indoors.' In this policeman
voice. And he and Luciana and Angel Rain all took their
shoes off.

Me and Mum sat on the stairs and took our shoes off too.
Only Mum was wearing long boots and it took ages to get
those off. Mum made these 'ARG!' noises and asked me to
help pull.

Once we'd put our shoes on the rack, Gus started
moving the shoes around, sort of tidying them up.

'This is his OCD,' said Luciana. 'He likes things to be in
their right place.'

'Nothing wrong with things being in the right place,'
said Gus. 'It's chaos, otherwise.'

'God, don't ever come round our house,' said Brandi.
'There are shoes all over the place. And none of them are in
pairs. It's well messy.'

Gus's lips went all thin and white. 'Why wouldn't you
keep your shoes in pairs?' he said.

But Mum didn't have to answer that, because Angel
Rain's twin brothers came bundling downstairs then.

The twins had big mops of curly, black hair, and wore
suits and waistcoats, like little lords. But they weren't acting

like lords. More like little lunatics, running around the hall and going 'AAAAAAAAARGH!'

Gus shouted, 'Boys! We have guests. For God's sake! Can't you be quiet for five minutes? Elodie? Elodie!'

Then Elodie ran downstairs after the boys, all skinny and worried. 'Ferdinand!' she shouted. 'Felipe! Stop, stop! I have begged you to stop!'

But Luciana said, 'It's okay, Elodie. We are having brunch now. You can have some free time.'

'We're not having the boys at the table, are we?' said Gus. 'I was thinking Elodie could take them out.'

But it was too late. Elodie had already shot out of the front door. She didn't take a bag or coat or anything.

So we all went into the dining room for our meal – me, Mum, Angel Rain, Gus, Luciana and the two boys, Ferdinand and Felipe.

I think we'll have to leave it there, Mr Lamb. Look – Mr Harvey is at the door with some parent-teacher people. They'll want this room to be private so they can talk about Mr Blowers behind his back. You can't argue with them and say you won't listen. Trust me, I've tried. And it's nearly time for the bell, anyway.

But did Miss Hussain tell you the good news? You can come tomorrow, if you like. Because there's a school trip and me and Dexter aren't allowed to go due to past bad behaviour.

So maybe I'll see you then?

SIXTEEN

Michael Lamb

I have decided to see Callum tomorrow. It is an additional interview day, but the more days we spend together, the more likely I am to get the data I need.

It is a source of frustration that Callum has shown himself to be very respectful towards women so far. But I'm sure, in time, I will uncover signs of toxic masculinity.

To further facilitate rapid data collection, I rode home through DeMontford Park. I wanted to gather information about the park and its surroundings, and cross reference these with Callum's recollections. It's important to verify geographical facts where possible to check the accuracy of a subject's memory (Boggis et al.)

When I reached the park cafe, I got off my bicycle and observed my surroundings, while autumn leaves danced and skipped.

A young couple were on a nearby bench, feeding

squirrels from a share-sized packet of Dorito Cool Original chips. One bold squirrel bounded close to the couple, making the girl screech with hilarious shock.

Ifeoma and I used to feed wildlife, I remembered. Except we fed swans, rather than squirrels. Ifeoma had a thing about swans. 'Royal birds', she called them, despite it being common knowledge that swans can break a person's arm.

As I watched the couple, I realised I'd never bought Ifeoma an ice cream from the park cafe. I had no idea why not, because she would have enjoyed the experience. Like Callum, Ifeoma would have chosen some wild, chaotic concoction of flavours. Whereas I would have opted for vanilla.

It was another regret to add to the pile.

While I considered ice cream flavours, it started to rain. The couple found this hilarious, but I didn't. So I cycled home.

As I hung my wet things in the utility room, I remembered Callum's 'Hug in a Mug' taking up unnecessary space in my bag. The charity collection people wouldn't come until next week, so I decided to put the mug in the kitchen cupboard. Then I thought I may as well make a cup of tea in it, since I was by the kettle.

As I carried my tea up to the office, I had a sudden urge to turn the heating on.

Which was curious.

The cold hadn't bothered me since Ifeoma left. But as I warmed my hands around the mug I thought, yes, heat is needed.

Ifeoma liked the heating on full blast, sometimes even in September. And certainly by October. Former residents of

African countries do not, as a rule, enjoy the English cold. It was a regular source of conflict. Ifeoma would turn the heating on, citing health benefits. I would turn it off, also citing health benefits. But truthfully, neither of us had concrete data to back up our claims. I was emulating my mother, who had grown up with coal fires and a belief that central heating led to financial ruin. Ifeoma, on the other hand, just liked to feel warm.

As the heating came to life, I noticed things around the house that hadn't previously caught my attention. The dust. The cobwebs. The black dirt around the windows. Mould spotting the net curtains and creeping around the cornicing. I didn't have any thick, velvet curtains anymore because they'd all gone rotten last winter.

Suddenly, I was overcome with intense dissatisfaction. My house wasn't a good space. It was a hard, cold, unloved space and this was unacceptable.

I made a decision.

From now on, I would turn the heating on every day throughout autumn and winter. This would also solve the mould problem, which was getting out of control. And I would order a sofa. And curtains. But first and foremost, I would give the house a good clean.

Dusting led to polishing. The polishing led to hoovering. Hoovering led to scrubbing.

As afternoon turned to evening, I became a man possessed.

I scrubbed mould from the cornicing, polished all the woodwork and taps, vacuumed the bare floorboards and cleaned the windows. Then I marched to the Co-op, replenished my cleaning products, and continued.

By 9pm, I had a sparkling, pleasant-smelling home.

True, there are still mould spots on the net curtains. They were beyond cleaning. But the house felt fresher and lighter.

It's not good to sit in a cold, dusty, mouldy house.

I don't know why I didn't realise this before.

SEVENTEEN

Callum Duffy interview transcript: *Wednesday 3rd October, 9.07am*

I'm really glad you came today, Mr Lamb. It's good we got this extra time, isn't it? Because I do have a lot to tell you. And I'm not sorry about missing the school trip, either. It's only a museum.

I was telling you about brunch with Angel Rain, wasn't I? And how posh Angel Rain's house was. Although in some ways it wasn't that posh. Because it was quite small.

Don't get me wrong. I'm not doing it down. The dining table was massive and there was a chandelier hanging over it. But you could only just fit eight people around the table, and it was a squash.

I got the feeling Angel Rain's twin brothers didn't sit down much at the table. Because they were kicking each other and all sorts.

Gus shouted at them: 'Behave! Or no chausson aux pommes.' And for a few seconds, the boys stopped kicking each other and sat still. But pretty soon, they started up again.

Gus was all like rubbing his eyes and saying, 'These two are a nightmare at the table. We've had to get unbreakable glasses.' And he picked up one of the tumblers and thumped it on the table. 'Kids are just chaos,' he said. 'No matter how hard you try. We've turned the study into a playroom, but they still leave toys everywhere. Even with my ten-toy system.' Then he turned to Mum and said, 'So what do you do, Bran-day? Do you work?'

'I'm a full-time student,' said Mum. 'And I work in my parents' pub in the evenings.'

'What do you study?' Gus asked.

'Beauty therapy,' said Mum.

'Oh,' said Gus. 'Right.'

There was a long silence, then. Only broken by the sound of Angel Rain's twin brothers kicking each other under the table.

Seeing Felipe and Ferdinand being so crazy, I understood why I annoyed people at meal tables. And these days, I don't move around half so much when I'm eating. Which I think everyone appreciates.

Angel Rain was like, 'I'm sorry about my brothers. They are quite badly behaved.'

I told Angel Rain not to worry. In our family, there is always a blazing row at meal times. More often than not, about bags for life. And Granddad is right – 36 bags for life is too many to keep in the cupboard under the stairs. Nana should remember to take them shopping and stop buying new ones.

Before we had food, Luciana sprayed the table with disinfectant stuff and wiped it down.

'Is that because of Angel Rain?' Mum asked. 'Callum told me she had a heart condition.'

'No, Luciana just likes things to be clean,' said Gus. 'If we go to a restaurant, she cleans the cutlery before we eat.'

'That's a good trick, Luciana,' said Mum. 'You spoke without moving your lips.'

Luciana burst out laughing. Then she looked at Gus and stopped laughing.

'How many surgeries has Angel Rain had now?' Mum asked.

'Four,' said Gus. 'She's due another one soon, but it's just day surgery. That's a walk in the park for us.'

'What's the surgery for?' Mum asked.

'Stomach', said Gus. And he said it in a really short, sharp voice like he didn't want to say anything else.

Luciana brought out the food, then. It was nice, but she kept apologising for everything. Like, she said sorry the pastries weren't homemade. She'd bought them fresh that morning, and she'd checked they'd been made that day. But she really should learn to make them at home.

'Everything is from Waitrose,' said Gus. 'I wouldn't touch Tesco with a barge pole. Shoppers there commit more insurance fraud than at any other supermarket. You wouldn't believe the number of claims we get for break-ins in Tesco car parks. And 80% of them just happen to have a pair of Gucci sunglasses on the dashboard.'

After pastries, we had a really small English breakfast, like a dwarf breakfast, with a tiny bit of scrambled egg, one sausage, a really small potato cake, one massive mushroom and half a tomato.

Luciana was all apologetic again because she said the plates didn't all look the same. But to be honest, she should have said sorry about the flavour. Because the food didn't taste of much. You can get loads of flavour out of a mushroom if you cook it right. But you got the feeling the food was more for decoration.

'Why does it all need to look the same?' Mum asked.

'Luciana has high standards,' said Gus. 'She wants our home brunches to be as good as the Connaught brunch in London. We went there for a work do once and it was the best meal we ever had. Wasn't it Luciana? And Luciana's brunches are very nearly there. Four out of five, I'd say.'

Luciana seemed quite happy with her star rating and she gave Gus a nice smile. But let me tell you, Mr Lamb. If Granddad ever gave Nana four out of five stars for a meal, he'd get a smack around the head.

Then Luciana said sorry about the orange juice because she hadn't made it herself. But me and Mum were like, don't worry. We have Sunny Delight for breakfast. This is a hundred times better.

Along with all the fancy food, were these dry, green pumpkin-seed and bran muffins. They looked out of place, and it turned out Gus made the muffins himself for his cholesterol.

Gus didn't strike me as much of a baker and he wasn't. Because the muffins tasted as bad as they looked. But on the good side, I got to use two new words from my Word of the Day for Kids app:

Cloying and bland.

And I think Gus was impressed.

While we were eating, Mum asked Luciana how she and Gus met.

'I was staying with an English family,' said Luciana. 'For my placement year. And they took me to a wedding reception. That is where I met Gus.'

'I was there with another woman,' said Gus. 'But when I

saw Luciana, I fell head over heels. Love at first sight. A month later, Luciana gave up her studies and moved in with me. And six months after that, we had our wedding in Barbados.'

'It was a fairy tale,' said Luciana.

'Before the kids came along,' said Gus.

Luciana did a nervous laugh and said, 'Angel Rain's heart condition has been very, very hard. For Gus especially. He likes everything to be perfect.'

'Angel Rain is perfect,' Gus snapped.

'I'm not perfect,' said Angel Rain. 'My new heart isn't working properly.'

'Don't be ridiculous, Angel Rain,' said Gus. 'Your heart is doing just fine and you're going to live a very, very long time. You have your goals. You're marching into the future.'

Luciana was a bit kinder. She gave Angel Rain a nice smile and said, 'You mustn't worry, my darling. Your heart is a gift from god. We just have to get the medication right. That's all.'

Gus's face went all tight. Then he said, 'Where do you live, Branday? Angel Rain says you hail from Great Oakley. Lovely little place.'

'Yes, Great Oakley is alright,' Mum told Gus. 'Me and Callum live at my parents' pub. The Great Oakley Arms.'

'So you and Callum and your parents all live in the same house?' asked Gus. 'In a pub?'

'Yes,' said Mum. 'And my cousin John Boy lives there too.'

'Four adults?' said Gus.

'It can be a bit mad,' said Mum. 'But there's a lot of love.'

There was another awkward silence.

Then Gus said, 'Tell me about school, Callum. What are you reading?'

'*Pip and Pop in Space,*' I said.

Gus frowned and said, 'That sounds a little young.'

'I'm not allowed proper books yet,' I said. 'Because I'm on the slow reader table. And it's well boring.'

'You mean really boring,' said Gus.

'No,' I said. 'I mean well boring. Which means really, really boring.'

Angel Rain gave a little giggle then. And we shared a smile. Which felt epic.

'Well, you know what they say, Callum,' said Gus. 'Only boring people get bored.'

'No one's ever called me boring before, Sir Gus,' I said. 'Especially not at school. I'm the kid who mucks around. But everyone does on the purple table. Because we never do anything fun. The silver and gold tables do soda rockets and baking. And the blue table gets interesting craft projects. But all we get is the purple book box and word searches.'

'It sounds like you're not being pushed hard enough,' said Gus.

'You're right there,' I said. 'We're not being pushed at all. Mrs Bullard ignores us most of the time. And if Danny starts screaming, our whole table gets sent to the Calm Corner. We spend all day there sometimes.'

'Someone needs to talk to your school,' said Gus. 'When Angel Rain started at St Mary's, they tried to fob us off with the bottom set. They said she was behind because of her surgeries. But I was having none of it. I must have had twenty meetings with that school, and they cracked in the end and admitted their mistake. They agreed that Angel Rain was a brilliant child. Now she's in the top set and thriving. Why haven't you talked to the school, Branday?'

Mr Lamb, your iPad has a message from someone called Bethany Balls. Do you want me to reply for you?

EIGHTEEN

Callum Duffy interview transcript:
Continued ...

Alright, no problem. Shall we just carry on then?

Mum hadn't spoken to the school about my reading, Mr Lamb. Which I know sounds bad, but it's a cultural thing. Mum is dead scared of school. Because the teachers talk down to her and she feels stupid and can never say what she means.

Mum said to Gus, 'I did try to talk to Callum's teacher once. Because Callum was finding the work so boring. But teachers don't listen when you're a young mum. And they're probably right not to listen, to be honest. I don't know anything about reading and writing. I'm dyslexic.'

'You're dyslexic, are you?' said Gus. 'When did that come to light?'

'When I failed all my GCSEs,' said Mum. 'I was a high-performing dyslexic. I went under the radar.'

'What's a high-performing dyslexic when it's at home?' asked Gus.

'One who gets their older, cleverer sisters to do their homework for them,' said Mum.

'Is Callum dyslexic?' Gus asked.

'No,' said Mum. 'He's been tested for everything. ADHD. Autism. You name it. But there's nothing wrong with him they can put a label to.'

'Talk to the school,' said Gus. 'Push harder. If you don't, who will?'

'There's no point,' said Mum. 'The teachers all look down their noses at me, because I had a baby at sixteen. It's different for you, Gus. I bet no one ever mistook you for a dinner lady.'

'It sounds like you've given up,' said Gus.

'It's not giving up,' said Mum. 'I just know when I'm hitting my head against a brick wall.'

'Maybe you could read to Callum more at home,' said Luciana.

'I do try,' said Mum. 'Half the time he runs away. By the time school is finished, he's had enough and I don't blame him.'

'He's too old to be on picture books,' said Gus. 'Something should be done.'

'I'm just a slow learner,' I said. 'I'm not ready for older books yet. Mrs Bullard says so.' Then I wanted to change the subject because being a slow learner is embarrassing. So I said, 'Angel Rain. Tell me about this operation. Are you feeling okay?'

'I feel all right, Callum,' said Angel Rain. 'It's just a small surgery to take something out of my stomach.'

'What are they taking out?' Mum asked.

'A growth,' said Gus, in a stiff voice. Then he put down his knife and fork and looked at his plate.

'I'm sorry,' said Mum. 'Is it serious?'

'It's nothing, this surgery,' said Luciana. 'Angel Rain has had big, big surgeries. This is simple. They take out the thing and it's done.'

'Still,' said Mum. 'You always worry, don't you?'

'Always,' said Luciana. 'Every minute of every day.'

Mum and Luciana shared a nice smile, then. And you could see Luciana was all right, deep down.

Then Luciana brought out a Spanish cake called torta something, which was the best part of the meal. I enjoyed the cake, even though it wasn't as fancy as everything else. But Luciana kept apologising for what it looked like. And pretty soon, Ferdinand and Felipe started chucking bits of cake at each other, and Gus said, 'You two. Upstairs. Now.'

So the twins went upstairs.

'Can me and Callum go play in my room?' asked Angel Rain.

'Callum and I,' said Gus. 'And no. Not your bedroom. You can play in the garden where we can see you.'

'Let's go, Callum,' said Angel Rain. And she grabbed my hand and pulled me out of the dining room.

Angel Rain's garden was quite small. Just a long yard really, with a load of empty plant pots and some uncomfortable-looking garden chairs. There was one tiny square of grass, about the size of a sandpit. A robot mower was going over the grass again and again. It must have been so bored.

'What's with all these empty plant pots?' I asked Angel Rain.

'That's my dad,' said Angel Rain. 'All the plants died

and he never got new ones. He's supposed to be in charge of the garden, but he doesn't really like gardening.'

'Tell your dad to grow a bit of ivy up the fence,' I said. 'Ivy will do well in a shady garden like this and it doesn't need feeding or watering or anything. You'll get a nice, green covering and a few birds, hopefully.'

Angel Rain looked really serious then and said, 'Callum, I need you to start reading proper chapter books. The ones without pictures.'

'Mrs Bullard says I'm not ready for those books yet,' I said. 'I'm too thick.'

Angel Rain chewed her lip then, and said, 'It is quite important that you read chapter books, Callum. Otherwise, my dad won't let me see you again. He doesn't like me being friends with children who might hold me back.'

'I won't hold you back,' I said. 'Being thick isn't catching.'

'That's not how my dad sees it,' said Angel Rain. And she looked really serious.

That's the bell for break, Mr Lamb.

It's going to be a really weird break today, because most of my mates are on this school trip. And Dexter has his piano lesson on Wednesdays. So I'll have to make some more friends, but I quite like doing that.

See you in a bit.

NINETEEN

I had a good break, Mr Lamb. The year threes made me their leader, and I helped them do a football match. They're not so bad, those year threes. I'm not sure Mr Rafferty is the right teacher for them, though. They run rings around him.

Anyway. Where was I?

Angel Rain said her dad wouldn't let us see each other if I didn't start reading chapter books.

'Dad thinks it's important for me to be around other good readers,' Angel Rain said. 'He read an article about it. The right friends are important for reading skills.'

I'm not saying I agree with Gus's point of view, which is quite stuck up. But if reading meant I'd get to see Angel Rain more – well, I was up for it.

So I said to Angel Rain, 'Alright. I'm well up for it.'

Then I did a handstand.

Angel Rain was impressed.

So I did another handstand and walked around on my hands.

Angel Rain thought that was brilliant.

'I wish I could do that,' she said.

'You can,' I said. 'It's really easy. You just start against a wall and keep practising.'

'I'm too scared,' said Angel Rain. 'I know it's silly. The doctors say I can run around as much as I like. But Dad gets worried. Because my heart is still quite new.'

'When will you be allowed to do handstands, then?' I asked.

Angel Rain shrugged. 'Who knows? Maybe never.'

Then Mum came out and said it was time to go.

'Can't we have a little bit longer?' I asked. 'Just five more minutes.'

Mum said she loved me very much, but half an hour was a long time to answer questions about school.

We went inside and said thank you for the brunch and all of that. But Mum had her hand on my shoulder the whole time, pushing me towards the door.

As we were leaving, I said: 'Angel Rain. Do you want to come to my birthday party at the end of August? It'll be in our pub garden and we're getting Mr Bubble-tastic. And I reckon some of my tadpoles will have turned into frogs by then. So you'll get to see a real frog.'

Angel Rain made this squealing noise and clapped her hands together.

But Gus said, 'I'm not sure about parties. Angel Rain is studying for an important exam.'

'Oh Gus,' said Luciana. 'Can't she go to a birthday party? If it's outside, we don't need to worry so much about germs –'

'Her operation is coming up,' said Gus. 'And we've talked about friendship groups.'

And I knew then. Angel Rain was right. Gus didn't want his daughter being friends with a thicko picture-books kid. And I wouldn't be invited for brunch again. Not unless I got my head around chapter books.

Luciana gave me a nice smile and said, 'It was good to meet you. And thank you again for your help in the hospital.'

Gus shook both our hands like he was trying to pump up a bike. But he didn't smile or say 'see you again' or anything.

On the way back to the car, I told Mum I was going to get better at reading.

'Even if I'm bored stupid for the whole summer,' I said. 'I'm going to get better. And I'm going to get on the silver table at school. And show Angel Rain's dad that I am good enough for his daughter.'

Mum sighed and said, 'Maybe if you had two parents and one of them could spell, you'd find reading easier. But all you've got is me. A thick, dyslexic young mum.'

I put my arm around her and said, 'That's lucky, isn't it?'

Mum looked a bit teary and gave me a big smile. 'You're the best thing that ever happened to me,' she said. 'You know that, don't you?'

And I did know.

When we got back from brunch, Nana had a cold buffet out in the garden in case we hadn't liked the food at Angel Rain's house. She'd made pheasant sandwiches with Hellman's mayonnaise and filled a few bowls with pork scratchings.

It all looked very nice, but I told Nana I didn't have time for buffets.

'I need to do school stuff,' I said.

'What school stuff? Nana asked. 'It's the summer holidays.'

'Reading and that,' I said. 'So Angel Rain's dad will like me.'

'You should never change for other people,' said Mum. 'If they don't like you for who you are, they can jog on.' Then she went upstairs to do her gel nails and put more blonde extensions into her hair.

'Seriously, Nana,' I said. 'Angel Rain's dad was well funny with me. He wouldn't let Angel Rain come to my birthday party. I need to get better at reading. Like today.'

Granddad popped his head up from the beer cellar and said, 'Did I hear someone say they wanted to do some reading?'

'Yes, Granddad,' I said. 'I need proper, long books. Can I borrow your *Little Neddy* ones?'

Granddad got a tear in his eye.

'This is the happiest day of my life,' he said. 'I always hoped you'd come around to *Little Neddy* in the end.'

Nana looked a bit awkward then. 'I've got a confession to make, Bob,' she said. 'I got rid of those *Little Neddy* books. It was revenge. Plain and simple. Because you threw away my fondue sets. But I don't think those books are Callum's cup of tea anyway. They're very old-fashioned. And you get the feeling Little Neddy is a right little racist behind closed doors.'

Nana and Granddad had an argument after that.

Granddad said Little Neddy was not racist and loved all God's people.

'You're right Bob,' said Nana. 'Little Neddy can't be racist. There's not a single Black or Asian person in those books to be racist to.'

Granddad admitted that the *Little Neddy* stories

probably did need more colour.

'But he still teaches wonderful lessons about mending clothes and making jam,' said Granddad. 'And lasting all day on one slice of bread and butter.'

Then Granddad said, 'Callum, I am taking you to the village library. We shall find *Little Neddy* there. Grab your library card. We are leaving this minute.'

But I didn't have a library card because I wasn't a member.

So Granddad called Mum downstairs for a telling-off.

'I am part of the Save Our Village Library Group,' Granddad told Mum. 'And the Books for Tots Campaign. And the Old Boy's Book Brigade. Yet my own grandson isn't signed up to our local library.'

Mum said she had dyslexia and hated the library and got spat at once by a librarian for eating a Dairylea Dunker.

'That librarian died years ago,' said Granddad. 'And she didn't spit. She hissed at you. You're making excuses.'

'All right, I'll sign Callum up to the library,' said Mum.

'No, I will sign Callum up to the library,' said Granddad. 'We shall go together and find *Little Neddy* and his adventures. Can you imagine anything more exciting, Callum?'

I definitely could. Like Disneyland or a massive waffle extravaganza at Kaspa's dessert parlour, with twelve scoops of gelato on six Belgian waffles. But I didn't tell Granddad that, because he was helping me out.

So Granddad put on his floppy sunhat and sprayed suncream on his white arms, legs, face and beard. Then he tried to put sun cream on me too like he always does. But I don't need it, because I'm naturally tanned and dark-haired like my dad. So I never burn.

After that, we were on our way.

TWENTY

Callum Duffy interview transcript:
Continued ...

On the way to the library, Granddad kept saying what a special day it was and how he wished he'd brought his camera.

'I'm going to smash it at reading, Granddad,' I said. 'I don't care how hard it is or how much I hate it. I'm going to read as well as Francois on the gold table.'

Which was a bit ambitious, to be honest. But I was all fired up, like Rocky when he runs up the steps to do his training.

'That's not the right way to look at reading, Callum,' said Granddad. 'You're supposed to enjoy it. And with *Little Neddy* by your side, I'm sure you will.'

When we got to the town library, there was a girl behind the counter with blue hair. She didn't look up when we came in because she was typing on a laptop.

Granddad said in a proud voice, 'My grandson is here to join the library.'

The girl looked really tired and bored and told Granddad he could set up my account on the self-service computer.

'But what about his library card?' Granddad asked.

The girl said they'd run out of cards, but she could send him a digital one for his Apple Wallet.

'That's not acceptable,' said Granddad. 'Callum needs his own plastic card. So he can feel proud to be a member.'

The girl said they might get some new library cards soon, but she didn't know when.

'Well, maybe you could help us find a particularly special book,' said Granddad. 'We are looking for *Little Neddy.*'

'We don't do racist books anymore,' said the girl. 'They've been banned.'

'*Little Neddy* is not racist,' said Granddad. 'He's a children's classic.'

'Loads of children's classics are racist,' said the librarian. Then she told Granddad to check for *Little Neddy* himself on the self-serve computer.

Granddad said he wouldn't look up books himself on principle.

The girl asked what principle.

Granddad said on the principle that if there was a trained librarian in branch, then that librarian should get off her backside and help him find a book.

The girl said she wasn't a trained librarian yet, but a part-time student. And if she helped everyone who came into the library she wouldn't finish her essay, which was due in on Monday.

'No matter, Callum,' said Granddad. 'I will find you *Little Neddy*.'

But Granddad couldn't find the *Little Neddy* books or any of the other books he wanted like *William's Magic Farthing* or *the Splendid Book of Children's Bicycle Adventures*.

While Granddad was complaining, I saw Miss Hussain by the hobby shelf reading a book about cupcakes. She had sparkly sunglasses on her pink hijab and looked happy and rested.

'All right, Miss Hussain?' I said. 'You're looking well.'

Miss Hussain gave me her lovely smile with dimples and said, 'It's good to see you in the library, Callum. Are you finding some lovely books?'

'Not yet,' I said. 'Granddad is helping me. I need some proper, long books, Miss Hussain. Without pictures. I don't care how boring they are. I'm going to push on through.'

'Reading shouldn't be boring, Callum,' said Miss Hussain. 'I know Mrs Bullard has her targets and charts and book boxes. But reading really can be fun.'

'I don't think I'll ever like books, Miss Hussain,' I said. 'Because I'm a thick special-needs kid. But I'm pushing on through. Like Rocky. I've seen that movie eighteen times now.'

'You should stop calling yourself those names, Callum,' said Miss Hussain. 'They are not true. Come with me. We're not in Mrs Bullard's class now. You don't have to put up with the purple-table book box. We have a whole library to explore. Let's find some stories to enjoy.'

Miss Hussain went along the shelves and pulled out lots of books with fun covers. The sorts of books that the silver and gold tables get to read.

'I think you'll like *Diary of a Wimpy Kid*,' said Miss Hussain. 'My nephews love this series. It's very funny.'

Miss Hussain also gave me a *Scare Town* book and a book called *Monster Quest* with an evil bird on the front cover. I said the evil bird looked a lot like Mrs Bullard, and you could see Miss Hussain wanted to laugh. But she didn't.

'These look like good books, Miss Hussain,' I said. 'But I do feel a bit intimidated.' Which was a word from my Word of the Day for Kids app. 'Because Mrs Bullard would say these books are too hard for me.'

'Well, that's where Mrs Bullard and I don't see eye to eye,' said Miss Hussain. 'I think you should be allowed to give anything a try.' Then she thought for a minute and said, 'Do you know what might help you, Callum? The library does free audiobooks these days. You might enjoy listening to a story while you're reading along. And even if you don't read the whole time, listening to stories is still very good for reading skills. You get all those lovely words.'

'How can I listen to stories?' I asked.

'You can download library audio books on your phone,' said Miss Hussain. 'I'm sure you have your phone with you, don't you? You usually do. I hope it's on silent though, Callum. This is a library.'

After I put my phone on silent, Miss Hussain helped me download a library book called *George's Marvellous Medicine*. And then Miss Hussain found me the paperback of *George's Marvellous Medicine* too, so I could read along at the same time.

'This is brilliant, Miss Hussain,' I said. 'I'm going to get good at reading over the summer holidays. And handwriting. I've decided.'

'What's brought all this on, Callum?' asked Miss Hussain.

'I've made a new friend called Angel Rain,' I said. 'I really like her, but she's too good for me. And her dad won't let me see her until I get better at reading.'

'No one is too good for you, Callum,' said Miss Hussain. 'You're a lovely little boy with a big heart.'

'This girl is too good for me, though,' I said. 'She lives by DeMontford Park. I had to go round there in my school uniform because I didn't have anything smart enough to wear.'

'Well, I'll tell you what,' said Miss Hussain. 'My sister is a bit of a shopaholic. My nephews have piles of fancy clothes they've never worn and have grown out of. What if I drop a few bags around the pub this evening? Then when you see this girl again, you'll have a whole smart wardrobe to choose from.'

'You can't do that, Miss Hussain,' I said. 'You should sell the clothes and put the money towards your wedding.'

'Oh, I don't have time for selling clothes,' said Miss Hussain. 'I'm too busy making table decorations. Think of this as an early birthday present. You've got a birthday coming up, haven't you?'

'Next week,' I said. 'Thank you, Miss Hussain. You are epic.' And I gave her a big hug. Which she said was allowed, because we weren't at school.

After that, Miss Hussain had to go. Because she was doing wedding cake tasting with her fiancé.

'I'm spending the afternoon eating cake with the man of my dreams,' she said. 'I'm the luckiest girl in the world.' Then she gave me her nice, dimply smile again and said, 'If you need any help in the holidays with your reading, you know my email address, don't you?'

'Thank you, Miss Hussain,' I said. 'But the holidays are

your free time to do your wedding. You're not paid in the holidays. I don't want to bother you.'

'Don't be silly, Callum,' said Miss Hussain. 'What a sad world it would be if we only helped other people when we were paid to do it.'

When Miss Hussain left, I showed Granddad the books Miss Hussain had given me. Granddad wasn't sure about them, because he said they looked American. But he also said I could take them out if I wanted, because part of the fun of reading was choosing my own books. And his parents hadn't been especially keen on *Little Neddy*, because Little Neddy wore a colourful neckerchief, which they said was sinful. So maybe he needed to get with the times.

Which was definitely true.

When we got home, I started reading *Diary of a Wimpy Kid.*

I couldn't read every single word, but Granddad said that was all right.

'Just guess at the words you don't know,' said Granddad. 'As long as it makes sense, you're reading.'

Which was a new one for me, because Mrs Bullard says you have to know every single word in a book before it is proper reading.

And guess what? *Diary of a Wimpy Kid* is a well funny book. I read a bit to my tadpoles, and they were all laughing away. It was so much better than *Gran is Bad*.

I stopped reading at tea time because I didn't want to overdo things. And after tea, Miss Hussain came round with two recycling bags of clothes.

'Happy early birthday, Callum,' she said. 'These are from my nephews, with love.'

I was so grateful. I told Miss Hussain she was the best

teaching assistant in the world, and I would buy her two boxes of Matchmaker chocolates at the end of next term. And I'd ask Nana to sort her out with a free Folkingtons's Rose Lemonade next time she came into the pub and an alcohol-free Becks for her fiancé. Because I know that's what they like.

Mum kept saying, 'Please let me give you some money, Miss Hussain. This is so kind.'

But Miss Hussain wouldn't hear of it. She said it was her pleasure.

'Your mum has been such a help with my wedding, Brandi,' said Miss Hussain. 'Getting me all those things from the cash and carry. I wouldn't dream of taking payment.'

Then she pulled some handwriting sheets from her Chanel bag and said, 'These are for you too, Callum. Because you want to get better at handwriting. And I know which letters you find a bit tricky, so I thought these sheets would help.'

I was blown away.

'These are brilliant, Miss Hussain,' I said. 'Thank you so much.'

And the handwriting sheets really were good. I did a few of them that evening, and I could feel my writing getting better.

It made me wonder why Mrs Bullard had never given me those sheets. But I knew why, really. Because Mrs Bullard isn't bothered about the purple-table kids.

After I'd done the handwriting sheets, I tried on the new clothes. They were well smart. Miss Hussain's sister had bought her kids designer stuff from Gap and Marks and Spencer. All in mint condition. I got some nice outfit combos together with jeans and trainers and I felt the business.

Don't get me wrong. I still loved my tracksuits and football shirts. But it was nice to have something smart to wear for my birthday party, which was coming up.

Anyway, that's the lunch bell.

Oh my god. Don't turn around Mr Lamb, whatever you do.

TWENTY-ONE

Michael Lamb

It was a shock. A terrible shock.

There was a boy at the window wearing Bart Simpson underwear, with his bottom pressed right up against the glass.

Callum didn't seem concerned, though. Nor did Miss Hussain, who marched up to the window and shouted, 'Stop that Dexter. No one likes it.'

The boy, Dexter, ran off then.

'That boy is extremely badly behaved,' I said.

'He's alright, Mr Lamb,' said Callum. 'I'd better meet him in the lunch hall or he'll do it again. See you later. Alright?'

And off Callum went.

'Are you coming to the staff room today, Mr Lamb?' asked Miss Hussain.

For a moment, I considered it. Then I thought of all the unfamiliar faces and decided best not.

'No thank you,' I replied. 'I need to order a sofa.'

'What sort of sofa?' asked Miss Hussain.

'I'm not sure,' I said.

'Well, what sort of house do you have?' Miss Hussain asked.

'Does it matter?' I asked.

'Of course,' said Miss Hussain. 'You want to match your furniture to your style of home, don't you?'

'I have a large, Victorian house,' I said.

'You'll want something traditional, then,' said Miss Hussain. 'I saw a beautiful Chesterfield sofa at the weekend. Upholstered in dusky pink velvet. Stunning. What's your budget?'

I felt embarrassed. 'Budget isn't an issue for me these days. I've been saving money for years. And I was lucky enough to write a series of mathematics books that do rather well.'

'Well, in that case, Period Home is your place,' said Miss Hussain. 'That's where I saw the Chesterfield. It's pricey, but everything there is so well made. It will last you a lifetime. They have a shop in town, but they're online too.'

I thanked Miss Hussain and sat down to browse the Period Home website and eat my tin of chickpeas. Since I have no clue about home furnishing, I took Miss Hussain's advice and ordered the Chesterfield.

While I was ordering the sofa, I noticed that the entire furniture suite represented better value, so I ended up purchasing the sofa, two easy chairs and a footstool.

You never know. I might have guests one day. And it's always nice to put your feet up.

TWENTY-TWO

Callum Duffy interview transcript: *Wednesday 3rd October, 1.31pm*

Sorry about what happened before lunch, Mr Lamb. But I did tell you not to turn around. Don't take it personally. Dexter is always flashing his underwear to people. That was just his way of being funny.

Dexter's alright really. He's just a bit of a show-off. You have to ignore him when he gets like that.

I'll carry on with the story, shall I?

After I saw Miss Hussain at the library, I read books every day and listened to them too. Even though it was the summer holidays and I had my birthday coming up. And do you know something, Mr Lamb? It wasn't half bad, reading in the pub garden under a parasol, with a cold J2o. I thought – if I could read books like this at school and not be stuck at a desk, I'd like it a lot more.

I even read on the morning of my birthday, because I wanted to know how *George's Marvellous Medicine* ended.

Birthdays in my family are epic, Mr Lamb. And mine is best of all because I share it with Nana.

Nana is quite old, but she's more of a kid than me sometimes. So we always have a good day, and she gets me the best presents.

That year, Nana got me loads of swish clothes because she saw how happy I was with the swag from Miss Hussain.

Nana is a snappy dresser and buys top-quality stuff. So she got me a Hawaiian shirt with bananas on it, a pink suit, a fedora hat and these well-cool sunglasses. AND she got me a new pair of Nike trainers and a karaoke microphone. She is dead generous, my nana.

The karaoke microphone was defo my favourite present. Even better than my signed football by Bukayo Saka – who is an England footballer and plays for the Arsenal, just in case you didn't know.

Mum said Bukayo had stopped by the pub to do the signature. But he'd had a few pints first so that's why he'd spelt his name wrong.

I was a bit confused, because Bukayo is clean living and doesn't drink. But Mum said Bukayo had made an exception to celebrate my birthday. So then it all made sense.

There was a bit of sad news before my party. The entertainer, Mr Bubble-tastic, called in sick.

John Boy was angry about it because he'd seen Mr Bubble-tastic in Wetherspoons the night before, doing bubble tricks and sambuca shots with a bunch of girls. So John Boy reckoned Mr Bubble-tastic was not properly sick, but hung over. He said Mr Bubble-tastic couldn't keep up with the girls, who were all soldier's wives. And when the bar closed, Mr Bubble-tastic had to be carried out.

'He couldn't even blow a bubble by last orders,' said John Boy.

I admit I had an emotional moment. Because Mr Bubble-tastic had let me down, and I have issues about that because of my dad. So I punched the 48-pack of Hula Hoops that Nana bought from the cash and carry and got sent to my bedroom.

Then Nana came upstairs and said, 'Right. Tantrum over. Wash your face and come downstairs. There's someone very special waiting for you in the garden.'

I thought maybe Nana had threatened Mr Bubble-tastic with violence and made him come after all. But Nana said it wasn't Mr Bubble-tastic. It was someone even better.

When I came downstairs, I couldn't believe it.

Angel Rain was in the garden holding a present with a bow. She had on a yellow dress with apples all over it, and one of those poofy Alice bands made of silky stuff.

I was blown away.

Angel Rain was the best birthday present I could have wished for. Even better than the signed football by Bukayo Saka.

Angel Rain looked a bit nervous. Probably because Dexter was tearing around our pub garden screaming his head off.

For a minute, I just stood there, staring like an idiot.

Then Angel Rain threw herself at me and gave me a big hug. Which was brilliant.

We hugged for ages. Then I said, 'What are you doing here? I thought your dad wouldn't let you come?'

Angel Rain said, 'Ooo, Callum! I think I'm squashing your present!' And she giggled in that way she did, like bubbles. Then she gave me her gift, which was a Barbie Fab Friends Hair Stylin' Head.

Some boys get funny about girls' toys, Mr Lamb. But I don't. Because I am a real man and can win fights.

Noah has called me a girl before and also a gay lord for wearing nail varnish.

I said to him, 'So what if I am gay? What's wrong with that?'

Noah said, 'Because gay people are weird.'

Which is prejudice.

We do Gay Pride in the pub every year and I make rainbow posters that say, 'Love is Love' and 'God Loves Gays'. And Granddad says God definitely does love gay people, because God loves everyone.

I always get loads of Skittles on Gay Pride night too, which is brilliant.

I told Noah, 'Do you know what's stupid? Your 1980s He-Man haircut.'

Everyone laughed at Noah then. And he stood around for a minute not knowing what to say. Then he shouted, 'Transgender!' And ran off.

I didn't bother chasing after him and rugby tackling him to the ground, which I could easily have done. I just thought, he'll learn the hard way. When he gets beaten up by transgender people as a teenager.

I was well happy with the Barbie Hair Stylin' Head that Angel Rain gave me.

'It's brilliant,' I told her. 'I've always wanted to learn how to cut hair. Do you want to come and see my tadpoles? I'm really sorry. They're still not frogs just yet. But maybe seeing you will encourage them.'

Angel Rain said she'd love to, but she'd better tell Elodie first.

'Didn't your parents come with you?' I asked.

Angel Rain looked a bit embarrassed.

'No,' she said. 'I didn't tell them it was your birthday party. They think it's a party for a girl in my class. That's why your present is a Barbie Fab Friends Hair Stylin' Head.'

I won't lie, I did feel hurt. I knew that Gus didn't approve of me, but it wasn't nice to have it hammered home.

Still, I tried to push bad thoughts aside and think about Angel Rain's feelings.

'It must have been a massive stress,' I said. 'Lying to your parents.'

Angel Rain said yes, it was stressful and worrying.

'But I didn't lie,' she said. 'I never lie. I just didn't tell the truth.'

'What's the difference?' I asked.

'A lie is a sin in the bible,' said Angel Rain. 'But if someone doesn't ask you for the truth, it's okay not to tell them. That's what my mum says.'

But that's lying too, really.

While all the other kids were arriving, I showed Angel Rain my tadpoles.

'There are only four left now,' I told her. 'The Rock, Juggernaut, Geronimo and Judge Dredd. Look at The Rock. He's a big tank, isn't he? I'm sure he'll get feathery protrusions first. Geronimo is big too, so I reckon he'll be next. Big G is a bit of a bully, to be honest, chasing Judge Dredd around. I love him as one of my own, but I don't like him all that much.'

'Do you really think these tadpoles will become frogs?' Angel Rain asked.

'Yeah, definitely,' I said.

'How will you feel if they don't?' Angel Rain asked.

'Sad,' I said. 'Because I want them to live their best life. And also, I want you to see a frog. It's one of your wishes.'

Angel Rain looked all thoughtful. Then she said, 'Maybe there will be other ways to see a real frog.'

'Yeah, there are,' I said. 'There are dozens of them squashed on the road down the dusty lane. But I want you to see a living one.'

Angel Rain gave me a big smile and said, 'You are so funny, Callum.'

Then Granddad started doing some games, so we went outside to play.

'You're going to have loads of fun today,' I told Angel Rain. 'We've got so many crisps it's unbelievable.'

After the games, I turned on my new karaoke mic and got everyone rocking out to 'Gangnam Style'. Then Angel Rain wanted me to sing 'Amazing Grace', which was her favourite song. Because her middle name was Grace.

'I'm not doing hymns,' I said. 'This is a party. Not a church.'

If you're a good singer, people are always asking you to sing stuff, Mr Lamb. But you have to draw the line somewhere. For me, it's hymns and anything by Maroon 5.

'Why don't you sing Amazing Grace?' I asked Angel Rain. 'I bet you have a brilliant voice.'

'No, I don't at all,' said Angel Rain. 'My choir teacher made me leave because I was making everyone else out of tune.'

'Well, I think you should try,' I said. 'Give it your best shot.'

So Angel Rain sang 'Amazing Grace' out of tune in a really loud voice, and we all clapped along.

Angel Rain looked dead happy and it was a great day.

I was sad when Angel Rain had to leave. Angel Rain was sad too. And so was Elodie, because she'd got into karaoke and was singing this French song about no regrets over and over again. Then she and John Boy did a duet – 'Islands in the Stream'.

'I wish my parents could see your pub,' said Angel Rain. 'It's really nice.'

'You should invite them here,' I said. 'We're doing a real ale festival on the bank holiday weekend. There'll be a live band and a barbecue and beer in two-pint mugs. Tell your dad I've joined a library and am reading proper books. Then maybe he'll let you hang out with me.'

'I'll tell my dad about the beer,' said Angel Rain. 'He likes beer.'

'Wait a minute,' I said. 'Your dad wants you to get into grammar school, doesn't he?'

Angel Rain said yes. That was his goal. And hers too.

'Well, the grammar school headmaster, Derek Badger, comes to our real ale festival,' I said. 'Your dad could meet him and put in a good word for you.'

'I'm not sure that's how grammar schools work,' said Angel Rain.

'Angel Rain,' I said. 'Many a deal has been done over two-pint mugs of beer at our real ale festival.'

So Angel Rain took a flier for our real ale festival and promised to show her parents.

Are you much of a drinker, Mr Lamb? If you drop by our pub, I'll get Nana to sort you out with a pint of whatever you want for free. Just say the word, alright?

TWENTY-THREE

Callum Duffy interview transcript:
Continued ...

I'm glad you're up for visiting our pub, Mr Lamb. Does Field Research come in a cask or a bottle? Real ales have all sorts of funny names, don't they? Even if we don't have Field Research when you come, I'm sure Granddad can sort you out with a pint of something similar.

Anyway.

Speaking of real ales, the weekend after my birthday it was the real ale festival. And I had no clue if Angel Rain and her family were coming or not, but I had all my fingers and toes crossed.

Around mid-morning, the pub garden started filling up with people. Everyone was talking and laughing and having a good time. Nana was throwing giant Bratwursts on the hanging sausage pit BBQ, Granddad was serving 20 different real ales from casks, and Old Queen, the best band ever, were stretching their leather trousers on stage. But midday came and went, and I couldn't see Angel Rain or her family.

I felt so disappointed.

'They're not coming,' I told Nana. 'I knew they wouldn't come.' And I was about to go inside and punch a football, when Nana said, 'Look over there, Callum.'

And like magic, Gus walked through our back gate looking like Santa's angriest elf with his bald head shining in the sun.

I was so happy.

Gus was wearing these wraparound sports sunglasses like he was about to do the Tour de France. And he was scanning our garden like a security guard.

I never thought anything could be worse than Gus's crimes-against-fashion jeans and shiny leather shoes, Mr Lamb. But I was wrong. Because that day, Gus wore a Chelsea shirt and shorts with white legs. And I think those things should never be seen together.

For a bad moment, I thought Gus had come on his own. But then Ferdinand and Felipe came tearing through the gate wearing cricket whites. And after that, Angel Rain and her mum came into the garden.

Angel Rain had on this spotty dress and looked all brown and nice, with her hair done like a princess. When she saw me, she gave me her big, nice smile.

I waved and waved, and she waved back. We were both smiling our heads off.

'Callum!' said Angel Rain. And she grabbed her mum's hand and pulled her over to me. Gus followed, arms crossed like a security guard, while Felipe and Ferdinand tore around the garden.

'You look like a pop star, Callum,' said Angel Rain. And she started giggling

Well, I couldn't argue with her, Mr Lamb. Because I was wearing the new Hawaiian shirt and fedora hat Nana had given me and I did look the business.

Gus appeared behind Angel Rain then, and said, 'So, where's Derek Badger?'

'He's here somewhere,' I said. 'Probably on the dance floor. He loves a dance after four pints or so.'

Gus looked me up and down then and said, 'What have you come as, Callum? Justin Timberton?'

'I think you mean Justin Timberlake,' I said. 'But you're a bit out of date there, Sir Gus. He's before my time.'

Then I offered to take the family for a tour of our garden.

Luciana loved Granddad's roses. She spent ages looking at those. And she liked the walled garden too, with all the ivy. But the flower and vegetable beds were her favourite. I explained how Granddad used this edger thing and scissors to get the lawn neat around the flower beds, and Luciana was impressed.

Of course, Angel Rain had to pretend she hadn't seen the garden before, which I know she found a bit difficult. But she managed to do it without telling a lie, which was good.

Once everyone had seen the garden, I said, 'Would you all like a sausage from the giant barbecue?'

You could tell Gus wanted to say yes. But he said, 'No. We won't. I have high cholesterol.'

'Go on,' I said. 'It's a bank holiday. And Nana is doing proper German Bratwursts with smoked cheese, chilli ketchup and crispy onions.'

'Oh, go on then,' said Gus. 'When in Rome.'

So I took everyone over to the sausage pit, and Nana

chucked on a few more Bratwursts and asked who wanted sauce.

Gus said, 'Why are the sauce bottles on chains?'

'Yorkie nicks them otherwise,' said Nana. 'He's one of our regulars. Pub regulars are like family, Gus. You love them dearly but you can't choose them. Now, can Bob sort you out with a beer?'

Gus said he'd have a pint of Heineken lager.

'We don't do pints today,' said Nana. 'Or lager. This is a real ale festival, not a student union bar. Everything comes in two or four-pint mugs. Gus, you'll have a two-pint mug of Ferret's Paw and you'll like it.'

Gus laughed and said, 'When in Rome,' again. And he had a two-pint mug of beer.

Then the band started playing, and Luciana clapped her hands and went, 'Woo!'

Gus frowned and ate his sausage. Then his eyes went all narrow and suspicious and he said, 'Why are all those David Lloyd gym towels over those beer barrels?'

'To keep the barrels cool,' said Nana. 'I always grab a few towels whenever I visit the gym. They're free that way.'

'They're not free,' said Gus. 'Taking them home is dishonest.'

'That's what Bob says,' said Nana, handing Luciana a two-pint mug of Sussex Rosy Russet Cider. 'But that gym membership costs me £110 a month and I never use the tennis courts. I have to make my money back somehow.'

You could tell Gus wanted to say something else about the gym towels. But instead, he frowned and said, 'I don't suppose you happen to know where Derek Badger is, do you?'

Nana pointed to the stage and said, 'There he is. Dancing to Old Queen. He's the one in the waistcoat with a pint of beer in each hand and the grey-haired woman on his shoulders.'

Luciana said, 'Gus, shall we go and dance?'

Gus didn't look too happy about that idea, but he went over to the stage with Luciana.

I felt sorry a bit sorry for him, really. Because trying to cover your ears with a two-pint mug and a sausage in your hand is difficult. But then Gus downed his beer and finished his sausage, and after that he was dancing with Luciana, Mr Badger and Mr Badger's new girlfriend.

While Gus and Luciana were dancing, I asked Angel Rain if she wanted to see my tadpoles again.

'They're still not frogs yet,' I said. 'But keep the faith. They'll turn soon.'

Angel Rain said she'd love to see my tadpoles. And she held my hand, which felt really nice.

Inside the pub, Juggernaut, Judge Dredd and Geronimo were zipping around to the music. But the Rock looked a bit slow. Probably because of the heat.

Angel Rain put her sausage on the bar and stroked the tank and told the tadpoles how nice they were. Then she gave me a serious look and said she had some important news.

Do you think we should finish things for today, Mr Lamb? It's a bit noisy now, isn't it? With those year fives, pretending to be Viking invaders.

TWENTY-FOUR

Callum Duffy interview transcript:
Continued ...

Alright, Mr Lamb. We'll carry on if you're okay.

Angel Rain's news really was important. She was due to have her stomach operation in four days' time. And after the operation, she was going to try some new drugs. Which meant she'd be in hospital for a month, or maybe more.

'What kind of new drugs?' I asked.

'To help my body accept my heart,' said Angel Rain. 'I'll be one of the first children to take them. So they want to keep me in hospital to make sure I'm okay.'

Which was a real worry, but I didn't say so. Because I didn't want Angel Rain to feel scared.

'Can I come and visit you?' I asked.

'I don't think so,' said Angel Rain. 'Because I'll be in London. And that is a long way away. Over one-hundred miles. But you will write to me, won't you? Letters cheer me up.'

'Of course I will,' I said. 'And when you get out of hospital, my tadpoles will be frogs. And you'll see them and get one of your wishes. I'm going to miss you so much.'

'Ooo, let's read the same books while I'm in hospital,' said Angel Rain. 'Then it'll be like we're in the same place.'

'You mean like a book club?' I said. 'My granddad used to be in one of those. He got annoyed with it, though. Because he was the only one who read the books. He said everyone else just drank wine and talked about their kitchen extensions.'

'But we really will read the books, won't we?' said Angel Rain.

'All right,' I said. But inside I felt nervous. Because although I'd been reading, I knew Angel Rain was a proper genius and read really hard books.

Then Angel Rain did a big, adult sigh and said, 'I don't like hospitals, Callum. I wish I didn't have to go back.'

'Well, you're not in hospital yet,' I said. 'Let's dance and enjoy the sunshine.'

'Dance?' said Angel Rain. 'Dad will say no, but ...' Then she got this stubborn look on her face. 'I am going to tell my dad. I am going to say, Dad, l will dance.'

'Come on, then,' I said. 'Let's go tell him.'

We went over to the stage, and Gus was dancing like a crazy person. It was so funny. Luciana was trying to get him to dance in time to the music, but it wasn't working.

Angel Rain giggled and said, 'My dad is so embarrassing.'

She was right. Gus was embarrassing. Sticking his arms and legs out and singing, 'They call me MR FAHRENHEIT!'

Like that.

Angel Rain walked right up to her dad and said:

'Callum and I are going to dance too.' Like we were going to do something daring.

But Gus stopped dancing and said, 'No, Angel Rain. Not until after your operation.'

Angel Rain crossed her arms and said, 'No. Not after my operation, Dad. I'm always having operations. I want to dance now. The doctors say exercise is good for me.'

Luciana took Gus's hand and said, 'Please, Gus. All of us are dancing. Even the twins.'

Ferdinand and Felipe were taking after their dad, chucking themselves about on the dance floor like madmen. They'd taken their cricket jumpers off and looked like proper rock stars with their big, curly hair flopping all over the place.

Gus sighed, rubbed his eyes and said, 'All right.'

So me and Angel Rain got to dance to Old Queen. Who are a brilliant band, by the way. And they prove that even if you have grey hair and need a little sit down every so often, you can still rock and roll.

Angel Rain really got into the dancing. She put her Alice band in her little handbag and started jumping around. When 'I Want to Break Free' came on, Angel Rain swung her hair and jumped all over the place.

After that, the band took a break. They sat on the stage with their flasks of tea and custard creams and talked about their health problems. And I thought it was a good time to tell Gus about my reading.

'Have you ever read *Monster Quest – Evil Bird from the Sand Kingdom?*' I asked Gus. 'It's about a boy called Tom who has a sword and kills a monstrous bird with a sword. And it is a proper chapter book, Sir Gus. Without pictures. I've read the whole thing.'

'*Monster Quest* doesn't sound very proper,' said Gus.

Well, that threw me.

'What sort of books are proper, then?' I asked.

'I'm probably a bit out of touch, these days,' said Gus. 'Ask your teacher when you get back to school.'

Which was a pointless thing to say. Because I knew Mrs Bullard would just tell me to read the purple-box books.

'What sort of books do you like, Sir Gus?' I asked.

'I enjoy the odd crime thriller on holiday,' said Gus. 'But most of the time, I'm too busy with real crime to read books. And believe me, crime is everywhere. In this pub garden, there'll be at least two insurance-fraud criminals.'

I thought Gus was being generous there. Truthfully, there were probably a lot more.

'What about when you were a kid?' I asked. 'What sort of books did you like then?'

Gus said he hadn't read much when he was younger.

'I didn't set goals back then,' he said. 'I should have done. You can see how goals are working for Angel Rain. Goals keep you going.'

'But you ended up all right,' I said. 'You're a big man in the insurance business. You have to be clever to be in insurance, don't you?'

Gus said not really. You just needed a suspicious mind.

'I was thinking,' I said. 'When Angel Rain goes into hospital, can I come and visit? I don't mind if the hospital is in London. Granddad can take me on the train.'

'No, Callum,' said Gus. 'Angel Rain is doing a drugs trial. She might have tubes coming out of her. It will scare you.'

'Angel Rain could never scare me,' I said. 'Even if she had a thousand tubes coming out of her, she'd still be the most beautiful girl in the world.'

I felt embarrassed then, because I hadn't meant to sound

so soppy. But Gus gave me quite a nice look. And he said, 'You keep up that reading, Callum. Keep it up.'

Then he strode off to talk to Mr Badger again. But he had to wait his turn because there was a crowd around Mr Badger going, 'Down it, down it!' And Mr Badger was knocking back a two-pint mug.

I went off to dance after that, because the band had started. And Angel Rain was by the stage with her mum and brothers, jumping around. We danced for the rest of the afternoon. But then fake Brian May started playing chords wrong because of his arthritis. So there was no more live music after that.

'I want to hear more music,' said Angel Rain. 'I liked the music.'

'I'll tell you what,' I said. 'How about I go up there and sing for you?'

'You never would,' said Angel Rain. 'Go up there and sing in front of everyone?'

'I really will do it,' I said. 'I've sung on loads of stages. I was in the church choir.'

'Go on then,' said Angel Rain. And she said it like I wouldn't do it. So of course, I had to get up on stage then and do my thing.

The gentleman in me wanted to ask Angel Rain for requests. But she might have asked for 'Amazing Grace' again, like she did at my birthday party. So I had a think, and I decided to sing 'Stay Another Day' by East 17. Which is an old song about missing someone who's going away. And it felt right because I was sad about Angel Rain going into hospital.

I sang the song quite well, and I think Angel Rain really knew that I'd miss her.

When I got down from the stage, everyone cheered.

And Angel Rain said, 'This has been the best afternoon ever.'

Then she hugged me tight and said, 'I'm never letting go!'

But she had to let go in the end, because her family were leaving. And I felt sad. And worried about Angel Rain's operation and the new drugs and all of that.

Before Angel Rain left, she took a fluffy notepad out of her bag and wrote down some books for me to read. I hadn't heard of any of those books, Mr Lamb, and they sounded old-fashioned and difficult. But I took the list and folded it carefully and promised Angel Rain I would look at it later.

'Do you have any books for me?' Angel Rain asked.

'Well, *Diary of a Wimpy Kid* is brilliant,' I said.

'I read that when I was six,' said Angel Rain. 'It was good. But not very challenging.'

'What about *Monster Quest*?' I asked. 'Have you read any of that series?'

Angel Rain said she hadn't. But she would try to get hold of *Monster Quest – Evil Bird from the Sand Kingdom* and read it while she was in hospital.

There goes the bell.

Well done for putting up with all that noise this afternoon, Mr Lamb. I reckon you're getting used to all the school madness now.

See you tomorrow. We're seeing a lot of each other this week, aren't we?

TWENTY-FIVE

Michael Lamb

After Callum left, I stayed in the Calm Corner and re-read some of his interview. The tales of kinship, home-cooked barbeque sausages and pub garden comradery were heart-warming. They made me want to be among friends, enjoying food prepared with love. It had been a very long time since I'd eaten anything that wasn't in a tin or packet.

On the way home, I decided to stop at Abi's Delicatessen. I haven't shopped there since Ifeoma left, but it felt like high time I bought something fresh.

As I slowed my bike to view the fresh bread in the window, Abi came to the door.

'Michael!' she demanded. 'Where have you been? I thought you'd died. Come inside immediately.'

I parked up my bike and followed Abi inside the shop. The fresh bread and olives smelt delicious and I remembered, fondly, the days I used to buy my lunch at the deli.

'It's been nearly a year since I've seen you,' Abi accused. 'What happened? Did you move?'

'No,' I said.

'Good god,' said Abi. 'You're still at the same place? I thought that house had been abandoned. Cut back your front garden, for goodness sakes. It's full of weeds. And wash your net curtains. Or better yet, throw them away and buy new ones. They're like rags. Damp-spotted, filthy rags.'

'I was thinking of ordering new net curtains,' I said.

'Well, stop thinking and get on with it,' said Abi. 'Now what can I get you? How about some fresh focaccia bread and a pot of those nice green olives you like?'

'Yes, thank you,' I said. 'Thank you very much.'

Abi picked up an especially fluffy looking focaccia loaf.

'Ifeoma tells me you two broke up last Christmas,' she said, in a brisk, no-nonsense tone. 'Is that why I haven't seen you in a while?'

'Yes,' I replied, hoping my tight voice would indicate the matter was now closed.

'She says you never called her,' Abi went on, wrapping the bread in wax paper.

'I texted,' I said, somewhat defensively.

'It's a shame.' Abi went on as though I hadn't spoken. 'Do you know Ifeoma's back at that god-awful block of flats? She misses you, Michael. Can't you at least be friends? You were together, how long?'

'Two years,' I said.

'Two years, and you can't even give the girl a call?' said Abi.

'I texted her,' I said, going slightly red. 'And I'd rather not talk about this, if you don't mind.'

'Alright,' said Abi. 'Let's talk about you instead. You look like death warmed up, Michael. Have you been eating? You need a good meal. Actually, twenty good meals. Thank god you're here.'

After Abi stickered and wrapped my olives, she put a lump of pale cheese on the scales and said: 'You need fattening up, Michael. Take some of this smoked mozzarella too. It is the best mozzarella you will ever taste.'

Since I rarely eat mozzarella, I guessed Abi was right.

'And take these.' Abi put more items on the counter. 'Sun-dried tomato paste. Smoked paprika. Make yourself cheese on toast with this lot and you'll gain ten pounds overnight.'

I offered to pay for the extra items, but Abi wouldn't hear of it.

'Seeing you put on weight will be payment enough for me.' Abi put everything in a brown bag and gave me a friendly slap on the hand. 'Come back, won't you? I hate to think of you living all alone. Look after yourself, Michael. And for God's sake, give Ifeoma a call.'

That last comment made me deeply uncomfortable. But I thanked Abi and promised I would return.

When I cycled onto Church Road, there was a Period Home van waiting outside my house.

I felt both excited and surprised.

Excited, because my new living room suite had arrived. But surprised, because the furniture people hadn't bombarded me with emails and text messages telling me they were coming.

Usually, delivery companies send a whole sequence of messages, detailing your item's journey from depot to depot. Often, they will even name your driver. But not so in this case. I'd had no messages whatsoever.

As I approached my house, I found two cheery delivery people on my doorstep.

'Doctor Lamb?' one asked.

'Yes,' I confirmed.

'We were passing, so we thought we'd give you a try,' she said. 'We have the love suite for you a few days early. If you open the door, we'll bring it inside.'

Which seemed like a reasonable deal.

I didn't know my furniture set was called the love suite, but the name seemed apt since the fabric was dusky pink.

Once my furniture suite was in place, I stood staring at my lounge, unsure if I was worthy of such beauty. The soft, velvet sofa, easy chairs and footstool had an instant, brightening effect on my shabby living room.

Cheered by the new items, I threw out my mouldy net curtains and resolved to order new window furnishings at the next opportunity. Then I headed to the kitchen with my large brown bag of deli goods. I was extremely hungry – a feeling I hadn't noticed in a while.

It was a grey day, so I turned on the lights downstairs and made grilled mozzarella cheese on focaccia bread with sundried tomato paste, paprika and sliced olives. Then I sat on my wonderful new sofa, eating the toasted mozzarella and feeling the softness and comfort of brushed velvet. Jolly pleasant, I must say.

After supper, I made a cup of tea in Callum's 'Hug in a Mug', returned to my sofa and listened to a Radio Four documentary about interior design. It felt like something had lifted from my shoulders. A weight I'd been carrying around without realising.

I don't want to live in shabbiness and cold anymore.

I'm not sure why I ever did.

TWENTY-SIX

Callum Duffy interview transcript: *Thursday 4th October, 9.02am*

You're looking well this morning, Mr Lamb. A bit more colour in your cheeks.

I imagine you'll want to know about Angel Rain's operation, so I'll get straight to it.

The Friday after the real ale festival, Angel Rain went into hospital.

I was so worried. I hardly ate anything on the morning of her surgery. Just one slice of beans on toast with no grated cheese, a bowl of Frosties, a Findus Crispy Pancake and a Munch Bunch Strawberry Fromage Frais.

And Mum was no help. She wouldn't phone Luciana and find out what was happening.

'That family have enough on their plate, Callum,' said Mum. 'Without us bothering them. Let's leave them be for a bit.'

But I kept going on, and the next day Mum did send Luciana a text asking how the surgery had gone.

Luciana messaged back saying thank you for our concern and the surgery had gone well and Angel Rain was starting her drugs trial.

My poor tadpoles – I spent the whole weekend at their tank, fretting.

'I'm so worried,' I told them. 'What if Angel Rain doesn't get on with the drugs and they make her really sick? You boys have to work extra hard at becoming frogs now. So you can cheer Angel Rain up when she comes home again and make her frog wish come true. Alright?'

Then school started again.

The first day back after the summer holidays is always hard, isn't it Mr Lamb? But this one was worse than ever, because Angel Rain was in hospital AND we had Bullard again for another year.

It was well bad.

The whole class booed when Mrs Bullard came into the room, and she told us off for being too noisy. Then she took ten house points off everyone on the purple table, because she said we were making the most noise. Which, to be honest, we were.

After the register, we had to stand up and talk about our summer holiday news.

I told the class about Angel Rain and her surgery, and that I didn't know what was happening and I really hoped she was okay.

Dexter stuck his hand up and said, 'My granddad had surgery. He died afterwards.'

I got a bit emotional then.

Miss Hussain told me to do calm breathing and asked

what I could do to keep busy while I waited for news about Angel Rain.

'I can look after my tadpoles,' I said. 'So they turn into frogs for Angel Rain. Because she really wants to see a real frog.'

'You still have the school tadpoles?' Miss Hussain asked. And her eyebrows went all pointy and surprised. 'They're still alive? In autumn?'

I said yes. Well, some of them. But they still weren't getting feathery protrusions. And that got me thinking. I'd been slacking on the encouragement front. So later that week, I decided to show my tadpoles next door's pond. You know... like, you could live in this posh pool with the metal-ball water feature, boys, if you grow some arms and legs.

Our garden fence is quite high, so I leant a wheelbarrow against it to give me a leg up. Then I lugged the tadpole tank into the garden. I spilt quite a bit of water, but those tadpoles were well brave, Mr Lamb. They'd been through worse in the school sink, so they were like US marines and they could stand anything.

By the time I got to the wheelbarrow, there wasn't much water left in the tank. So I knew I had to be quick.

I managed to climb up on the wheelbarrow, but that's when it all went wrong. Because wheelbarrows have wheels, and wheels move. Well, you live and learn, don't you?

When that tank fell, Mr Lamb, my heart was in my mouth. I honestly thought my boys were done for. But luckily, the tank landed the right way up in the flower bed.

I wasn't all right, though. I whacked my head on the fence and my ankle bent back on itself. There was blood everywhere.

Mum came running out, shouting at me. And Granddad

tried to put me in the recovery position. Except, it was a bit difficult because I was sort of lying on the wheelbarrow.

I felt sick and dizzy, just like when I got hit by the baseball bat. And it turns out, the big cut on my head had opened up again and that's where all the blood was coming from.

'This looks like another trip to A&E, Callum,' said Granddad. 'Your ankle is the size of a Scotch egg.'

'Oh my god,' said Mum. 'I can't take him there again. They'll give us a season ticket.'

'Well, he has to go, Brandi,' said Granddad. 'He'll need stitches and a plaster cast.'

I cheered up a bit then because I've always wanted a plaster cast.

Mum carried me to the car, while I called out, 'Granddad, my tadpoles! They'll want a bit of food for the trauma. Maybe one pea to share and a couple of fish flakes. And their castle broke. Someone should take it out of the tank. They might cut themselves.'

Then it was off to hospital.

I got seen a lot quicker this time, because there was no one else with a head injury. And you'll never guess which doctor I saw.

It was Dr Chang again.

I said, 'Don't you ever go home, Dr Chang?'

And Dr Chang gave a crazy laugh and said, 'Not much!'

Dr Chang said I needed staples for my head because it was more split than last time. But no one could find the staples, so they had to use butterfly stitches and a big Mr Bump bandage.

Then Mum wrote Silly Sod on my bandage in eyeliner. Which she thought was funny, but I didn't.

Dr Chang said I might need an operation on my ankle

because it was a complicated break. That was exciting. I would have been happy if I hadn't felt so dizzy.

I was given a proper wheelchair too, which was brilliant. And then a lady called Nurse Leakes wheeled me to the children's ward, while Mum went to get a cup of tea.

Nurse Leakes was a very tall, big lady and sort of bulgy looking. She sighed a lot and I think she used too much gel in her hair, because it looked like it needed a wash.

When we got to the children's ward, Nurse Leakes couldn't make the bed go up and down. She sighed a bit more. Then she got really angry and said a child had probably broken the bed, because 'children can't leave buttons alone.'

I did offer to help because I'm quite good with electrical things, but Nurse Leakes snapped that I'd done enough already. Because I'd accidentally wheeled over her foot, trying to get the hang of my wheelchair. And I'd made a screeching noise, pretending to be a Formula One car.

In the end, Nurse Leakes couldn't work the bed, so she pressed the emergency button to call for help.

Then Nurse Gibbons came running over, and you could tell she was annoyed with Nurse Leakes for pressing the emergency button. And Nurse Gibbons said, 'You mustn't keep using that button like a telephone, Karen.'

But Nurse Leakes said it was an emergency because a patient was waiting.

Then Nurse Kolawole walked past, rolled her eyes at Nurse Leakes and said, 'Dear god, Karen. If only that was an emergency.'

What's wrong, Mr Lamb? Where are you going?

TWENTY-SEVEN

Michael Lamb

I should have terminated the interview the moment Callum talked about the children's ward. It was inevitable that he would meet Ifeoma on that ward. But stupidly, I'd let him continue.

Perhaps deep down I was hoping Callum would mention Ifeoma. But when he did, I felt like I'd been given an electric shock.

'We cannot discuss the children's ward any further,' I said. 'It would be unprofessional for me to continue.'

Unfortunately, Callum kept talking.

'Why are you stopping things there, Mr Lamb?' he asked. 'It'll be ages before the bell goes.'

'I need to speak with Bethany Balls,' I explained. 'As a matter of some urgency. Researcher ethics have been compromised. I know one of the people you just referred to.'

I tucked the iPad into my leather shoulder bag and bid Callum farewell. But Callum followed me into the corridor.

'Are you talking about Nurse Kolawole?' Callum asked. I flinched.

'I should have remembered,' said Callum. 'She's your ex-girlfriend, isn't she? Why can't we talk about her?'

'It would be very wrong to discuss Ifeoma during this interview process, Callum,' I said. 'I could use you to find out things about her. Like if she's seeing anyone. Or ... or living with anyone. And that wouldn't be right.'

I felt a sharp, painful lump in my throat.

'Nurse Kolawole isn't seeing anyone or living with anyone, Mr Lamb,' said Callum. 'At least, she wasn't when I spoke to her. And that wasn't so long ago – just last month when I was on the children's ward. She's living on her own. And she doesn't like it because she can't afford a good place to live and her flat gets damp. She has storage heaters, you see. And they get too hot at night, but in the daytime they're freezing.'

The lump in my throat eased.

'She was seeing a man called Benjamin not so long ago,' Callum continued. 'But he didn't want to commit. She thinks she went on too much about marriage and scared him off. But I told her. Nurse Kolawole, if a boy really likes you, nothing you say will scare him away. And if he's decent, he will want to marry you.'

'But what if the boy ... I mean, man, doesn't believe in marriage?' I asked.

'Then he should get over it and do what the girl wants,' said Callum. 'Because for some girls, weddings are really special. And boys have to understand that. Why did you two break up, anyway?'

'Because I didn't want to get married,' I admitted.

'But you love her, don't you?' Callum asked.

'Yes,' I said. 'Desperately.'

'Then why not try to win her back?'

'It would be too difficult,' I said. 'This is intolerable. For nearly a year, I've avoided Ifeoma to the point of inappropriate footwear. Yet here she is, walking back into my life without permission and looking after sick children right in front of me.'

Callum was patient as I began to hyperventilate. He patted me on the arm and took deep breaths in a demonstrative way.

'You shouldn't avoid difficult things, Mr Lamb,' said Callum. 'You should face them.'

'Running away is a sensible and natural response to danger,' I said.

'No way,' said Callum. 'You've got to face your fears.'

I got rather irate then. 'Masculinity and courage are constructs. That's what this whole research project is about.'

But Callum was shaking his head. 'It sounds like you've made a right dog's dinner of this, Mr Lamb. But Nurse Kolawole is a very forgiving person. She believes in Jesus and all of that. Maybe if you tell her you made a mistake, you could win her back.'

'I have to go now, Callum,' I said. 'I need to speak to my tutor and explain that my researcher ethics have been compromised.'

I strode out before Callum could lure me into answering any more questions with his sincere, brown eyes. Then I cycled at speed to the university.

Luckily, Bethany Balls was in her faculty office with the door wide open. She was sitting at her desk, eating a burrito over a polystyrene container. There were a can of Irn-Bru and two open ketchup tubs by her keyboard.

Bethany looked as casual as ever in a hooded jumper

and ripped jeans, with two black pigtails hanging over her shoulders.

'Everything alright, Michael?' Bethany asked, lowering her burrito.

Normally, I would have launched into my ethical dilemma. But I remembered Callum's use of 'ice breakers' and began with, 'How are you, Bethany? Are you well?'

'I'm surviving, Michael,' said Bethany, giving her burrito a vigorous dip in ketchup. 'Thanks for asking. What can I do you for?'

'I have an ethical research dilemma,' I said. 'I believe my research has been compromised. There is an overlap between my life and the life of the subject matter.'

'So?' said Bethany.

'It's unethical,' I said. 'I could use the research to find out personal details about someone I know.'

'We've all done it,' said Bethany. 'I bet Weber did too. What's the overlap, anyway? I bet it doesn't even matter.'

'It certainly does matter,' I said. 'Callum was cared for by my ex-girlfriend, Ifeoma Kolawole. Whilst in hospital.'

'Michael,' said Bethany. 'You're taking this far too seriously. This is qualitative research. Think sociology, not mathematics. And half the staff don't even think sociology is a real subject. It doesn't matter that your ex-girlfriend has popped up in the research. She's not the one you're interviewing, is she?'

'But I feel wretched about it,' I said. 'I have worked very hard to avoid my ex-girlfriend.'

'Why is that?' said Bethany. 'Did she dump you?'

'I wouldn't use the word dumped,' I said.

'Well, what word would you use?' asked Bethany.

'Left,' I said. 'It was an overreaction in my opinion.'

'When did this happen?' Bethany Balls asked.

'On Boxing Day last year,' I said.

'So that's one, two, three ...' Bethany began counting on her fingers. 'A lot of months, Michael. SUMO. Shut Up and Move On.'

'It's exactly nine months and seven days,' I said. 'And I have moved on. I hardly ever go out anymore. I avoid everywhere we might bump into each other.'

'That's not moving on,' said Bethany Balls. 'That's running away. This is the world forcing you to face your fears, Michael.'

'Why does everyone keep saying that?' I raged. 'Ifeoma isn't a fear. She is just a person who makes me deeply uncomfortable. I would like your permission to terminate this interview process.'

'Permission denied,' said Bethany, taking a swig of Irn-Bru. 'Carry on with the interviewing. And if your ex-girlfriend's name comes up, you'll just have to deal with it. The world is sending you a message. Face your fears, Michael. Face your fears.'

It was like she and Callum were in cahoots.

I left then. Bethany Balls had spoken, albeit in a nonsensical, non-data-driven way.

TWENTY-EIGHT

Callum Duffy interview transcript: *Tuesday 9th October, 11.06am*

You're back, Mr Lamb. I'm so glad. You're later than usual, but better late than never. That's what my mum always says.

I was worrying all weekend, thinking you might not carry on with our story. So well done for being here.

I will try not to mention Nurse Kolawole too much, Mr Lamb. Because I know it upsets you. But I'll have to mention her name once or twice, otherwise things won't make sense.

Like, remember I was telling you about the broken bed on the children's ward? Well, Nurse Kolawole was one of the three nurses who tried to fix it. But no one could get the bed working, and Nurse Gibbons said they had no chance because someone had thrown the instructions away. And that same person had thrown the instructions away for the staff coffee machine. So now no one could make frothy drinks, like choco-milk or cappuccino. And you got the feeling Nurse Gibbons was talking about Nurse Leakes.

While the nurses were trying to get the bed to work, Mum came back from her cup-of-tea mission looking all excited.

'Guess what?' said Mum. 'This hospital has a Starbucks. One of the nurses told me after I lost my change in the tea machine. So I can get us both a Frappuccino. What do you fancy? Cookie Crumble or Strawberries and Cream?'

'You can't go wandering off again,' I said. 'I have suspected concussion.'

'Callum,' said Mum. 'You're in a hospital with one, two three nurses fixing your bed with their bottoms in the air. And you're in a wheelchair. Even you can't get in trouble in this setup. Just stay put. I'll be five minutes.'

Mum was loads more than five minutes. And in the end, the nurses gave up on fixing my bed and went away to help patients with more urgent needs. So I got bored. You know how you do.

There was a TV on an arm over the bed. But it would only work with a card, and I didn't have one of those. So I thought I'd take the wheelchair out for a little spin, up and down the ward. Not too far. And I'd watch out for people's feet this time.

On my travels, I found this cool play area with a TV and all these squashy rainbow pillows. Which was dead good. A real find. The sign said, 'Harry Hippo's Play Area'. And there was Shaun the Sheep on the TV, so I parked up my wheelchair and watched that for a bit.

Just as I was thinking about heading back, I heard Nurse Leakes say, 'Slowly, Angel Rain, slowly. Just a few more steps.'

I thought I'd heard that wrong. Nurse Leakes couldn't

have said 'Angel Rain'. Because Angel Rain was in a London hospital, hundreds of miles away.

Then Nurse Leakes said, 'That's it, Angel Rain. This way.'

Well, I had to have a look then. Because Angel Rain is a very unusual name. So I wheeled myself down the ward and saw Nurse Leakes and Nurse Gibbons helping this dark-haired girl to a bed.

I couldn't see that well, but from a distance the girl did look like Angel Rain. She had on a nighty down to her ankles and a tartan dressing gown, which is the sort of nice-young-lady thing Angel Rain would wear.

Then I saw Gus and Luciana behind the nurses. So then I knew for sure.

I had all sorts of emotions, Mr Lamb. Mega excitement. Because Angel Rain was here, in the same hospital as me. But I was also worried, because Angel Rain didn't look well.

Gus said, 'I'll put the school books on this table.'

Then Nurse Leakes pulled the curtain around Angel Rain's bed and said, 'Have a little sleep, now. You've had a long journey.'

But Angel Rain said, 'I'm not especially tired.'

'Sleep is a good idea,' said Nurse Leakes. 'You've not been very well.'

Then all the nurses came out from behind the curtain and headed to the nurse's station.

A few minutes later, Gus and Luciana came out from behind the curtain too, holding hands, looking upset. They went towards the quiet room, and I heard Luciana crying in a strange way, like an owl hooting.

I was so worried. My stomach felt like a screwed-up bit of paper.

No one was around, so I wheeled myself over to Angel Rain's curtain and whispered, 'Angel Rain?'

It was quiet for a bit.

Then Angel Rain said, 'Callum?'

Hearing her voice was just brilliant.

'Yes, it's me,' I said. 'I don't want to tire you out or anything. But just tell me. Are you okay?'

'Yes, I'm okay,' said Angel Rain. 'I feel quite sick, but I'm okay. What are you doing here?'

'I'm in hospital too,' I said. 'I bashed my head and broke my ankle, trying to show my tadpoles next door's garden.'

Angel Rain laughed and said, 'You're so funny.'

'I'm not joking,' I said. 'I did do that.'

'Oh,' said Angel Rain.

'How come you're here?' I asked. 'And not in London?'

'They moved me,' said Angel Rain. 'We're doing the drug trial here now. It's better for Mum and Dad too, because we're nearer home.'

'It's like the stars are bringing us together,' I said. Then I felt a bit stupid. So I added, 'I'm going to go now. And leave you to rest.'

Angel Rain said, 'Don't go. I don't need to rest. I've been resting all day.'

But I was like, 'Nurse Leakes said you needed sleep.'

'She only said that because I was sick in the ambulance,' said Angel Rain. 'But that was just travel sickness. Tell me about your ankle.'

So I stayed outside Angel Rain's curtain for a few minutes and told her about my accident and my complicated ankle break.

I tried to sound all tough and manly. But then I remembered that Angel Rain had just had surgery, so compared to her, I wasn't manly at all.

Angel Rain said her surgery went well, and now she was taking the new drugs for her heart. And she was being monitored, which means watched. But they were short on beds in London, so they decided to move her nearer home.

'Should I come inside the curtain to talk to you?' I asked.

'I don't look very nice today, Callum,' said Angel Rain, in a serious voice.

'Don't be silly,' I said. 'You're always beautiful to me.'

Angel Rain didn't say anything then, but I knew she was smiling. So I opened the curtain and there she was. And even though she looked quite grey and tired, she was still stunning.

We smiled at each other for a bit. Then Angel Rain said, 'It's very good to see you. I have been quite bored. I am reading Heidi for the eighth time now.' And she pointed to a big, brown book on her bedside table with a leaf on the cover.

'What's Heidi about?' I asked.

'Oh, it's a wonderful story,' said Angel Rain. 'It's about a girl who goes to live in the snowy mountains with her grandfather. And her friend is sick but she gets better. Heidi is one of the reasons I want to go skiing so much.'

'It sounds a bit soppy for me,' I said. 'Is there any fighting in it?'

'Not really,' Angel Rain admitted. 'What are you reading right now?'

'Nothing,' I said. 'All my books are at home.'

Angel Rain folded her arms and said, 'Callum. How can you have a good reading habit if you don't have any books with you?'

'I don't have a good reading habit,' I said. 'Reading is quite a new thing for me.'

'If you want to be a good reader, you should have books

with you all the time,' said Angel Rain. 'Then you will have a good habit.'

And Angel Rain is right about that, Mr Lamb. So I always have books with me these days.

It was a bit gloomy sitting behind the curtain. So I said, 'Shall we pull this curtain back?'

'Why?' asked Angel Rain.

'Then you can see the window,' I said. 'It's good to see the sunshine.'

There was a mackerel sky that day. Which is when the clouds are puffy and make lines, like fish scales. And when I pulled Angel Rain's curtain back, I said, 'Mackerel sky, mackerel sky, never long wet, never long dry.'

Then I felt a bit embarrassed. 'That's just something Granddad says,' I explained. 'When the sky looks like this. We watch the sunset together sometimes, me and Granddad. Granddad calls it looking into the heavens.'

'I've never watched the sunset before,' said Angel Rain.

'What, never?' I asked.

'No,' said Angel Rain. 'I've seen it. But I've never watched it.'

'Let's watch it tonight,' I said. 'There's a really good west-facing window in the Harry Hippo play area. We'll see the most amazing colours. Granddad says that people pay loads to go to Disneyland, but they miss the greatest wonders of all, like the sunrise and sunset. If you watch the sky every day, you know there's something magic out there looking after you and you're never alone.'

'Your grandfather sounds like a very wise man,' said Angel Rain.

'But what about your dad?' I asked. 'He's not that keen on me, is he? Will he let us watch the sunset together?

Maybe you could lie and say you're going to the play area to do reading.'

'Lies are wrong,' said Angel Rain, looking all serious.

'Not always,' I said. 'A white lie can be kind. Like when I told Nurse Leakes her BMI was all right.'

'No,' said Angel Rain. And she looked quite cross. 'Lying is wrong. And you must never, ever lie to me, Callum, because otherwise, I won't trust you. And trust is important.'

'I might have told you a lie,' I admitted. 'About how I hurt my head. Because I wanted to sound brave. But I'm very sorry and I won't lie to you again. I can see that the truth is important to you.'

Angel Rain thought for a minute, then said, 'I forgive you.'

'I'll come by tonight and ask your dad if we can see the sunset together,' I said. 'At 8pm. I can't believe you've never watched the sunset before.'

'My family don't sit and watch things,' said Angel Rain. 'We're too busy studying and cleaning and writing reports.'

And that's so bad, isn't it, Mr Lamb? Because what's the point of having a big fancy house and passing exams and getting good jobs if you don't stop to look at the sunset?

It's like that Center Parcs advert says:

'A poor life this, if full of care, we have no time to stop and stare.'

When I got back to my hospital bed, Mum was there with two frothy, whippy drinks from Starbucks and a nice surprise.

Nana had come to visit me.

'Look who I found in the Starbucks queue,' said Mum. 'Sorry I took so long. There were about twenty doctors and nurses ordering triple espressos.'

Nana was holding an extra-large Starbucks cup and a giant picnic bag.

'I came to bring you emergency provisions, Callum,' said Nana. And she started unloading yellow-sticker food all over my bed.

'I found a surprise person here too,' I said. 'Angel Rain.'

Mum looked at me like I was mad. Then she turned to Nana and said, 'We'd better get Dr Chang. I think he has concussion.'

But I said no. Angel Rain really is here. She got moved from the hospital in London. And thank you very much for this Frappuccino, Mum, it looks well nice.

'I always said you were born under a lucky star, Callum Duffy,' said Mum. 'It's just like you to end up with a friend in hospital.'

'I've already set us up a sunset date tonight,' I said. 'Nana, could you sort me out with some refreshments?'

Nana said of course.

'You'll be doing me a favour, really,' said Nana. 'I've got six Tesco's Finest pork pies that will go off by tomorrow.'

So I hobbled over to Angel Rain's bed to ask if she liked pork pies.

Angel Rain looked a bit shocked to see me at first. She had her massive, brown *Heidi* book on her lap and she stuffed it under her blanket like she'd done something wrong.

'Sorry,' I said. 'Am I bothering you?'

Angel Rain took the book out then and said, 'You're not bothering me, Callum. I thought you were Dad.'

'Why are you hiding books from your dad?' I asked.

'Because Dad says I should read Animal Farm today,' said Angel Rain. 'But I am fed up with reading books I don't like. So I am taking a break and reading Heidi again. When

I finish, I will have read it eight times. And then I will lend it to you.'

'You shouldn't read books you don't like,' I said. 'That's what's made me hate reading.'

'I have to,' said Angel Rain. 'For my goal. You'd better go now, Callum. My dad will be back soon. But come back at 8pm for our sunset date.'

So I went back to my bed.

It felt like a long wait until 8pm. But I did get an evening meal while I was waiting, which was Patak's mild chicken curry with white rice, and thick and creamy Yeo Valley yoghurt for dessert.

After the evening meal, Nurse Kolawole asked Mum if she wanted a folding bed to sleep on. And I'm sorry for saying her name, Mr Lamb, but I've got to tell you all the facts.

Mum said thanks but no thanks to the bed. She was looking forward to a quiet night at home with a rom-com double bill and a tub of Ben and Jerry's.

I was a bit offended, because most of the other mums were staying over. But Mum said, 'None of them are single parents, Callum. We take our breaks where we can get them.'

'I don't mind if you go,' I said. 'But please look after my tadpoles. They'll be missing their dad. And tell me if any of them get feathery protrusions. I want to be the first one to know.'

When Mum and Nana finally left, I wheeled myself over to Angel Rain's bed. It was five minutes past eight by then, which was bad. Because you should never leave a lady waiting on a date.

I called through the curtain, 'Angel Rain? Sorry I'm late, but Mum and Nana took their time leaving.'

Then I heard Gus say, 'It sounds like that Callum boy.'

It was like climbing Rapunzel's tower and finding the wicked witch at the top.

The curtain twitched a little bit, and I saw Gus's angry elf face poke out. Then the gap closed up, really quickly.

Angel Rain said, 'Callum hurt his ankle. He's in hospital too.'

'I thought we'd had enough bad luck to last a lifetime,' said Gus.

Luciana said, 'Shush, Gus. He'll hear you.'

'I can hear all of you,' I said. 'This is a curtain, not a wall.'

Luciana opened the curtain then, a bit red in the face. Her eyes were red too, and she looked skinnier than the last time I'd seen her, but her hair and makeup were still perfect.

'Hello, Callum,' said Luciana. 'How are you?'

'I'm all right,' I said. 'Except I broke my ankle and split my head open.'

'What on earth is that written on your bandage, Callum?' asked Gus.

That's when I remembered I had 'Silly Sod' written on my head.

'This?' I said, feeling my bandage. 'One of the nurses wrote it as a joke.'

'Which nurse?' asked Gus. And his eyes got all narrow.

'Nurse Leakes,' I said. Because I didn't want to get Mum into trouble.

I could tell Gus wasn't sure if I was lying or not. But he didn't ask me any more questions. Then he said, 'This is family time, Callum. Go back to your bed.'

'But I've come to ask if Angel Rain can watch the sunset with me,' I said.

'Angel Rain isn't well enough for anything like that,' said Gus.

But Angel Rain sat up in bed and said: 'If I'm not well enough to watch the sunset, then I'm not well enough to do school work.'

'School work is different, Angel Rain,' said Gus. 'It's your goal.'

Then Angel Rain said, 'NO!' And knocked all her school books off the bedside cabinet.

Gus and Luciana looked shocked.

Luciana put her hand on Angel Rain's arm and said, 'Calm down, Angel Rain. It's not good to get upset.'

Angel Rain crossed her arms and said, 'If you want me to do school work, then you have to let me watch the sunset with Callum. I promised Callum I would do it and it is wrong to break a promise.'

Luciana said, 'She is right about promises, Gus. Please. Can she do this? She has been through so much.'

Gus's eyebrows went a bit flatter and he said, 'Oh, if it's going to turn into a big scene.'

Me and Angel Rain looked at each other, really happy. And I said, 'YES!'

Gus's eye got all twitchy and he said, 'Only until 9pm. After that, it's bedtime.' Then he checked his watch and said, 'I need to get back, Luciana.' And then he left.

Which was brilliant.

'Just one hour, Angel Rain,' said Luciana. 'Okay?'

When Luciana's mum left, me and Angel Rain did happy dances with our arms.

Angel Rain said, 'Sunset adventure!'

And I said, 'Epic!'

Then we went to the Harry Hippo play area together and got ourselves settled on the rainbow cushions.

Angel Rain really loved the sunset. She said it was the most beautiful thing she'd ever seen, and she would watch it whenever she could from now on.

'I can't believe it's been here my whole life,' she said. 'And I never stopped to look. It's even better than reading books. And I love books.'

'Granddad says the sunset is probably what heaven looks like,' I said.

Angel Rain went all serious then and said, 'Do you believe in heaven, Callum?'

'Not like Granddad does,' I said. 'But I do have some ideas about what happens when we die.'

'I don't believe anything happens to us after we die,' said Angel Rain. 'We just go in the ground and that's the end of things. Mum and Dad say we go to heaven. But it doesn't make sense to me. Because if heaven was in the sky, we'd have found it with space rockets. What do you think happens when we die?'

I had a good answer to that, because Granddad is always talking about death. And I'm interested in how things work. So between the two of us, we talk about dying quite a lot.

'We definitely go up to the sky when we die,' I said. 'And that's science because of water vapour. And after that, I reckon we become a bit of everything. Like clouds and trees and birds, or whatever we want really. And we float around as energy, looking after people we care about. And that's sort of heaven.'

'I like that idea, Callum,' said Angel Rain. 'If I can still be around everyone I care about, dying will be all right. I am quite scared of dying.'

'I'm not surprised,' I said. 'I probably would be too if I'd had all the operations you've had. You're so brave. Even braver than my cousin John Boy, and he's been shot at. But you're not going to die any time soon, Angel Rain. That's a Callum promise. You're going to live to be an old lady and I'll be the old man who takes care of you.'

And we smiled at each other and held hands.

After a bit, I said, 'How about we go outside tomorrow? Get a bit of sun on your face? We could go frog hunting at the hospital duck pond. And if we're really lucky, you might see a frog. Then one of your wishes will come true. Because my tadpoles aren't showing a lot of promise right now, to tell you the truth.'

'What duck pond?' Angel Rain asked.

'You must have seen it,' I said. 'It's sort of tucked around the side of the hospital. There are willow trees and grass and a bench. It's nice.'

'Dad won't let me go outside,' said Angel Rain.

'So don't tell your dad,' I said.

Angel Rain thought for a moment. Then she said, 'Okay. But we can't leave the ward by ourselves. The nurses won't let us.'

'There's always a way,' I said. 'Don't you worry about that.'

'Do you really think I might see a frog in the pond?' Angel Rain asked.

'Let's keep our fingers crossed,' I said. 'It's a very sunny pond and frogs don't usually like that. But you never know. It's worth a try.'

'Callum,' said Angel Rain. 'You are well exciting.'

I said, 'Did you just say well exciting?'

'Yes,' said Angel Rain. 'It means really, really.'

And we both smiled at each other.

While we were chatting away, Nurse Kolawole came over and said we looked a picture, sitting in the nice pink light.

'I have good news,' said Nurse Kolawole. 'I've fixed the frother on the drinks machine. Two hot choco-milks are going spare for children who see the wonder in God's green earth. I'll bring them over.'

Then Nurse Kolawole went away and came back with two foamy hot chocolates in plastic cups.

The drinks were nice. It was only the foam that tasted of bleach.

Me and Angel Rain said thank you to Nurse Kolawole and drank our hot chocolates holding hands and watching the sunset. We didn't talk much at first. Because you don't always need to talk when you're with good friends. And someone should tell Dexter that, really.

After a while, I said, 'I hope my tadpoles are doing all right. I feel like a rubbish dad tonight because I'm missing their tuck-in.'

'You are a brilliant dad, Callum,' said Angel Rain. 'Your tadpoles should have died a long time ago. You should be proud of yourself.'

'I don't feel proud at all,' I said. 'I just feel bad about the ones that died. A good dad wouldn't let that happen.'

'Sometimes, nature isn't kind,' said Angel Rain. 'Like me being born with a bad heart. But it's not anyone's fault. It's something that is.' Then she looked at me with her big, golden eyes and said, 'You've never told me about your dad. Do you still see him?'

I wanted to lie, like I usually do when people ask about my dad.

Sometimes, I say Dad is a long-distance lorry driver who drove away and never came back. Or I'll say I was born with no dad, like Anakin Skywalker.

But I'd promised Angel Rain I would always tell her the

truth. So I said, 'I don't see my dad. He's not a very good person.'

'Why not?' said Angel Rain.

I took a deep breath and said, 'Because he hit my mum. I feel angry with my dad. And also, like, ashamed.'

'You shouldn't feel ashamed,' said Angel Rain. 'You're not his parent. He's the one who should feel ashamed.' Then she squeezed my hand and gave me the biggest smile and it felt brilliant. But then we had to go back to our beds, because Nurse Leakes wanted to Dettol spray the rainbow cushions.

Luciana was waiting for Angel Rain, wiping the sheets with disinfectant wipes. She'd unfolded a Z-bed and got out ear plugs and an eye mask and a special neck pillow and this lavender 'natural antiseptic' spray stuff too.

I had to go back to my own bed then, except the nurses still hadn't worked out how to make my bed go down, so I climbed in like a wounded commando.

Once I was all tucked up, I called out, 'Night, Angel Rain.'

And Angel Rain called back, 'Night, Callum.'

Then Angel Rain read a bit of Heidi to me through her curtain, but I didn't understand it all that well. And I sang her the special song Nana sings me sometimes that goes, 'I like driving in my car, it's not quite a Jaguar'.

Then we went to sleep. Or at least tried to.

Have you ever stayed overnight in a hospital, Mr Lamb? The nurses say it's 'lights out' at nine o clock. But they don't turn the lights out. They just turn them down.

Then you've got the night nurses, who don't keep their voices down. Or walk quietly. Or put their phones on silent. They just act like it's daytime.

I don't sleep much at the best of times, Mr Lamb. But in

that hospital, I hardly slept at all. Which is how come I heard Angel Rain crying late at night, when everyone else was asleep.

Sorry. Can you give me five minutes? I just need to get myself in order.

Actually, there goes the lunch bell. That's good timing.

I'll see you after lunch, alright? I'll have gotten myself together by then.

TWENTY-NINE

Michael Lamb

I felt a twinge of something in my chest, seeing Callum getting so emotional. I wanted to comfort him. To reassure him that we all go through painful experiences with loved ones. To tell him that I understood. But unfortunately, Callum bolted out of the Calm Corner before I could express any of these sentiments.

Sharing emotions with another human being hasn't happened to me in a long time. Not since Ifeoma left. I've never been too keen on empathy. It can be a painful business. But on this occasion, I felt honoured that Callum was sharing these difficult feelings with me.

Normally at lunch time, I'd hide away in the Calm Corner with my tinned tuna and hope none of the teachers noticed me. But today, I fancied a change.

Callum had become emotional. And I hadn't seized up or spasmed at the sight of it. Nor had I become distressed when he mentioned Ifeoma. If I could manage to do these things, perhaps I could manage the company of others.

Ifeoma used to say, 'Socialising is good for you, Michael. But it's like jogging. You won't get any better if you don't practise.'

Certainly, I had not practised socialising in a while. For the last nine months, my usual social encounters started with something like, 'Do you have a loyalty card?' And ended with, 'Would you like a bag? They're 20p now.'

So I headed towards the gentle hum of human voices with trepidation. It was rather like approaching an ice bath. Probably good for me, but also painful.

The staff facility was a small, shabby room of saggy, fake-leather sofas, chipped mugs and half-opened biscuit packets. But for all its shabbiness, it felt warm and friendly. And I was pleased to see Miss Hussain smiling away as I teetered at the threshold.

'Hello, Michael,' said Miss Hussain. 'I'm glad you found us. I was starting to worry about you.'

Other staff members eyed me politely, and one or two even smiled.

I wondered if the staff room had unwritten rules, like my old school. Did the teachers call each other Mr and Mrs in their free time? Who owned the biscuits? Should I have brought my own mug? Which seat belonged to whom?

While I was having these thoughts, a dark-haired man with pronounced front teeth pulled himself up from a sofa.

'Come and sit here, mate,' he said. 'It's not good for my back, this sofa. I'm Mr Rafferty. Mark Rafferty. You're the researcher, aren't you? Miss Hussain's been telling us. What's your study about?'

The man sounded just like Ringo Starr.

'It's about toxic masculinity,' I said, as I was sucked into the sofa's foamy innards.

Mark Rafferty nodded sagely. 'Men are an oppressed group these days. We run around in circles trying to please women, but whatever we do is wrong. My ex-wife told me to help around the house. But whenever I did, she ended up re-doing. Then she said she didn't fancy me anymore because I'd got too fat.'

Mark chomped a biscuit while he spoke and crumbs flew out of his mouth.

'Let's not talk gender roles in the staff room again, Mark,' said Miss Hussain. 'The last time we did, you threw a mug.'

'What do you reckon, Mikey?' Mark asked. 'Do men have it harder than women these days? They definitely commit suicide more. Fact.'

The old, saggy sofa had formed something of a sinkhole around my body. Perhaps it was designed that way on purpose. To prevent people from leaving in the middle of awkward conversations. If so, it was highly effective.

'My partner left me for not being manly enough,' I admitted. 'I said I'd run away if I saw her getting mugged.'

The silence became absolute, so I added, 'Perhaps I wouldn't run away. No one knows what they would do under pressure. I was just trying to be honest. In a fight or flight situation, I pick flight.'

'It sounds like you miss your partner,' said Miss Hussain.

'Does it?' I said. Because nothing I'd said had indicated anything of the sort. I must have done something non-verbal that gave the game away.

'I do miss Ifeoma,' I admitted. 'I miss her terribly. I would do anything to get her back.'

'Have you tried talking to her?' Miss Hussain gave me a kind smile and dropped two Jaffa cake biscuits into my hand.

'I have talked to her,' I said. 'I ended up ruining my shoes with washing-up liquid.'

There was another awkward silence.

After that, the teachers talked about OFSTED and I resumed my usual role of observer. It was not unpleasant. Then the bell rang, and Miss Hussain helped pull me out of the sofa.

'You have to be a bit careful with this one,' said Miss Hussain. 'Some of our larger guests have got stuck before.'

All in all, I enjoyed having some company at lunchtime. From now on, I would join the staff during my lunch break. It really was preferable to eating alone.

THIRTY

Callum Duffy interview transcript: *Tuesday 9th October, 1.02pm*

You look happy, Mr Lamb. I hope you had a nice lunch break. I saw you in the staff room, chatting with Mr Rafferty. He spits when he talks, but he's alright, deep down.

Sorry about earlier. I got a bit upset. But I played a bit of football at lunch time to calm myself down. Exercise is good for that. So I'm all better now.

I was telling you about Angel Rain crying at night. I could hear her really clearly, and she sounded so sad. But Luciana was wearing those earplugs. She couldn't hear anything.

So I called out, 'Angel Rain? Are you alright?'

Angel Rain didn't say anything at first. Then she called back, 'Callum, I'm scared.'

'Did you have a bad dream?' I whispered.

'Not exactly a dream,' said Angel Rain. 'I thought my

heart had stopped beating. I'm scared, Callum. What if I die in my sleep and leave everyone behind?'

'You're not going to die,' I said. 'You're just worrying. Because you're in hospital.'

'Will you come over and keep me company?' Angel Rain asked.

'Of course I will,' I said. 'Give me a minute.'

It was hard getting out of bed, because I was still really high off the ground. In the end, I just sort of threw myself on the floor, which did hurt. Then I got up on one leg and hopped towards Angel Rain's bed.

When I got to Angel Rain's curtain, I thought it best not to open it. Because of privacy and that. So I just patted the curtain instead and said, 'You're going to be all right.'

'No, I'm not,' Angel Rain sniffed. 'My new heart isn't working the way it should. I know it isn't.'

'So the doctors will give you another one,' I said. 'A better one.'

'It's not as simple as that, Callum,' said Angel Rain. 'What if I go back to sleep tonight and never wake up again?'

'That's not going to happen,' I said.

'But it might,' said Angel Rain.

'No way,' I said. 'Dying is something that happens to older people. Get a good night's sleep. Everything will look better in the morning.'

I was about to hop back to my bed, when Angel Rain said, 'Callum. Will you stay here until I fall asleep?'

I said of course I would. Although, to tell you the truth, standing on one leg was hurting a bit.

It took ages for Angel Rain to go to sleep. I was hanging on the curtain in the end, to stop my leg from going numb. But after a while, Angel Rain's breathing turned into sleeping breathing. So I knew she was all right and I could leave her to it.

It was really difficult hopping back to bed. I nearly fell over, because my leg didn't have any strength left in it. And one of the night nurses shouted at me for making a noise, which was hypocritical. Because she'd been on her phone for ages, texting with keyboard sounds.

After that, I decided to stay up all night. Just in case Angel Rain woke up crying again.

I knew a few tricks for staying awake, because Cousin John Boy was in the army and he told me his night-watch secrets. Like shining a torch right in your face and drinking energy drinks.

One time, cousin John Boy had to stay up for three nights in a row. And by the third night, a giant, talking ladybird walked into his tent and told him he hadn't cleaned his rifle properly.

After that, John Boy told his commanding officer that he was a danger to himself and others, so he got ten minutes' sleep on a rusty camp bed. But it wasn't worth it, because the other lads roughed him up for getting special treatment. The next time John Boy saw the giant ladybird, he didn't tell anyone and just had a chat with it instead. And the ladybird told him there would be a delivery of jam doughnuts to the mess tent the next day, but that turned out to be wrong.

I didn't have any energy drinks or a torch, so I just held my eyes open with my fingers for a long time and watched my tablet.

It hurt after a while, but it did work.

Luckily, Angel Rain didn't wake up again. I checked on her a few times, just to make sure. But then the night nurse shouted at me for being noisy on my crutches. Which again was hypocritical, because she'd just been shouting on her

phone, telling her partner off for getting a signed-for
delivery that day when she needed to sleep.

It was a long night, but I got through it.

I finally dozed off around 6am, but then Nurse Leakes
came on shift and went on and on about a missing KitKat in
a loud voice. She was looking around the ward saying, 'If
one of you children ate it, you should know it's theft.'

While Nurse Leakes was looking around my bed, I told
her I had good news.

'Have you found my KitKat?' Nurse Leakes asked.

I said no. But I did have a multipack of special offer mint
KitKats that Nana had put in my bedside cabinet. They
were out-of-date, like a lot of Nana's food, but no one minds
that with chocolate.

'You should probably give me all of those KitKats,
Callum,' said Nurse Leakes. 'For all the trouble you've
caused me with this bed.'

'I can't give you all of them,' I said. 'That's more than a
portion. And eating too many portions is unhealthy. And
that's probably why you're overweight, no offence.'

'I'm tall, Callum,' said Nurse Leakes. 'You're getting the
two things confused.'

'Maybe your BMI is alright,' I said. But she definitely
was overweight.

'Don't you want to hear my good news, then?' I asked,
while Nurse Leakes was sitting on my bed, eating the mint
KitKats.

'I thought the good news was you had KitKats for me,'
said Nurse Leakes.

'No,' I said. 'My good news is that I'm dizzy and sick and
have double vision. So I'll have to stay here another night.'

Which was a lie and I know that's wrong. But I wasn't
an improved child at the time.

'You won't want your breakfast then,' said Nurse Leakes. 'If you're feeling sick.'

I said, actually, a fry-up could sort me right out. And could Nurse Leakes pop down to the canteen and get me a five-item with three sachets of brown sauce?

Nurse Leakes said no, and I should count myself lucky to get Coco Pops for breakfast. Except hospitals don't do real Coco Pops, Mr Lamb. They do fake ones, and you can tell because they don't make the milk as chocolatey.

After Nurse Leakes left, I managed a little doze. But then my family turned up at 7am. It's just typical, isn't it? The one day I could do with a lie-in. Nana woke me up by putting her heavy picnic bag on my bad ankle.

'I couldn't sleep for worrying about your breakfast,' said Nana. 'I brought you some real butter and five boiled eggs and a Terry's Chocolate Orange. And those pork pies I promised you.'

'Didn't you say those pork pies would be out of date today?' I asked.

'Oh, best before dates are just a guideline,' said Nana. 'Let's not get obsessive.'

When Nurse Leakes told Mum that I was staying another day, Mum looked well suspicious.

'You're absolutely fine, Callum,' said Mum. 'Why did you tell the nurses you had double vision?'

'I want to stay another night with Angel Rain,' I said. 'She needs me.'

'You shouldn't be taking up a bed, Callum,' said Mum. 'Hospitals are short of beds.'

'They're not short of beds, love,' said Granddad. 'They're short of doctors. Look – five beds are going free on this ward.'

Which was true.

'I promised Angel Rain we'd go frog hunting today,' I told Mum. 'At the hospital duck pond. Please let me stay.'

'What am I going to do with you, Callum?' said Mum.

'You're going to tell him what a good boy he is,' said Nana. 'And let him stay one more day.'

Mum said all right. One more day. But I had to buy the nurses a box of chocolates out of my pocket money and be very well behaved.

'And don't ask the nurses for anything, Callum,' she said. 'No ringing the bed buzzer like this is a hotel.'

'As if I would,' I said. 'I'm the one doing room service around here. Nurse Leakes has had all my mint KitKats now and half of that squashed box of Quality Street with the special offer sticker on it.'

Nana said I was a good boy for sharing. Then she told Grandad, 'You see, Bob? It pays to buy special offers. Those hard-working nurses have benefitted.'

Granddad asked if the hard-working nurses wanted to share the two kilograms of gone-off pork sitting in their fridge. Then he and Nana had a big row. Which always happens when Granddad mentions the fridge. But there's no point trying to stop Nana and Granddad when they argue. You may as well just turn up the iPad and let them get on with it.

While Nana and Granddad were going on, Dr Chang turned up. He wiggled my foot around and said my bones looked like they were going back into place all by themselves. And wasn't my body clever? So I wouldn't need an operation.

'My body is not clever,' I said. 'If it was clever, it would know I want an operation and a plaster cast.'

Dr Chang said I'd have to make do with a moonboot. But I would get crutches, so that was something.

After breakfast, Gus and Luciana arrived with the twins. The whole family were dressed up, on their way to church.

Luciana had on a purple hat with net stuff on it, and Ferdinand and Felipe were wearing bowler hats like Dr Watson in Sherlock Holmes. But they didn't stay long, which was brilliant. Because it meant me and Angel Rain could have our big adventure and go frog hunting. Which I will tell you about next time, because I have to go now.

We're having a special sex education assembly this afternoon, which is absolutely not to be missed. I guarantee you that Gary Glover will faint, because he always does when he gets embarrassed. And then on Thursday morning, we're having a visit from the water people about what we should and shouldn't flush down the toilet.

So the next time I'll see you will be Thursday afternoon. Alright?

See you then.

THIRTY-ONE

Callum Duffy interview transcript: *Thursday 11th October, 1.07pm*

Hello Mr Lamb. I hope you've had a good few days. Thanks for asking how I've been. I appreciate it.

I was telling you about me and Angel Rain going on a frog hunt, wasn't I? So let me get right back into it.

When our families left the hospital on the Sunday morning, I hopped over to Angel Rain's bed.

I said to her, 'Are you ready for an adventure?'

But Angel Rain had piles of school work on her bedside cabinet, and she looked really sad and stressed.

'I'm sorry Callum,' she said. 'But I have too much to do. I promised Dad I would read 50 pages of Animal Farm.'

'You can get free audiobooks from the library these days,' I said. 'Why don't we listen to this Animal Farm book outside in the fresh air? Then we can frog hunt at the same time.'

Angel Rain frowned and said, 'Maybe that would be okay. But you have to help me understand the concepts.'

'What are concepts?' I asked.

'They are a sort of hidden story,' said Angel Rain. 'Something the writer is trying to say. You get them in difficult books.'

'I get it,' I said. 'Like that movie, Babe. When they're telling everyone to be vegetarian. Nana hates that movie. She thinks it's brainwashing children.'

'You're good at spotting concepts,' said Angel Rain. 'I think you'll be a great study partner.'

So I downloaded Animal Farm to my phone. Then I showed Angel Rain my cunning escape plan – which was basically shooting dinky cars into the children's ward security doors.

It worked like a charm, too. The first porter who went out with a bag of medical waste – BAM! I shot a toy car into the door jam, and it stopped the doors closing.

Then me and Angel Rain stuffed our beds with pillows and made a run for it. Which was difficult on crutches, but I managed.

Once we got out of the children's ward, it was easy. We just walked down the corridors, down the stairs and right out. Acting confident, you know? Then we were outside, giggling like maniacs. It felt so good to be in the sunshine.

'I'm so proud of you,' I told Angel Rain. 'You did it.'

Angel Rain looked up at the sky with a big smile and her eyes closed. Feeling the sun on her face. Then she got a bit panicky and said, 'Maybe we should go back now. We don't want to get into trouble.'

'No way,' I said. 'We're going frog hunting. Come on. Before someone sees we're not with parents or carers.'

So we went around the side of the hospital to the duck pond, with the willow tree and the bench and the grass.

Angel Rain loved the ducks. 'Quack, quack, quack!' she said. 'Quack, quack, quack!'

We sat on the bench and the ducks came right up to me, because I was very still and calm and quiet. They quacked right around my feet, like we were old friends.

I have no trouble keeping still around animals, Mr Lamb. They calm me right down. But Angel Rain was the opposite. She was so excited and kept jumping up and pointing and talking.

I told her, you have to be still. Be one with the animals. Otherwise you'll scare the ducks away. And the frogs too.

Angel Rain went silent then, and watched the water with really serious eyes. Then, after about a minute, she whispered, 'I don't think the frogs are coming.'

'It might be a bit sunny for them today,' I said. 'They usually like shade.'

'That's a shame,' said Angel Rain. 'It would be a perfect day if we saw a frog.' Then she smiled and said, 'But it's already a perfect day, really.'

And I smiled back because I felt the same way.

After that, we gave the ducks names and pretended they were our kids.

We did have a small falling out over the names, because Angel Rain wanted serious king and queen names, like Elizabeth and Harold. And I wanted more fun names, like Sky, Tenerife, Clover and Ocean.

Angel Rain said no one would take our children seriously if they had those names. And I said Elizabeth and Harold sounded like they'd be boring and go on about politics all the time.

Then Angel Rain crossed her arms and wouldn't speak

to me for five minutes. So I said, 'Let's meet in the middle. I'll choose one of your names and you choose one of mine.'

Angel Rain said that sounded fair, and she chose Sky. And I chose Harold, because Harold could be Harry. And Prince Harry sounds like a right lad under all the royal stuff, so that might work out.

Then I played *Animal Farm* on my phone and helped Angel Rain spot some concepts.

Animal Farm wasn't what I thought it would be, Mr Lamb. It was very complicated, but quite interesting too, with some violence.

I think one of the concepts was about people letting power go to their heads. It was a pity Old Major died, because he sounded all right. But Napoleon was a nightmare. Totally brutal. They should never have let him take charge.

It's the same at our school, Mr Lamb. They made Francois Head Boy. And it's gone to his head and now he takes away house points from kids who laugh at his haircut.

After we'd listened to *Animal Farm*, Angel Rain said she'd learnt enough and we should just talk instead. So we talked about all sorts of things. Like the hospital dinner, our families, going into space in a rocket. And I said I wanted to go up in a rocket at the end of this October, because there was a meteor shower and it would be mega exciting to see that from space.

Then I had a thought.

'Angel Rain,' I said. 'I'm sorry you didn't see a frog today. But what if you got to see a shooting star instead? That way, one of your wishes would still come true.'

'I don't think you can really plan to see a shooting star,' said Angel Rain. 'They're too magical.'

'You can,' I said. 'There are always loads of them during

a meteor shower. You just need to be somewhere really dark, like the nature reserve. Why don't we go to the nature reserve on meteor shower night? They've got a big telescope there. And there'll be food vans.'

'Ooo!' Angel Rain clapped her hands together and got so excited. 'Callum, that would be … WELL EPIC!'

'You work on getting better and getting out of hospital by the end of October,' I said. 'And I'll sort out the rest.'

'Deal,' said Angel Rain.

We stayed under the canopy for a long time, holding hands and looking at the sky. But we couldn't stay forever, even though we wanted to. We had to go back, and that was hard. Because we were having such a nice time.

When we got to the ward, it all kicked off.

(Inaudible)

But I'll tell you about that next time, Mr Lamb. Because Miss Hussain says I have to go back to class for a minute. We're making bread and they need me for the dough. No one else punches it hard enough.

THIRTY-TWO

Callum Duffy interview transcript: *Thursday 11th October, 2.12pm*

I'm baaaack. Thanks for waiting, Mr Lamb. I wasn't sure if you would, because it's not long until the end of school now. But I'm glad you did wait.

Sorry I'm a bit covered in flour, but that's always the way when you bake in school, isn't it? The good news is, we'll both get a fresh bread roll when we leave. I made an extra one for you, with an L on top for Lamb. I think you'll really like it.

Anyway, back to the story.

When me and Angel Rain got back to the children's ward, the toy car had gone from the door jam and the security doors were locked tight.

Angel Rain was worried, but I was like, 'It's all right. I've got a plan.'

And I pressed the intercom buzzer and said in a high, screechy voice, 'I am Brandi Duffy and I am here to see

Callum. I hope he's behaving himself because he can be a very naughty boy.'

I can do a spot-on impression of my mum, Mr Lamb. Me and Angel Rain were cracking up.

A second later, someone buzzed us in.

'See?' I told Angel Rain. 'Nothing to it.'

When we got past the reception desk, I thought we were home and dry. But then Nurse Leakes appeared behind us like a big dragon.

'WHERE HAVE YOU CHILDREN BEEN?' she said. 'We've had the whole hospital looking for you.'

It was a real 'uh oh' moment.

Poor Angel Rain. Her head was all bent over and she looked so upset.

I was used to breaking rules and getting into trouble. But Angel Rain wasn't. She was nearly in tears. And I knew I'd been inconsiderate, which means not thinking about other people. And I know that word, not because of my Word of the Day for Kids app, but because Granddad says it about Mum when she puts her face wipes in the paper recycling.

'Nurse Leakes,' I said. 'This was all my idea. Don't blame Angel Rain for it. She didn't want to go frog hunting at the pond. It was all me.'

Nurse Leakes went even more mental then. She said she hadn't realised we'd gone OUTSIDE the hospital and she was horrified.

'I put my trust in you this morning, Callum,' she said. 'And you have let me down.'

Then Nurse Leakes said I'd committed fraud because I'd pretended to be Mum on the intercom and I was lucky not to go to prison.

I didn't feel scared, because John Boy says kids can't go to prison. It's only when you turn twelve you have to watch out. But Angel Rain didn't know that, and I could see her crying even harder.

'Listen,' I said. 'It's not Angel Rain's fault. I kidnapped her against her will.'

'On crutches?' said Nurse Leakes.

'That's right,' I said. 'I threatened Angel Rain with my crutches.'

While we were getting told off, the worst thing happened.

Angel Rain's parents turned up.

Gus said, 'What is going on, here?' In this big, booming voice.

'Something extremely serious,' said Nurse Leakes. 'This young man stole my door pass and took Angel Rain OUTSIDE the hospital.'

'I don't steal,' I said. 'Not everyone with shaved hair nicks stuff.'

And I tried to explain about the dinky cars and my dastardly scheme. But in those days, I wasn't as good at managing my emotions. And when I got accused of stuff, I got upset and sounded guilty.

Angel Rain tried to stick up for me. She said I hadn't stolen anything. But she was crying and gasping so no one could hear her.

Then Gus said he wanted Angel Rain moved to a private bedroom, away from bad influences.

Nurse Kolawole walked past then, and said there was a private room available. But it cost £112 a night and had a tiny window with a view of the bins. And it was a funny shape, so they could never really clean it properly. And also, it was by the toilets. And by and large, when people saw and smelt the room, they decided to take their chances on the ward.

But Gus said he'd take the room.

'Who will look after Angel Rain at night?' I said. 'She might get scared again.'

Gus's nostrils went all big and flared and I could see right up his nose.

'Her family will look after her,' he said.

'But Luciana wears ear plugs,' I said. 'She won't hear.'

I was getting more and more upset.

Nurse Leakes was angry. Gus was angry. I was angry and upset. And Angel Rain was crying her eyes out.

Then Mum and Nana turned up and things went from bad to worse.

Gus got all puffed up and said to Mum, 'Do you know your son has taken my daughter out of the hospital without permission?'

'How could I know that?' said Mum. 'I've only just got here.'

Which made Gus even redder and angrier.

'I don't want your son seeing my daughter anymore,' Gus shouted. 'He is a bad influence.'

'No he is not,' said Nana. 'He is a lovely little boy.'

'We beg to differ,' said Gus.

I wanted to say, please don't stop me from seeing Angel Rain. She is the best thing that ever happened to me. But I was upset. So instead, I shouted, 'Go back to Santa's workshop you stupid, fat elf!'

And that made things loads worse.

'Callum!' said Mum. 'Say sorry right now.'

'Why should I say sorry?' I shouted. 'He is stupid. He doesn't know anything. Angel Rain loved seeing those ducks.'

'Come on, Angel Rain,' said Gus. 'I think this boy has

just proved why you can't be friends.' And he took Angel Rain away to the private room.

I called out, 'I'll write to you, Angel Rain. I'll send you letters.'

But Gus barked back, 'No, you will not. Any letters from you are going straight in the bin.' And he carried on walking.

Luciana was a bit nicer. She said, 'Everyone is upset. I hope we can all calm down.' Then she went after Gus and Angel Rain.

'Can't you do something?' I asked Mum. 'Angel Rain will be miserable in that private room.'

But Mum said we had to respect Gus's wishes, because he had a sick child.

'I'm a sick child too,' I said.

'You're not that sick, Callum,' said Mum. And she gave me her telling-off eyes, so I kept quiet after that.

For the rest of that day, Angel Rain was shut up in her private room, like a princess in a tower.

I missed her so much. We couldn't have our dinner together – which was a special Sunday one of chicken sandwiches with chicken crisps. Or watch the sunset. And I couldn't sing her the car song at bedtime. Or listen out in case she woke up at night.

It was even worse the next day, because I had to go home without saying goodbye. I was heartbroken.

I did try and sneak down the hallway and knock on Angel Rain's door before I left, but Nurse Leakes caught me and told me I'd caused enough trouble for one week. So I had to hop back to my bed.

Then Mum drove me home.

Back at the pub, I went straight to my tadpole tank. And there was even more bad news.

The Rock was floating around dead at the top of the tank.

It was a total shock, because the Rock had been doing so well. He always got the Wotsit before any of the others. He was a real winner. I thought he'd be the last one to pop his clogs.

And Geronimo had all these manky, black patches on him and was being all slow and tired. Like he had some sort of disease. Juggernaut was nowhere to be seen. I looked and looked. And I got Granddad to look too. But we couldn't see him anywhere.

'I imagine Juggernaut was eaten by one of the others,' said Granddad. 'Tadpoles get stressed in tanks, Callum. And when animals get stressed, they do terrible things.'

I have to admit, Geronimo did have a guilty look on his face. But I couldn't believe he'd do something like that, no matter how stressed he was.

Granddad told me not to get upset about my tadpoles. Because they'd all be dead soon. But I was upset. One tadpole was dead, one was missing and one was manky. And I will never see Angel Rain ever again.

So that's the end of my story, Mr Lamb.

Angel Rain is still in hospital, as far as I know. But I can't visit or write to her or anything.

I know it has a sad ending, but sometimes stories with sad endings can still be good. Like Titanic.

Do you want your iPad back now?

THIRTY-THREE

Michael Lamb

I was in shock.

Utter shock.

Callum's story could not end this way. It was perfectly obvious that Callum and Angel Rain's friendship must continue, for everyone's sake.

'When was the last time you saw Angel Rain?' I asked.

'Nearly a month ago,' said Callum. 'All this happened just before you started interviewing me.'

'You must see your friend,' I said. 'Not just for my continued research, but for your continued happiness. And Angel Rain's too.'

'But there's no way,' said Callum. 'Her dad won't let me see her.'

'Have you tried talking to her father?' I asked.

'No,' said Callum. 'He'll just tell me to get lost, won't he?'

'It's still worth a try,' I said. 'He might have calmed

down by now. Tell him you're sorry. Throw yourself at his mercy. Beg if you have to.'

'Alright,' said Callum. 'It's worth a try. Will you come to the hospital with me? And then you can apologise to Nurse Kolawole at the same time.'

I let out something like a splutter. 'Pardon me?'

'That's where we'll do the apology, right?' said Callum. 'At the hospital. Because Sir Gus goes there every day to see Angel Rain, and he can't close the door on me like he would if we called round his house. And you can help me say sorry with your big university words. Sir Gus will like that.'

I thought for a moment. 'I suppose visiting the hospital would count as field research. And if I were able to observe your interactions with Angel Rain and her family, it would go down very well with Bethany Balls. She believes in observing first-hand where possible'

'Yeah,' said Callum. 'And you could talk to Nurse Kolawole too. And make your own apology. You know, for not marrying her and that.'

'Let's not get our purposes crossed over,' I said. 'I will help you make your apology. But if I see Ifeoma on the children's ward, it is best I avoid her. Because she is not part of this research.'

And I was 90% sure I would avoid Ifeoma if I saw her. Probably at high speed.

'Will your university be okay with interviewing me outside of school, Mr Lamb?' Callum asked.

'Yes,' I said. 'My tutor, Bethany Balls, is okay with everything. Even intravenous drug use, at one point in time. As long as safeguarding is observed, Bethany will have no problem.'

Callum left then, promising to discuss the hospital visit

with his family. We need a safeguarding parent or guardian on the visit – of that I was quite insistent.

'I'll text you when I find out who's going to take me,' said Callum. 'I've got my own phone.'

I told Callum that, under absolutely no circumstances, should he text me.

'We must follow safe-guarding protocol,' I said. 'I am an unfamiliar adult. Have your parent or guardian call me.'

'But you're not unfamiliar,' Callum insisted. 'We've talked for weeks, now. You're a mate. Well, pretty much. I'm not loving the socks and sandals, but I can sort you out with some trainers. Just say the word.'

I must say, Callum's gentle acceptance felt very nice.

On the way home, I stopped at Abi's Delicatessen and bought fresh pasta, organic tomatoes, parmesan and fragrant basil.

When I got to my front door with my bag of deli goods, there were two, large flat packages stacked up in my porch and a note:

'More by your shed.'

According to estate agents, I don't have a shed. I have a summer house. But I forgave the note-maker their error and found a pile of homeware parcels, large and small, in the back garden.

After a comforting meal of steaming hot ravioli in tomato sauce, I got to work, lugging packages inside and unpacking them with my parcel tool.

Some of the furniture items required assembly, but the velvet curtains fell from the packet in soft, red folds, ready to hang. And hang them I did. The effect was cheering and my house felt warmer and happier.

While I was enjoying my newly dressed windows, I received a phone call from an unknown number.

It turned out to be Callum's Aunt Juliette, who had been 'roped in' to the hospital visit at the weekend.

'Callum's mum wants a lie-in on Sunday morning,' Juliette explained. 'So I'm helping out. Callum is a very brave boy, trying for this apology. I can't see it going well. Angel Rain's dad is a Nazi. Lucky you're around to help. I thought Sunday at 9am would be good. Does that work for you?'

'Yes,' I said, having uneasy visions of a confrontation with Angel Rain's father. 'But I'm not helping, as such. I am just an observer.'

'That's a shame,' said Juliette. 'Callum might need backing up.'

'I'm not the right person to back anyone up,' I admitted. 'I am something of a coward.'

'Oh,' said Juliette. 'Right. Well, it's brave of you to admit that, at least.'

Then she told me about herself. She was a single mother, she said. With a two-year-old daughter, Daisy, who would be coming with us to the hospital. And Juliette loved Callum like a son, but she was glad he wasn't her son because he couldn't sit still.

I am to meet Juliette and Callum at the Great Oakley Arms on Sunday morning.

Juliette will drive us to hospital. She warned me about her car, which will be covered in: 'crumbs, dribble and other toddler detritus'.

I told Juliette that I didn't mind detritus in the slightest. I was just grateful for the lift and the company. We parted on pleasant terms, and I don't think she held the coward comment against me.

As the evening went on, I stacked and packed old

cardboard in my alleyway and assembled furniture. I went on well into the night, whistling while I worked.

I am looking forward to Sunday.

Not because I might see Ifeoma. But because I can now also observe Callum's family in their home setting, and then his interactions with Angel Rain, thus gathering valuable data.

Of that motive, I am now 85% certain.

THIRTY-FOUR

Michael Lamb

This morning, I cycled to the Great Oakley Arms for Callum's hospital visit.

Callum's family pub was a large, traditional Tudor-beamed building with 'Best Pub' prize stickers in the window and hanging baskets around the doors. It was cheerful and welcoming.

Through the well-tended beer garden, I found the back door to Callum's living accommodation.

I knocked.

After some shouting and stomping, an older lady in a sparkly dressing gown and leopard print slippers opened the door. She had bleached blonde hair, a friendly face and a large body.

'Sorry, love,' she said, eyes glued to my Velcro trekking shoes. 'I don't hold with religion so don't bother trying to convert me. My husband has been banging on about Christ for 40 years and I'm still not convinced.'

It took a while, but eventually I persuaded her that I wasn't a born-again Christian.

'Oh, you're the *researcher*,' the lady bellowed. 'Callum did say something about your sandals. I should have known.' Then she stuck out a large hand and said, 'Shirley Duffy. Family matriarch. Come on inside, I'll do you a bacon sandwich.'

Shirley shook my hand until I feared my shoulder joint would come loose. Then she led me upstairs, where Callum and the rest of his family were gathered in a large, modern kitchen.

Callum's mother, Brandi, introduced herself with a hug and thanked me for taking Callum off her hands.

'Don't get me wrong,' said Brandi. 'Callum's my life. But sometimes, I need a break.'

Brandi was very young, and wore an obscene amount of makeup for 9am on a Sunday morning. She also wore flamingo-patterned pyjamas and giant, pink fluffy slippers.

Despite the rather crowded environment, the living accommodation was warm and cosy, with Tudor beams and a wood-burning stove.

Shirley Duffy barked orders at her husband, Bob, and her nephew, John Boy, and the two men furnished me with a bacon sandwich and a Sunday newspaper.

Callum seemed happy to see me, but confessed he was nervous about the hospital visit.

'Do I look alright?' he asked. 'Am I smart enough?'

'You look the business, mate,' said John Boy, who was shirtless and displaying a plethora of tattoos. 'All you need is a Rolex watch and you'll look like a millionaire playboy. You can borrow mine if you like. Don't worry about losing it. It only cost twenty quid and it doesn't always tell the right time. But you've got your phone for that.' Then John Boy turned to me and said, 'And I've got something for you too, Mr Lamb. Wait there.'

John Boy left the kitchen and reappeared with a pair of bright blue New Balance trainers.

'Callum wanted me to get you these,' said John Boy, handing me the trainers. 'To say thank you for going to hospital with him.'

I was overwhelmed.

'Thank you,' I said. 'This is extremely generous.'

'Put them on now, Mr Lamb,' said Callum. 'And I'll bin your sandals.'

I hesitated. The trainers were rather bright for my taste and I feared a headache. But I didn't want to offend Callum or his tough-looking cousin, so I slipped the shoes on.

'They're the business, aren't they?' said Callum, dropping my trekking shoes into the bin with a resounded clang.

'Wait!' I said. 'I can still use those as slippers.'

'Don't you even have slippers, Mr Lamb?' Callum asked, sounding very sorry for me. 'Your feet must get well cold while you're watching the football. It is deprivation to be cold. You are living in poverty.'

Shirley clicked her fingers. 'John Boy!

John Boy disappeared again, and reappeared with a box of Arsenal slippers in plastic packets.

'One of the regulars found this in an unlocked warehouse,' Shirley explained. 'Take a couple of pairs if you like. One for upstairs, one for downstairs.'

This seemed excessive, but I accepted one pair of slippers with gratitude. They did look comfortable.

While I was lacing up the New Balance trainers, Callum's aunt Juliette arrived.

Juliette was an attractive lady with piles of blonde curls

and a healthy, curvy figure. There was a passing resemblance to Callum's mother, but Juliette had more natural blonde hair, more clothes and less makeup.

Leaving the pub turned out to be quite difficult. I had to decline Shirley Duffy's offer of a full English breakfast no less than three times. Then, we had to get Juliette's two-year-old daughter, Daisy, into the car. This also proved difficult, because Daisy wanted to drive which, of course, was not possible.

Daisy became rather red in the face and angry about being relegated to the back seat, and screamed for the whole car journey.

As we neared the hospital, I could tell Callum was nervous. His seat kicking reached new heights of irritating, and eventually Aunty Julesy turned around and shouted at him. Which was a relief.

At the hospital car park, Callum asked, 'Are you worried about bumping into your ex-girlfriend, Mr Lamb?'

Juliette said, 'What ex-girlfriend?'

'Mr Lamb went out with Nurse Kolawole,' Callum explained. 'But she dumped him. So maybe he can win her back today.'

'That's not why I'm here,' I said, feeling deeply embarrassed. 'I am here to observe how Callum interacts with Angel Rain. And to support him while he apologises to her father.'

Which, at that point, I felt to be 80% true.

I admit that, when we reached the children's ward, I had a quick scan around for Ifeoma. And yes, I felt disappointed not to see her. But mainly I was preoccupied, trying to stop Callum from kicking anything medical.

Additionally, Daisy had become rather a menace, tearing off at speed and trying to climb inside vending machines. So all in all, I was rather distracted. And it was a surprise to hear Ifeoma's familiar voice say, 'Michael?'

Something like happiness flickered in my chest. I'd been avoiding Ifeoma for months. And yet, I wanted to see her. Quite desperately.

'Michael?' Ifeoma asked again, this time in an angrier voice.

I turned around, finding Ifeoma's stern, brown eyes. She was so beautiful, dressed in her blue nurse's uniform, holding a pile of cardboard vomit receptacles.

'What are you doing here, Michael?' Ifeoma demanded.

I wanted to give a full and useful explanation of my research, and how it had, coincidentally, led to this visit. However, all I could manage was a strange, quacking sound from the back of my throat.

It was rather awkward. But luckily, Callum saved a little of my dignity by saying, 'Mr Lamb is studying me for university, Nurse Kolawole. So that's why he's here. To observe me and that. And he's going to help me talk to Angel Rain's dad with his university voice. Because he's sad that me and Angel Rain can't be friends anymore.'

Ifeoma's face softened. 'Oh. I ... if I've got things wrong, I apologise.'

'No need to apologise, Nurse Kolawole,' said Callum. 'That's my job today. Something happened, you see. I took Angel Rain to the duck pond.'

'Yes, I heard about that,' said Ifeoma. 'Nurse Leakes has taken all the dinky cars out of the Harry Hippo play area.'

'Is Sir Gus around?' Callum asked.

'Not yet,' said Ifeoma. 'I think the Pegg family must be caught in traffic. There is a Vegan Society event in town this morning. A lot of staff have arrived late with plant-based bacon samples. Angel Rain is back on the ward if you want to see her while you wait.'

'She's back on the ward?' said Callum. 'That's good news.'

'Yes,' said Ifeoma. 'By a big window, with a good view of the sunset.'

I gave a little cry of delight, and Ifeoma looked at me strangely.

'Sorry,' I said. 'I'm just happy that Angel Rain can see the sunset.'

Ifeoma smiled then. A full, beautiful smile. 'We share that happiness, Michael.'

For a moment, our eyes met and it was magical.

Then Juliette said, 'Callum shouldn't see Angel Rain just yet, Nurse Kolawole. Not until he's said sorry to her parents.'

'But Angel Rain's family aren't here yet,' said Ifeoma. 'And I say Callum is good medicine for that little girl. So this is nurse's orders, Callum. Say hello to your friend.'

Callum shot off down the children's ward like a limping rocket. Then Daisy wiggled free of her mother and ran after him, so Juliette followed at speed.

'You can go too, Michael,' said Ifeoma.

'Don't I need permission from Angel Rain's parents?' I asked.

'You have my permission to be with Callum on the ward,' said Ifeoma. 'As Callum's guardian.'

I felt overwhelmingly happy.

'Ifeoma?' I asked.

'Yes, Michael?' Ifeoma looked at me, her eyes large and earnest.

I wanted to tell Ifeoma that I missed her terribly and

wished I'd taken her to the hospital duck pond. And bought her ice cream. And watched the sunset with her.

But instead I said, 'Blart.' Which was just a noise.

'Off you go, Michael,' said Ifeoma. 'You have research to do.'

When I caught up with Callum, he was sitting by Angel Rain's bed, grinning like a lunatic.

I knew it was Angel Rain, because she had neat, brown plaits and a book on her lap. She reminded me of a little old lady, with grey bags under her amber-brown eyes, but she was smiling away at Callum. I'd never seen two children look so happy.

'Alright, Mr Lamb?' said Callum, as I approached the bed. 'Angel Rain, this is Mr Lamb. Don't mind him. He's just here to do research. And he's going to help me say sorry to your mum and dad.'

'Oh,' said Angel Rain. 'That's probably a good idea. Dad is still quite angry.'

They carried on smiling at each other.

Behind us, I could hear Juliette, shouting at Daisy.

'NO Daisy. The beds are NOT climbing frames!'

'Nurse Kolawole says there's bad traffic,' Callum told Angel Rain. 'And your parents might be a while. So I can talk to you a bit first. What have you been up to?'

'Nothing much,' said Angel Rain. 'But I have good news. The drugs are working very well now. So the doctors say I can go home in a few weeks.'

Callum looked absolutely delighted. His eyes were shining with joy.

'That's so good, Angel Rain,' said Callum. 'Just brilliant. The relief.' And I could tell emotion was getting the better of him. Hopefully, I can square things up with your dad today, so he'll let me take you out. If you're out in a few weeks, I can take you to the nature reserve to see shooting stars.'

'That would be a dream come true,' said Angel Rain.

'I don't want to oversell it,' said Callum. 'Shooting stars can be a bit meh sometimes. But we will have a good time.'

Angel Rain reached forwards then and grasped Callum's hands in hers.

'Callum,' she said. 'I will go star gazing with you and see the meteor shower. No matter what.'

'But what if your dad says no?' asked Callum.

'We will find a way,' said Angel Rain.

They both smiled at each other then. It was a beautiful moment.

For a second, I understood why people take photographs of these sorts of things.

Then I felt a tap on my shoulder.

THIRTY-FIVE

Michael Lamb

It was an extremely hard tap on the shoulder. More of a poke, actually. My body tensed, sensing some sort of confrontation.

I turned around and saw a short, balding man. He had something of *The Lord of the Rings* about him. A Mordor Orc, perhaps.

'Who are you?' demanded the man. 'And what's this boy doing here? I've told him before, he's not welcome.'

Normally, in situations like this, I would have apologised. It's a good idea to apologise in the face of conflict. But I felt incensed on Callum's behalf.

This boy.

'Are you Angel Rain's father?' I asked, my voice surprisingly clear and firm.

The man looked a little taken aback. 'Who wants to know?'

'I am Michael Lamb,' I said. 'A university researcher. I am here to observe Callum, who is a bright, sensitive and highly intelligent child.'

Gus's eyes widened in surprise. Then he stuck out his hand and said, 'Gus Pegg. You're a university man, are you? I'm hoping Angel Rain will go to university one day.' Then he turned to Callum and said, 'But you still shouldn't be here. I made it clear you're to stay away.'

'Yeah, I know,' said Callum. And he started kicking Angel Rain's bed.

'STOP KICKING THAT BED!' shouted Gus. And Callum stopped.

It was all very stressful, and I struggled to take a breath. But I managed it. Then I took another breath and said:

'I must ask you not to shout. Callum is highly empathetic and sensitive to stress. And you, sir, are causing stress.'

Gus stared at me.

'I am quite sensitive,' said Callum.

'And here was me thinking you were a little menace,' said Gus. 'Taking my daughter out to the duck pond without permission.'

'I've come to apologise for that, Sir Gus,' said Callum. 'I shouldn't have done it. But Angel Rain did need a bit of fresh air. It was good for her.'

Gus crossed his arms over his big, barrel chest and said, 'I've just spent twenty minutes cleaning soy milkshake off my car. I don't need your backchat.'

'Can I at least say sorry?' Callum asked.

'All right,' said Gus. 'Make your apology and hop it.'

'I can't do much more than hop, Sir Gus,' said Callum. 'Not with this moonboot on.'

I gave a snort of laughter, but Gus remained stony faced.

'Where's Luciana?' Callum asked. 'She should hear my apology too.'

'She's still cleaning soy milk off the car,' said Gus. 'She likes to be thorough. But you don't need to wait for her. Come on then. Get on with it. Say you're sorry.'

Callum gave a big, important cough and said, 'Dear Mr and Mrs Pegg. I am deeply, terribly sorry for the upset I have caused. I should not have taken Angel Rain to the duck pond. And I definitely shouldn't have called you a fat elf, Sir Gus. That was out of line. Please forgive me.'

Gus said, 'Well, that was well-rehearsed. Right. You've made your apology. Now hop ... off you go.'

I found myself stepping forward then.

'Mr Pegg,' I said. 'Callum and Angel Rain have been discussing a star gazing trip at the end of October. Might you give permission for –'

'No way.' Gus crossed his arms. 'What do you know about astronomy, Callum?'

'I know loads about astronomy,' said Callum. 'My granddad has binoculars and we sit in the garden all the time looking at stars. And he tells me all about them, even though sometimes I don't want to know.'

'Please, Dad,' said Angel Rain. 'I want to go with Callum and learn about stars.'

'You don't need to learn about stars,' said Gus. 'You need to learn about fractions and grammar. Remember your goal, Angel Rain.' Then he checked his watch and said, 'Right. Time to say goodbye now, Callum.'

'Wait,' said Angel Rain. 'I want to give Callum something.' And she took an old, brown book from her bedside cabinet.

'This is *Heidi*,' said Angel Rain. 'You should read it for our book club, Callum. It's my favourite book. And when you read it, you'll know why I love mountains and snow and want to go skiing. Heidi is like you, Callum. She loves nature and being outside. So I think you will like her a lot.'

Callum looked at the book with trepidation. It was quite the tome.

'I will try my best,' said Callum. But as he took the book, Gus snatched it and put it back into the bedside cabinet.

'You can't go lending this out, Angel Rain,' said Gus. 'It's a first edition. It cost over two hundred pounds.'

'That book looks a bit hard for me anyway, Angel Rain,' said Callum.

'Please, Callum,' said Angel Rain. 'I really want you to read it.'

'Right,' said Gus. 'Home time. Now.'

Callum looked sad. He reached out his hand to Angel Rain, and she reached out hers to his. And they held hands while Gus glared at them.

Then Ifeoma appeared with a blood-pressure cuff.

'Look at you two friends, holding hands,' said Ifeoma. 'It brings me such joy.'

Gus said, 'Callum was just leaving.'

'What a shame,' said Ifeoma. 'Callum is so good for Angel Rain.'

'Did you give this boy permission to come on the ward?' said Gus. 'Nurse Cola Bottle, or whatever your name is? Who gave you the right? You're not a doctor.'

I felt a fury like I'd never known. Both at the casual racism and the slight on Ifeoma's medical integrity.

I threw my shoulders back, drew myself up to my full height and barked at Gus: 'This lady's name is Nurse Ifeoma Kolawole. She is a highly trained and competent medical practitioner. And you will talk to her with ... with ... respect!'

Everyone stared at me.

I would have stared at myself too, if I were able.

Ifeoma gave me another marvellous smile. Then she said, 'Let's all stay calm. Callum. Perhaps it's better if you go now. But we'll see you next week to take that moonboot off. Maybe you can see Angel Rain then.'

'No,' said Gus. 'That won't be happening. He's a little menace.'

I wanted to say, 'How dare you.' But I was so enraged by then that the words came out like this: 'H – h – h – how ...'

Breathing became difficult, and I feared if I talked anymore, I wouldn't be able to breathe at all.

'It's time you were leaving,' Gus told Callum.

'Mr Pegg,' said Ifeoma. 'Do not tell people on *my* ward when to leave.' Her brown eyes were steely and utterly terrifying. How magnificent she was.

Gus seemed to shrivel on the spot.

'Visitors are good for Angel Rain,' Ifeoma continued. 'Don't you want what's best for your daughter?'

Gus couldn't look Ifeoma in the eye. 'All right,' he said. 'A five-minute catch-up when Callum visits to have his moonboot taken off. I can live with that.'

'Good decision, Mr Pegg,' said Ifeoma.

I watched her retreating back with awe.

'Callum,' said Angel Rain. 'You should read *Heidi* by the time you come back. And then we can talk about the story.'

Callum looked worried. But he nodded.

Then Gus said, 'What are you standing around for, Callum? Off you go.'

Angel Rain mouthed, 'Book club!' to Callum and made a heart sign.

Callum made one back, which was rather sweet.

I admitted defeat, and headed back down the ward with Callum. Juliette waited for us by the nurse's station with a howling Daisy under her arm.

'How am I going to read Heidi in just over a week?' Callum asked. 'It's going to be well hard, isn't it?'

'You will find a way, Callum,' I told him. 'And you will show Gus what a bright, sensitive, intelligent little lad you are.'

'Is that what you think of me, Mr Lamb?' said Callum.

I hesitated. Truthfully, I'd said those things to put Gus in his place. Did I really believe them?

'It doesn't matter,' said Callum quickly.

And I felt sorry I hadn't said yes.

Juliette seemed happy to see us. 'Are you two ready to go?' she said. 'Daisy keeps chucking pillows around.'

'Yeah,' said Callum. 'We have to leave now, but I'm dead happy. Because I'll see Angel Rain again when I have my moonboot taken off.' Then he gave me a look. 'I'm glad you stood up for Nurse Kolawole just then, Mr Lamb. But you really missed your chance to make up with her.'

'Are you alright, Mr Lamb?' Juliette asked. 'You look a little red in the face.'

'Fine,' I said. 'Very good. I'll make my own way home. Callum – I'll see you at school on Tuesday.'

Outside the hospital, I went to the duck pond and sat on the bench. The bench was dedicated to someone called Beryl, who apparently liked mallards. And it really was a lovely spot. I could see why Callum and Angel Rain had such a nice time here.

While I was sitting, I thought of Ifeoma. I could walk

right back into the hospital and ask her to live with me again. I could apologise, as Callum had, and say I would marry her and commit to a life of change and uncertainty.

Maybe she would say yes, and I would be happy again.

Or maybe she would say no and I would be more miserable than ever.

In the end, I decided not to take the risk.

THIRTY-SIX

Callum Duffy interview transcript: *Tuesday 16th October, 9.05am*

It's really good to see you again, Mr Lamb. Thanks so much for coming with me at the weekend. It was brilliant, wasn't it?

Did you hear the news about the Calm Corner? They're starting renovations today, so we have to be out of here by 10am. And the renovations will take at least a week. Maybe longer, because you know what schools are like.

I'm guessing Mr Blowers didn't tell you, Mr Lamb, because you look surprised and disappointed. Which is how I felt, when I found out. I like coming here and talking to you, and a week is a long time. But maybe you could come to hospital with me again, at the weekend? When I get my moonboot taken off?

Anyway, we'll talk about that at the end.

Guess what? I'm reading *Heidi*. Well, not the real *Heidi*.

An easy version. But I think Angel Rain will be okay with it, because I'm still reading the story.

I feel dead proud of myself for getting a copy of *Heidi* so quickly. I was on the case straight away, Mr Lamb. As soon as I got back from our hospital visit. When we got back to the pub, I asked my granddad if he'd heard of *Heidi*. And he got well annoyed, and was all like, 'Of course I've heard of *Heidi*. It's one of the best books ever written.'

'Do you have a copy, then?' I asked him.

Granddad said he'd had a mint-condition copy of *Heidi*, once upon a time. Not so much as a crease on the spine.

'But then your grandmother cleared the office to make room for a ZX Spectrum computer,' said Granddad. 'She promised she'd use that computer for the pub accounts, but instead, she played Dan Dare and Chuckie Egg for hours on end. And then we had the leak in the shed and my box of books was ruined.'

'So how am I going to get a copy of Heidi?' I asked.

'You'll have to read my second copy,' said Granddad. 'I'll go get it for you.'

Well, I don't know if you've ever read Heidi, Mr Lamb. But there are hundreds and hundreds of pages. Back then, that book felt well scary. Like someone had let the words overgrow and they were strangling each other.

I did give *Heidi* a go that night, but I had no chance when I was tired. The words were so close together and half of them didn't make sense. So I shoved the pages in my Smiggle rucksack and thought I'd try at school on Monday morning, while Mrs Bullard was reading the register.

Which I did.

Dexter called me a nerd and a boffin and all sorts when he saw me reading for fun. And that is another reason why it's hard to learn on the purple table, Mr Lamb. Because you get teased by the other kids, who are jealous.

But the reading wasn't fun, and I wasn't a nerd or a boffin. Because I couldn't get my head around all those words, Mr Lamb. No way.

Heidi is a well difficult book. There are words like misanthrope and ascends and inhale. And no pictures. I kept losing my place, even with a ruler.

At break time, I asked Mrs Bullard if she could help me with my reading.

But Mrs Bullard wasn't up for it.

'Every child gets five minutes of reading time with me once a week,' said Mrs Bullard. 'You will have to wait your turn. If I gave you extra help, I wouldn't have time to help the gold table with their advanced learning.'

'Please, Mrs Bullard,' I said. 'I need to read this book for my friend's book club. But it's mega difficult. There are hardly any full stops and it's doing my head in.'

'Callum, some children are natural readers,' said Mrs Bullard. 'And some are not. You cannot manage a book like this. Now, why don't you go and run around outside?'

'Because I'm on crutches,' I said.

'Well, walk up and down on your crutches, then,' said Mrs Bullard. 'You'll need strong arms to stack shelves in the Tesco shop when you're older, won't you?'

I hopped away on my crutches then, feeling sad and angry.

Luckily, Miss Hussain noticed I had a bad look on my face and came to talk to me.

'How are you feeling?' Miss Hussain asked.

'Like I want to knock things off Mrs Bullard's desk with my crutches,' I said.

'Why do you feel like that?' Miss Hussain asked.

'Because I'm trying to get better at reading and Mrs Bullard won't help me,' I said. 'She says I'm too stupid to read *Heidi*. But I need to read it, Miss Hussain. I really, really need to read it.'

I started getting upset then.

'*Heidi* is quite a difficult book,' said Miss Hussain. 'It has a reading age of eleven. Why not pick something else?'

'I need to read this one, Miss Hussain,' I said. 'Angel Rain wants me to understand why she likes mountains and snow.'

Miss Hussain thought for a minute. Then she said, 'I have an idea. We have a whole shelf of simple children's classics in the school library. Some clever person has taken big stories, like *Heidi*, and made them smaller and added pictures. So children find them easier to read. Shall we go and see if *Heidi* is one of them?'

I was well up for that.

So Miss Hussain took me to the library during her break time, which was nice of her. Because she had to eat her choc chip Tracker bar while we were looking for books.

The school library is this room, by the way, Mr Lamb. The Calm Corner. So it took a while for Miss Hussain to find the right books, because they were hidden behind first aid boxes and sensory toys. But just as the break bell rang, Miss Hussain said, 'Ah-ha!' and pulled out a book with a blonde girl and snowy mountains on the front.

'There you go, Callum,' said Miss Hussain. '*Heidi*. It's still rather long, but a good deal smaller than the full version. Pop this in your school bag and return it when you've finished.'

'But Mrs Bullard won't let purple-table kids take library books home,' I said.

'Well, I'm overruling her,' said Miss Hussain. 'I pick my

battles with Mrs Bullard, Callum. And this one is worth fighting.'

I was so happy.

'Thank you, Miss Hussain,' I said. 'You are the best teacher in the world.'

Miss Hussain got all embarrassed and said, 'Oh, I'm not a teacher, Callum. Just a lowly teaching assistant.'

'Well, I think you're better than Mrs Bullard,' I said. 'Any day of the week.'

I got stuck into easy *Heidi* the minute I got home last night. And by tea time, I'd read four pages and was feeling pleased with myself. Then after tea, I read another four pages.

Easy *Heidi* is still quite a hard book. I'm guessing a lot of words. So far, I've read about a girl going up a mountain to see her grandfather.

Everyone says Heidi's granddad isn't a nice man, but he seems alright really. Because he gives Heidi bread and cheese and lets her sleep in a hayloft, which is awesome. And there's a boy called Peter who has goats and hits them with a stick. And Heidi doesn't like that and tells him off. So she's alright.

Hopefully, by the time I see Angel Rain at the weekend, I'll have read the whole thing. I'm going back to hospital to have my moonboot taken off this Sunday, Mr Lamb. I've got the day marked on a calendar, because it's very special.

I know Angel Rain's dad isn't keen on me seeing her. But Nurse Kolawole will sort him right out, won't she? And will you come with me to hospital again? Because you were well helpful, last time. And otherwise, we won't see each other until next Tuesday. And maybe, if you come to hospital, you'll see Nurse Kolawole again and you can finally say sorry and win her back. Mum is taking me this time, so just call at our pub at 8am on Sunday, alright? And I'll ask her to give you a lift.

I'd better go back to class now, Mr Lamb. The decorators are here.

THIRTY-SEVEN

Michael Lamb

Perhaps it was the bitingly cold wind and the vertical rain, coupled with my rain poncho springing multiple leaks, but as I cycled home, I found myself longing for community and companionship.

And I decided – yes. I would meet Callum on Sunday for a second observational hospital visit.

Perhaps I would see Ifeoma again. I felt both excited and terrified at the thought. This time, I would apologise. And then, perhaps, maybe, I might suggest we give things another go. Depending on how angry she looks.

The rain seemed to intensify as I reached my street, and I felt happy that I'd soon be inside my now much warmer house with soft furnishings.

Some of my neighbours had already decorated for Halloween, I noticed. Normally, I would have treated the plastic pumpkins and gurning skeletons with derision. And possibly an internal monologue about the march of capitalist consumerism. But as I cycled past my neighbouring houses, I felt surprisingly warm towards the festivities.

The plastic nonsense would bring smiles to the faces of local children. Children like Callum. Moreover, the Halloween symbolism brought the community together.

On a whim, I popped into Gudram's Goods corner shop and bought a large tub of glow-in-the-dark lollies for trick or treaters. Then, on the way out, I noticed a 'light 'em up' plastic pumpkin and a 'shimmering neon' skeleton. They were charming. So I went back to the counter and purchased them too.

'I thought you hated Halloween, Mr Lamb?' Gudram queried. 'Last year, you complained about me selling ... what did you call it? Over-priced, sugar-filled nonsense?'

Last Halloween, I had complained about Gudram's Halloween stock. And I'd hidden in my bedroom on Halloween night, reading with the door closed, while Ifeoma gave sweets to the hordes of noisy trick or treaters. Even though I'd instructed her not to encourage them.

'I have had a change of heart about children,' I told Gudram. 'They're not all bad. I want to be a good community member. So it's my mutual responsibility to make sure children have too much sugar on festive occasions.'

'Very good, sir,' said Gudram. 'Happy Halloween.'

Halloween is, of course, over two weeks away. But I accepted the greeting with a smile and a wave.

At home, I changed into dry clothes and hung the skeleton on my door. Then I thought about what else I could do to bring cheer this Halloween. The internet seemed the answer, as it often is. And via Amazon and several other online merchants, I purchased a good deal more plastic tat to decorate inside and outside my house. Including a monster doorbell that made roaring noises.

Then I looked around the inside. My new furniture has certainly cheered the place. As has the central heating. But my paintwork is still chipped and stained, and the colours extremely dated.

It occurred to me that I should decorate my house. I enjoy methodical jobs like painting, and it would give me some much-needed physical exercise.

Yes.

A spot of DIY.

What a good idea.

After a quick supper of macaroni and cheese with a dressed salad, I headed to the HOME! Superstore, which is open surprisingly late these days.

Despite its redundant exclamation mark, the HOME! Superstore was very practical, and had many paint choices. So many, I feared being overwhelmed. But it turns out, home decor is quite simple. One only needs to study pictures in DIY store catalogues, then buy the listed paints and wallpapers and apply them.

By the weekend, I'd painted the lounge in warm colours, with a flock wallpaper feature wall. It looked very nice and I'd done a meticulous job, if I do say so myself.

I did consider tackling the front and back gardens on Saturday, because the brambles really have reached frightening heights. But I ached with physical exertion, and besides, the haunted house look will do well for Halloween. I would hang my new bats and floating spectres on the overgrowth.

Externals aside, my home is looking good. There is still the hallway and upstairs to paint, the gardens to do and the carpets to order. But things are coming together and I am thoroughly enjoying the space.

Maybe I'll even throw a Christmas party this year and invite the neighbours round for mince pies and sherry.

It is high time I let the world in.

THIRTY-EIGHT

Michael Lamb

The hospital visit came around quicker than I expected. I was so busy assembling and decorating that the time flew by. Then there were all the Halloween decorations to assemble and arrange. And before I knew it, I was cycling to the Great Oakley Arms to see Callum again.

Brandi greeted me at the back door and explained she would be driving Callum and myself to hospital.

'Only, we're running a bit late, Mr Lamb,' said Brandi, in an overly formal voice. 'That's why my hair is wonky. You know how it is with kids. You never have time to do your hair right.'

Then Brandi inclined her head to the staircase and screeched, 'CALLUM! YOU ARE KEEPING EVERYONE WAITING!'

She turned back to me and said, 'Excuse me, won't you? I will just go and get him.' And darted upstairs.

Five minutes later, Callum appeared at the top of the

staircase, looking considerably smarter than the last time we'd met. And a lot less likely to commit a violent offence.

'You're wearing new clothing,' I observed. 'And you've changed your hair.'

'That's right,' said Callum. 'I'm wearing the smart clothes Miss Hussain gave me. And I've had a new hairdo at the barbers. I've gone for the Prem footballer look. No razor this time.'

As Callum came downstairs, he bumped a pink suitcase behind him.

I enquired as to its purpose.

'It's full of presents for Angel Rain,' said Callum. 'I went a bit mad in the Age UK Shop. You can get a lot for your money there.'

'You'd better not have your Nerf gun with you, Callum,' squawked Brandi, clattering downstairs in dangerously high heels. 'We're going to a hospital. There are sick kids. And maybe use a bit less of John Boy's Lynx Africa spray next time. Not everyone is a fan.'

We headed to Brandi's car, which was a pink Kia with false eyelashes on the headlights. Then Brandi drove us to the hospital, speeding up at yellow lights, taking corners at speed and abusing other road users.

As we neared the hospital, my car sickness began to subside and I asked how Callum's reading was getting along.

'Brilliant,' said Callum. 'I've read all of *Heidi* now.'

'That's astonishing,' I said.

'It was the easy version of *Heidi*,' Callum admitted. 'With pictures and that, remember? But I still read the whole thing.'

I remained impressed, and told Callum so.

'How are your last two tadpoles?' I asked.

'They're alright, Mr Lamb,' said Callum. 'I take each day as it comes.'

At the hospital, Callum had an ankle X-ray to check his bones had healed the right way. Then he saw Dr Mulder, who was in charge of moonboot removal.

Dr Mulder was a cheerful doctor. She did cold water swimming, which she said did wonders for her mood. She'd even done an ice swimming competition in Finland and won a gold medal, because no one else turned up.

After a brisk examination of Callum's ankle, Dr Mulder told Callum he didn't need the moonboot anymore.

'Which is good,' said Dr Mulder. 'Because we're rather short of them.'

Then she sprayed the moonboot with disinfectant, gave it to a nurse and said, 'Whizz this down to the girl in bay four. She's been waiting rather a while.'

Callum was elated to have the moonboot removed. He looked like a baby giraffe, stumbling around on awkward, new legs.

'You can go home now, Callum,' said Dr Mulder. 'Mind your step on the way out, won't you?'

Because Callum had fallen over twice already.

'I can't go home yet,' said Callum. 'I'm visiting my friend, Angel Rain, on the children's ward.'

My heart quickened at the thought of seeing Ifeoma.

This was it. My chance to make amends and possibly win back the love of my life. And I would make good use of it.

'Hang on,' said Dr Mulder. 'I've just put two and two together. Are you the young man who took the heart donor girl for a jolly time by the duck pond? We've had to rethink the whole security system because of you.' Then she gave Callum a wink and said, 'Well done for getting that girl out in the fresh air. Best thing for her. I'm about to head up to the children's ward. Do you want to come with?'

'Yeah!' said Callum. So Dr Mulder showed us up to the children's ward, while I wheeled Callum's pink suitcase.

Callum had one bare foot, because no one had thought to bring a second Nike. But he didn't seem to mind.

'I can't wait to see Angel Rain,' Callum kept saying. 'I can't wait.'

But as we made slow progress through the hospital, I was overcome with anxiety. By the time we reached the children's ward reception, my heart pounded and I feared a panic attack. I couldn't talk to Ifeoma. I just couldn't.

Luckily, Ifeoma was nowhere to be seen.

Callum put a kind hand on my arm. 'I don't think Nurse Kolawole is here today, Mr Lamb,' he said.

My physical symptoms eased, but I wasn't relieved.

'Why don't you give her a call?' Callum suggested. 'And offer to take her to a nice restaurant or something?'

How could I explain to an innocent, optimistic child that things with adults are complicated? And that a meal in a nice restaurant wouldn't fix two years of resentment? Or that I was born a coward and would almost certainly die one?

'You mustn't worry about me,' I told Callum. 'Put your energy into walking in a straight line.'

Because Callum had crashed into a few beds on his way through the ward.

Angel Rain was at the end of the ward by the big window, just like before. Her curtain was wide open and she had books all over her bed.

Callum called out, 'Angel Rain!' and went hobbling towards her.

Angel Rain's face lit up. She waved and waved.

'Callum!' she said. 'Callum!'

Brandi and I hurried behind Callum, trying to stop him careering into beds and patients.

'Where are your mum and dad?' Callum asked, as he reached Angel Rain's bed.

'They're at home,' said Angel Rain. 'Helping Elodie. Because Elodie is upset.'

'What's she upset about?' asked Callum.

'Felipe and Ferdinand,' said Angel Rain.

'So me and you get a visit, just the two of us?' said Callum. 'What a result.'

Brandi said she'd go and get a cup of tea. So I sat myself by an empty bed and tried to look invisible. Which I'm quite good at.

'How are you feeling, Angel Rain?' Callum asked.

'I'm very well and ready to go home,' said Angel Rain. 'Dr Mulder says I can leave next week. So ... So ...' She looked all excited, like the smile was going to burst out of her face. 'I can go star gazing with you and see shooting stars!'

Angel Rain and Callum both squeezed their fists and made strange, excitable noises then.

Like, 'Neeeeeeee!'

'That's brilliant news,' said Callum. 'But what about your dad?'

'I have a plan about that,' said Angel Rain. 'Now let's talk about something else.'

'Alright,' said Callum. 'I've brought a few bits and pieces for you.' He snapped his fingers at me like a Mafia boss and said, 'Mr Lamb. The suitcase.'

Obligingly, I wheeled the suitcase over and opened it up.

Angel Rain's eyes grew enormous when she saw the contents, which were:

. . .

A stick-on nail set.

Glow in the dark hair beads.

Plastic jumping frogs.

Three *Scare Town* books.

Board games and jigsaw puzzles.

A hair clip with a frog on it.

'These are … the best presents … I've ever seen!' said Angel Rain. Then she held up the hair clip and went, 'Ribbet ribbet! Frog says thank you so much!'

Callum helped Angel Rain use the stick-on nails, then chose the Fairy Sparkle set for himself.

'Fake nails are well glam,' said Callum. 'But I don't know how Mum manages with them all the time, especially on the toilet.'

After the fake nails, Callum helped Angel Rain do the hair beads and jump the plastic frogs around. Then he said, 'I've got one more surprise for you.' And he pulled a karaoke microphone out of the suitcase.

'I thought we could do a bit of karaoke,' Callum explained. 'I know you like singing.'

Angel Rain looked extremely happy. 'Oh, Callum,' she said. 'This is brilliant. Will you sing me a song? You're a much better singer than me. I think you will be a famous singer when you're older.'

'It's an option,' said Callum. 'I don't think I will be a vet, Angel Rain. I'm trying very hard with the reading, but it's still a struggle. I'm just not clever enough.'

'You are clever,' said Angel Rain. 'You know about frogs and stars and flowers. And you know lots of unusual words. You have a very good vocabulary.'

I shouldn't have interjected. I was just an observer after

all. But I couldn't help it:

'Yes, you are clever, Callum. You are a bright, sensitive, intelligent boy. And I'm sorry I didn't affirm those things when you asked before. But I have spent a lot of time with you now, and I know for certain they are true.'

Callum gave me a marvellous smile. But then his face fell, and he said, 'Mrs Bullard doesn't think I'm clever. One time, she asked our class what we wanted to be when we grew up. And I said I wanted to be a vet. But Mrs Bullard said I'd have to pass lots of exams to be a vet. So I should think of a backup plan.'

Angel Rain crossed her arms and said, 'You will pass exams, Callum Duffy. And you'll be the best vet in the world. Your teacher doesn't know you at all. You can do anything you set your mind to.'

Callum's face lit up. It was lovely to see. But I felt thoroughly saddened that his teacher, whose job it was to nurture Callum's fragile spirit, had so badly let him down.

'Well, I suppose miracles can happen,' said Callum. 'I am liking reading a lot more now. And guess what? I read *Heidi*.'

'That's brilliant!' said Angel Rain. And she looked so excited. 'Let's do our book club.'

'Alright,' said Callum. 'Well, Heidi is a blonde girl who loves the mountain and her grandfather and –'

Angel Rain interrupted him. 'Heidi isn't blonde,' she said. 'She has curly, dark hair. Are you sure you read the right book, Callum?'

'I definitely read *Heidi*,' said Callum. 'But it wasn't like your big, brown book. It was an easy reader. And there were pictures of a blonde girl.'

Angel Rain looked a little disappointed.

'Callum, you should read real *Heidi*,' she said. 'Otherwise, we can't do book club properly.'

'But real *Heidi* looks hard,' said Callum. 'It's a massive book. And I'm not a genius like you.'

Angel Rain gave Callum serious eyes and said, 'Callum Duffy. You are the cleverest person I know.'

'Here, here,' I said.

The pride and happiness on Callum's face was quite overwhelming.

Then Angel Rain said, 'Let's do karaoke.'

'All right,' said Callum. 'Ladies first.'

So Angel Rain sang, 'Amazing Grace.'

I must confess – Angel Rain was not a natural singer. In fact, Nurse Leakes said she would take away Angel Rain's lunchtime jelly pot if she didn't quieten down. Which was rather unkind.

Callum, on the other hand, was quite something.

At first, Angel Rain wanted Callum to sing, 'Amazing Grace' too. But Callum was dead against it.

'I won't sing church songs, Angel Rain,' said Callum. 'I told you already.'

'Why not?' asked Angel Rain.

'Because of a trauma,' said Callum. 'I got teased something chronic when I was in the church choir and had to wear a white dress.'

In the end, Callum sung a song called 'Tsunami', which he called 'an epic tune'.

Personally, I didn't care for it because the lyrics made no sense. How can a rollercoaster get stuck inside a maze?

I was in the minority, though. Children and staff members formed a crowd at the end of Angel Rain's bed, and there was a lot of clapping when Callum finished.

I must admit, Callum was an excellent singer and quite

the showman. The children had requests when he finished and so did some of the nurses. But then Brandi returned and said it was time to go home – after Callum had sung 'I Will Survive', which was Nurse Leake's special request.

As we were leaving, Angel Rain told Callum that she'd write and tell him when and where to pick her up for star gazing.

'But don't write back,' she said.

'Why not?' Callum asked.

'Sometimes it's best not to ask too many questions,' said Angel Rain.

Callum accepted this with a small nod of his head.

Outside the hospital, Callum said, 'They're a bit behind on the Calm Corner renovations, Mr Lamb. Did you know? So it'll be after Halloween before we see each other again, I reckon.'

'But Mr Blowers said the Calm Corner would be operational again after this weekend,' I said, feeling deeply disappointed.

'No, they haven't even chosen the paint yet,' said Callum. 'The people doing the decorating can't find their arses with both hands. And that's not me swearing, Mr Lamb. Because Mr Holland, our caretaker, said that. Not me.'

'How can there be such a delay?' I asked. 'It's only painting.'

'That's schools for you, Mr Lamb,' said Callum. 'However long they say it will take, you have to double it.'

Which, in my experience, is an accurate observation of the public sector.

'Maybe you can use the time to call Nurse Kolawole,' said Callum.

'I'm not sure I can manage that, Callum,' I said. 'But I

will spend my time wisely. I am learning how to bake pumpkin-shaped shortbread biscuits for Halloween trick or treaters. They are turning out quite well. I will bring you one next time I see you.'

Callum expressed his gratitude. Then we parted ways.

THIRTY-NINE

Callum Duffy interview transcript: *Tuesday 30th October, 1.45pm*

How have you been, Mr Lamb? Thank you very much for the Halloween biscuit, I'll look forward to that. You are a very good baker. This looks just like the pictures in Great Nana Joan's Woman's Own magazine.

I won't eat the biscuit now, because of the crumbs. We've had a vermin problem in here because of Mr Rafferty's biscuits. But I do really appreciate it, Mr Lamb, and I'm sure it will be delicious.

What do you think of the decoration job on the Calm Corner? They just finished this morning. Well you know that, because we weren't allowed in here this morning.

Mr Holland is so angry about the colour. It is bad. He says it looks like a 1970s dessert. And they got paint on the floor over there. And there. And there. And they've missed a bit over there. And there. And there, see?

Anyway.

A lot has gone on since I saw you at the hospital, Mr Lamb.

A lot.

I've been up and down like a rollercoaster. But I'll start with the good news. Me and Angel Rain got to go star gazing. And she saw a shooting star and had a life wish come true. Which was magical and amazing.

Then it all went wrong and I am quite heartbroken.

They say you shouldn't have regrets in life, and I don't regret the star gazing. But I do regret what happened afterwards.

You'll understand better when I tell you what happened.

You remember Angel Rain said she was leaving hospital quite soon? Well she did, pretty soon after we visited her. And on that day, she sent me a brilliant letter.

Angel Rain said she felt really well and could come star gazing. She asked if I could pick her up at 7pm from her house, with a parent or carer.

'I must be home no later than 9pm,' Angel Rain wrote.

She underlined that bit.

No later than 9pm.

Which should have set alarm bells ringing, but it didn't.

I was so happy. I went running around the pub, shouting my head off. Until Mum took the wind out of my sails.

'I can't take you star gazing on Friday night, Callum,' she said. 'It's the Halloween spooky spectacular in the pub. I'm doing the witch's brew, mixing all the pub spirits that haven't sold. And Nana and Granddad will be busy too. Nana is a war-time zombie nurse, doing toffee brandy shots. And Granddad is dressing up as a druid and boring everyone about the real history of Halloween.'

'But Halloween isn't until next week,' I said. 'Can't

Nana and Granddad move their spooky spectacular? Please, Mum. Angel Rain asked me to pick her up.'

Mum said sorry, no. The posters had all been printed now. But John Boy could take me, as long as the star gazing didn't go on too late.

'We don't need a one-legged vampire until later on,' Mum explained.

So I begged John Boy to take me star gazing, and of course he said yes. Because John Boy is a soft touch. He'd do anything for anyone.

The only problem was John Boy's rusty old Land Rover. It needed sprucing up before I could take a nice young lady for a night out. So on the Friday afternoon, me and John Boy cleaned the McDonald's wrappers out, scrubbed the rude stickers off the dashboard and hung a sherbet-scented air freshener on the mirror. Then I put Mum's fluffy cushions on the back seats and a disco ball on the floor. And everything was looking good.

I was so excited, driving to Angel Rain's house. Because I couldn't wait to show her the nature reserve and the telescope and the food vans and all of that. And Nana had given me twenty quid to buy us both a nice meal, too. So that was good.

When we pulled onto Angel Rain's road, John Boy said, 'There are some fancy cars around here, aren't they?'

Angel Rain's street is full of brand-new BMWs and Mercedes and Teslas, Mr Lamb. And Teslas are like the most expensive cars you can buy.

Our knackered 1980s Land Rover was a bit out of place, especially when it backfired. But as John Boy said, it's the inside that counts. And inside our car were fluffy cushions and a disco ball. So when you look at it that way, we had the best car on the street.

I was nervous, walking up to Angel Rain's front door. Because what if her dad had changed his mind and cancelled our date? But I took deep breaths and gave the doorbell a really good press. Maybe a bit too good of a press, because Elodie shouted something in French, and I don't think it was a nice thing.

In the end, Ferdinand opened the door with no clothes on. He threw an apple at me and ran off screaming.

Then Elodie came into the hallway, looking stressed. She had a bit of loo roll on her shoulder, but I didn't ask why.

I put on my best voice and said, 'Good evening. I have come to take Angel Rain out, please.'

Elodie said, 'You are taking all the children? Yes?'

I said no. I would not be taking Ferdinand and Felipe, due to them being very young and a bit mad.

Elodie put her hand on her head and said, 'I know they are mad. This is why I want you to take them.'

But I said I couldn't, because me and Angel Rain were going to star-gazing. And Ferdinand and Felipe would probably knock over the big, expensive telescope, then scream their heads off while we were trying to watch the stars.

Elodie called up the stairs, 'Angel Rain! The boy is here. What is happening? I thought he was taking all of the children?'

Angel Rain came to the top of the stairs then. She looked stunning, Mr Lamb. Like a Disney princess. She had on this black dress with glitter all over it, and sparkly shoes and tights.

I said: 'You look like the night sky.'

Angel Rain got all shy and couldn't stop smiling. Then she told me she'd put extra sparkles on the dress with glue spray and a tub of glitter. Which I thought was dead clever.

'You'll need a jumper, though,' I said. 'It's cold outside.'

'I have a jumper and gloves in my bag,' said Angel Rain. And she turned around and showed me her backpack. It was a funny, green frog backpack with boggly frog eyes, which I thought was brilliant.

'What about a coat?' I asked her.

'Yes,' said Angel Rain. 'I have my ski jacket in my bag too.'

'I thought you'd never been skiing,' I said.

'I haven't been skiing,' said Angel Rain. 'But Mum and Dad like me to keep warm. Because of my heart. So I have lots of ski clothes.'

Elodie was getting a bit upset by then, because Ferdinand and Felipe were trying to wrap her in toilet roll. She said, 'Tell me what is happening, Angel Rain. Are you taking the boys or not?'

Angel Rain came downstairs and said, 'It's just me and Callum going out. I'm coming home at 9pm.' Then she gave me really serious eyes and said, 'And we must be back at exactly 9pm, Callum. Or I will turn into a pumpkin, like Cinderella's carriage.'

Which was a joke, but Angel Rain looked quite stern, like she meant it.

When we got outside, John Boy opened the car door for us, like a proper limousine driver. He made sure our children's seats were right, then got the disco ball going on the back seat.

Angel Rain loved the disco ball. She was like, 'Wow!' And followed the lights with her finger.

Then John Boy started the car and put on tunes that

were child friendly and didn't have swearing. Disney songs, basically.

Angel Rain thought the music was brilliant. We wound down the windows and sang, 'A WHOLE NEW WOOOOOORLD!'

Like that. So everyone outside could hear. Then she said, 'The sky goes on forever.'

And it really did, Mr Lamb. You could see so many stars that night.

Your iPad is going off again, Mr Lamb. Who is this Bethany Balls person? She's not a girl you're seeing, is she? I thought you liked Nurse Kolawole.

FORTY

Callum Duffy interview transcript:
Continued ...

I'm glad you're being faithful to Nurse Kolawole, Mr Lamb. That's important if you want to win her back.

Anyway, let me tell you about the nature reserve, so you can have a picture in your head when I talk about it.

The nature reserve is all these trails you can walk along, and hides you can sit in to watch birds. And there's a gift shop selling bird houses and real honeycomb, which Granddad says is over-priced.

I don't know if you've ever been to the nature reserve on a star gazing night, Mr Lamb. But there's an outdoor star gazing bit with benches and a massive telescope. And on extra special nights, like meteor showers, there are food vans doing fancy stuff, like Mexican lasagne and posh kebabs. All sorts. And they hang fairy lights around the food vans and put out hay bales wrapped in more fairy lights. So you can sit on hay bales wrapped in fairy lights and eat your food under the stars.

Angel Rain looked so happy when she saw the sparkly hay bales.

'Callum,' she said. 'I have never seen anything so magical.'

And the food area did look special, under all those stars.

Angel Rain wanted to know where the telescope was. Because it's a bit hidden, away from all the lights and everything. But I said, 'Why don't we have something to eat first? And then go look.'

And Angel Rain was up for that. But she was like, 'Ooo, Callum. I don't know what to have. There's so much to choose from.'

'You'll love Bohdan's wood-fired pizza,' I told her. 'He might even do you that pizza you like with the egg on top.'

So I took Angel Rain over to see Bohdan, who is a top bloke. And Bohdan told us all about his mini wood-burning pizza oven, like he always does. And how it's a real Italian oven from Naples, and he had to argue with Ryanair to get it on the plane. And they charged him more than the flight to put it in the hold. But it was worth it, because it makes the best pizza in the world.

Bohdan told us about the pizza special, which sounded a bit rank to be honest, because it was something called fungi. But I just smiled and nodded, like you do, and ordered pepperoni.

Bohdan could do Angel Rain's favourite – pizza Florentine. He got an egg from the gourmet burger van next door. They owed him a favour, Bohdan said, because he let them use his fridge for their cheese slices.

Angel Rain was worried that Bohdan's pizza Florentine

might be different from the pizza Florentine she had in town.

But Bohdan reassured her.

'Yes, it will be different,' he said. 'It will be so much better.'

Which made Angel Rain smile.

'Look, you can't go wrong with a fried egg,' I said. 'Fried eggs make everything better. Go for it. And if you don't like it, I'll get you something different.'

Angel Rain gave me a big smile then, and squeezed my hand and told me she felt really looked after.

I said a special thank you to Bohdan for sorting us out and told him his usual bottle of Budweiser would be on the house next time he came into the pub.

John Boy didn't join us for pizza, because he had a Ginster's pasty in the glove box with his name on it. But he did get a cup of tea and a massive slice of sponge cake from the nature reserve cafe. Then he sat behind me and Angel Rain on his own hay bale and he put his earphones in and listened to the football. Which was really thoughtful.

So me and Angel Rain sat on our hay bale with pizza boxes on our laps and fizzy Italian cherry drinks at our feet. And it was brilliant, having a bit of food together under the stars.

Angel Rain panicked about dropping crumbs at first. And she wanted a coaster for her fizzy drink. But I said, 'It's all right. The animals will eat whatever we drop.' And she calmed down a bit about the mess.

When Angel Rain tried her pizza, she said, 'This is the best pizza in the whole world.'

Which made me feel so happy, like I'd cooked it myself.

After our meal, me and Angel Rain went over to the star gazing area. We got ourselves settled on a bench, with blankets and that. And John Boy brought us over two cups of hot apple juice with cinnamon sticks to warm us up. He left us to it, but sort of hung around in the background, like a bouncer.

After a bit, we went over for a turn on the telescope.

I don't know if you've ever seen a real star-gazing telescope, Mr Lamb. But the one at the nature reserve is massive. Like, the size of a chair. Angel Rain was so excited to have a go. I let Angel Rain go first, because I am a gentleman.

And guess what, Mr Lamb? The moment Angel Rain looked through the telescope, she saw a shooting star.

I saw it too, with my naked eye. Which is not a rude thing to say. It just means I was looking without a telescope.

Angel Rain was so excited. She jumped up and down going, 'That was amazing! The most amazing thing I've ever seen.'

I was so happy for her.

'You should make another life wish,' I said. 'You definitely get an extra one now. Honestly. It's not cheating.'

Angel Rain looked a bit tired and said, 'I'm not sure I'll have time for any more wishes, Callum.'

'What are you talking about?' I said. 'You have your whole life ahead of you.'

'I'm very happy to see a shooting star,' said Angel Rain. 'Now all I have to do is see a frog and go skiing and that's enough for me. Although skiing is very unlikely.'

'The best wishes are the unlikely ones,' I said. 'So when they do come true, you know it's real magic.'

Just then, another shooting star went overhead.

Angel Rain said, 'Wow!'

'You definitely get another wish now,' I said. 'It's a sign. Come on. Wish for something. Disneyland. Anything.'

Angel Rain closed her eyes and said, 'I wish that when I die, I turn into the stars and the frogs and the snow. And be with you at sunset forever, because I love you.'

I was totally stunned.

Because the 'I love you' came out of nowhere and had nothing to do with Disneyland. The thing about dying was a bit unnecessary, but it was still the best thing I'd ever heard, so I wasn't complaining.

I got this stupid grin on my face and said, 'You love me? Really?'

And Angel Rain nodded.

I went all shy for a minute. And I was about to say, 'I love you too, Angel Rain. To the moon and back.'

But then a bad thing happened.

This dark figure came marching up to us, all stiff and angry.

At first, I thought we were going to get told off for hogging the telescope. Because we were standing by it and not looking through it. But then Angel Rain said, 'Oh no. It's my dad.'

'Your dad?' I said. 'Why would he be here?'

'I didn't tell my parents about star gazing,' said Angel Rain. And she swallowed like it hurt. 'But Dad must have found out.'

That was a shock, I can tell you.

'Why didn't you tell them?' I asked.

'Because I knew they would say no,' Angel Rain whispered.

Then I heard Gus's big, angry voice shout: 'Angel Rain! Angel Rain, come here right now.'

And it was another 'uh oh' moment.

Gus came storming up to us, pointing his big hammy finger at Angel Rain.

'I told you there would be no star gazing,' said Gus. 'And I told you to stay away from this boy. We are going home. Right now.' And he grabbed Angel Rain's hand and started pulling her.

That made me angry.

'Steady on,' I said. 'No need to grab her like that. She's not long out of hospital.'

Gus put his big, beardy angry elf face near mine. I could see right up his nose.

'Do not come near my daughter, again,' he said. 'Or I will call the police. Do you understand me?'

I saw red then. And I would have gone for him, but John Boy appeared out of nowhere and got in the way.

'All right,' said John Boy, in his soldier voice. 'Everyone calm down.'

John Boy is very good at stopping fights. He's not scared to walk right in the middle of a bust up, because he's been punched in the face so many times.

'Who are you?' said Gus. 'Oh wait. You must be the so-called chaperone.'

'What's a chaperone?' asked John Boy.

'The adult,' barked Gus. 'In charge of these children. The one who took my daughter out without permission?'

'I did have permission,' said John Boy. And he looked all confused.

Gus pointed a finger at John Boy and said, 'I don't want my daughter with the likes of you. You're lucky I haven't punched your lights out.'

'I wouldn't try it, mate,' said John Boy. 'I might be a raspberry ripple, but I keep fit. And what do you mean, the likes of me?'

Gus looked a bit guilty then, and said he had nothing against disabled people. But Angel Rain shouldn't be here. It was cold and she had a heart problem and they were going home.

Angel Rain looked so upset.

'Come on, Angel Rain,' said Gus. 'We're going.' And he pulled Angel Rain away, towards the visitor centre.

I wanted to run after her, but John Boy put a hand on my shoulder and said best not.

'He's worried about his daughter,' said John Boy. 'We'll work all this out another day.'

By the time me and John Boy got to the car park, I thought Angel Rain and her dad would be long gone. But Gus was having trouble with his BMW, because the key was on his mobile phone.

John Boy shouted, 'Do you need a hand, mate?'

But Gus said, 'No, I am quite capable.' And he did get his car open in the end.

Angel Rain gave me a really sad wave when they drove away. She looked like a puppy in a dog pound van. It broke my heart.

Then it was just me and John Boy and the car park and a galaxy of stars. And I looked up at that big sky that went on forever and wished and wished for another shooting star. Because I wanted to undo everything that just happened. But I didn't see one. Which is typical.

John Boy was well nice on the drive back. He said that stressed adults don't always act right.

'I saw it all the time in the army,' said John Boy. 'A lad misses his girlfriend or Heineken beer or KFC chicken or whatever. So he takes his mood out on everyone else. But one day it might be you in the army mess tent, punching a bag of Lays potato chips because you really, really want a bag of Walkers. There but for the grace of God and all that. You have to be forgiving.'

I did try to be forgiving, but I am still proper heartbroken.

I think we'd better leave it there for now, Mr Lamb. Because Francois is here for his violin lesson, and it will be hard to talk with all that noise going on. So you go on home to do your university things. And I'll just put some Blu Tack in my ears and wait for the home bell.

It'll be after Halloween when we see each other again, won't it? The kids are going to love your pumpkin-shaped biscuits. Well done, Mr Lamb. I am very proud of you making an effort for Halloween. Because honestly, when we first met I didn't think you'd be the type.

FORTY-ONE

Michael Lamb

What a Halloween it's been.

I realise All Hallows' Eve is supposed to be unusual, but this one was odd beyond belief.

I thought the most surprising part of the day would be my novelty monster doorbell.

How wrong I was.

The first Halloween shock came when trick or treaters rang the aforementioned doorbell at 4pm.

I hadn't expected the festivities to start so soon, and was still baking biscuits. But the two families on my doorstep informed me my house was too exciting to pass by.

Who'd have thought my 'spooky spectacular' front garden would be so popular? It was only an unkempt pile of weeds and brambles with ghouls, bats and cobwebs hanging at strategic places. And true, I did invest in a smoke machine, but it was only a small one.

'Yours is the best house on the street,' one of the children said. 'We've been waiting all week to come here. We got changed as soon as school finished and ran all the way.'

After that, I was inundated with trick or treaters.

I ran out of pumpkin-shaped shortbread biscuits early on. The glow-in-the-dark lollies went next, so I had to make an emergency dash to Gudram's Goods to clean him out of novelty Halloween chocolates, sweets and toys.

By nine o'clock, I thought it best to pack things away and send the message that children should go home to bed. The socio-demographic makeup of the street was changing and pub-goers were stumbling back from town.

In fact, one drunk man mistook one of my floating spectres for a friend and started having a chat. So I folded away the ghosts pretty quickly after that and put the boggly eye spiders back in their boxes.

Now we come to the oddest event of the night.

As I was unhooking a rubber bat from my bramble bush, I saw two young boys walking down the street. They didn't look old enough to be on their own, and I couldn't see a parent with them. So I kept an eye out, because that's what good community members do.

When the boys neared my front garden, I got the shock of my life.

One of them was Callum.

'I think we've gone the wrong way,' I heard Callum say. 'I don't remember this road at all.'

His friend, a skittish looking blond boy, said, 'No, this is the way to the train station. Trust.'

I recognised the boy, I realised. He was the one who showed me his underpants at the Calm Corner window. Dexter.

It was absolutely surreal. There was no reason for Callum to be in town, let alone on my street. He'd already told me he'd be in Great Oakley for Halloween. And where was his parent or guardian?

I didn't know what to do. For safeguarding reasons, I couldn't approach Callum out of the interview setting. But it sounded like he and his friend were lost.

While I was watching, three teenage boys crossed the street. They'd been hanging around outside Gudram's Goods for a while and looked up to no good. And they began to tailgate Callum and Dexter, shoulders back, hoods up.

I didn't like it. Not at all.

When Callum and Dexter passed my garden, the teenagers moved in front of them, forcing them to stop. One of the older boys pushed Callum's shoulder, and Callum stumbled back.

Safeguarding protocol went out the window.

I leapt over my garden wall and shouted, 'Hey! What are you doing? Get away from those young boys! Get away!'

'Mr Lamb?' said Callum.

The older boys looked startled too, but they didn't get away, as requested.

One of the teenagers said, 'Who are you, Jesus?'

'I am Doctor Michael Lamb,' I said. 'A concerned community member with two PhDs.'

'Leave it, Mr Lamb,' said Callum. 'We'll just give them our phones. It's not worth getting hurt.'

I felt both terrified and furious.

How dare these boys try to steal from Callum?

In my rage, I grabbed a scythe from a floating sceptre and charged at the boys, much as one might charge up to a group of geese to scare them away.

The teenagers ran, and one shouted over his shoulder, 'You're a mental case!'

Which I didn't take personally, because I did look rather unhinged.

Once the teenagers were gone, I sagged over my front wall taking deep breaths.

'Are you alright, Mr Lamb?' asked Callum.

I swallowed quickly. The urge to vomit was there, but passing quickly. Eventually, I turned to Callum and Dexter, certain I looked as white as the remaining ghoul in my garden.

'I'm fine,' I said. 'Are you two alright?'

'Yeah!' said Callum. 'You saved us, Mr Lamb. You're a hero. If they'd taken our phones, we would have been totally stuffed. We don't know where we are.'

'Never mind that,' I said. 'What on earth are you doing here, Callum? Why aren't you in Great Oakley?'

'It's a long story,' said Callum. 'But me and Dexter have to get the train now.'

I checked my watch. 'The next Great Oakley train is in fifteen minutes,' I said. 'And you're going the wrong way.'

'We don't know where the train station is,' Dexter piped up. 'We're lost.' Then he gave a crazed laugh.

'Follow me,' I said. 'But not too closely. This is totally against safeguarding protocol. You must not talk to me or interact in any way. Do you understand?'

'Can you keep quiet, Dexter?' Callum asked his friend. 'For once in your life?'

Dexter nodded, and the pair followed me down the road like junior muggers in training.

At the station, the train was waiting. Callum and Dexter jumped on board, just as the guard blew his whistle. I hopped on too, and saw the boys safely home.

'You won't tell Mum what happened, will you?' Callum asked, when we reached the Great Oakley Arms.

'I'm not sure I could if I wanted to,' I said. 'I have no idea what happened. What on earth were you doing in town?'

'I'll tell you at school,' said Callum. And he went indoors.

I am still mystified by the whole experience. But also, rather proud.

I met three muggers and I didn't run away. I was heroic. Who'd have thought?

FORTY-TWO

Callum Duffy interview transcript: *Thursday 1st November, 9.02am*

Here he is! The man who chases off muggers!

Alright, Mr Lamb? You're a hero, do you know that? Thank you so much for helping us out on Halloween. We would have been stuffed if it hadn't been for you.

I know you're wondering what me and Dexter were doing in town. And I will tell you. But let me fill in the blanks first.

I wasn't looking forward to Halloween this year, Mr Lamb. Or Bonfire Night. Because I was heartbroken after the star gazing and all that. I just wanted to stay at home with my tadpoles. But you can't miss Halloween when you have a friend like Dexter.

At school on Wednesday, Dexter was like, 'You can't miss the best night of the year. Think of all those sweets. Sweets are better than a girl, any day of the week.'

But I was like, 'No way. Angel Rain is better than Extra-

sour Fizzy Twangers, Mega Lick'em Stick'em Dip'ems and
Squashy Drumsticks all mixed together. She is the best girl
in the world. But I'm never going to see her again. I'm
heartbroken.'

Dexter put an arm around my shoulder and said, 'Why
don't you text this girl and see if she'll have you back? You
can use my phone if you're out of credit.'

Which was decent of him, because Dexter is on pay as
you go and his text messages cost 20p each.

'I didn't get dumped,' I said. 'Angel Rain's dad won't let
us see each other anymore. If I see Angel Rain again, he'll
call the police.'

Dexter thought for a minute. Then he said, 'Your
problem is her dad, then.'

Which was true.

'So if you were invisible from her dad, there'd be no
problem?' Dexter went on.

'Dexter,' I said. 'There is no such thing as an invisibility
cloak. Let it go.'

'I've got a better idea than that,' said Dexter. 'A really
epic, amazing idea.'

'This isn't about putting cling film over toilets again,
is it?'

'No,' said Dexter. 'It's about helping you see this Angel
Rain girl without her dad knowing. If I make that happen,
will you stop being all miserable and help me egg some
houses?'

I said yes to the first bit, but no to the second. Because I
am a changed man with a new haircut and a book on the go,
and I don't want to be a hooligan.

'But I can't see Angel Rain,' I said. 'Her dad will call the
police.'

'That's where my genius idea comes in,' said Dexter. 'It's Halloween. Right? What do we do on Halloween?'

'We put cling film over your mum's toilet seat,' I said. 'And she falls for it every year.'

'Yes,' said Dexter. 'And?'

'We go around the village asking for sweets,' I said. 'And you take it too far and start threatening people.'

'You're missing the most important bit,' said Dexter. 'Costumes. On Halloween, we wear costumes. Which are like disguises. Right? So why don't we go and see your girlfriend in Halloween disguise? Then her dad won't know it's you.'

Which actually wasn't a bad idea. You can see where this is going, can't you, Mr Lamb? Are you putting the pieces together?

I said to Dexter: 'But Angel Rain lives in town, by the big park. How will we get there?'

'You can drive us,' said Dexter. 'In your cousin's car.'

I had to be honest with Dexter then, and tell him I'd lied about being able to drive.

'But we could take the train,' I said. 'It stops near DeMontford Park.'

Me and Dexter looked at each other. And we both knew we were going to do a crazy plan and probably end up in loads of trouble. It was well exciting.

I'll say this for Dexter. He's a doer, not a dreamer.

'Let's go for it,' I said. 'We'll get really good disguises and take the train into town.'

Dexter started jumping around, going, 'Wooo!'

He gets like that sometimes. Usually, after he's eaten a packet of Skittles.

I know it's dangerous to catch a train on your own without an adult, Mr Lamb. And I would never tell a younger kid to do it. But me and Dexter had a proper plan with train times and everything. And we both had phones. So we thought it would be okay.

On Halloween, I went to Dexter's house for tea. We had fish fingers and chips, because that's what Dexter's mum always does. And I appreciate it, Mr Lamb, because some parents try to cook fancy things on play dates, and they can be hit and miss. But you can't go wrong with fish fingers.

After tea, me and Dexter put on our costumes.

Dexter had a Squid Games costume, which was way too big for him. It turns out, violent TV programme costumes don't come in kids' sizes. So Dexter had to use loads of masking tape to make it fit.

I had a frog costume, because I thought Angel Rain would like that. I strapped big papier-mâché flippers to my shoes, which looked brilliant. And the costume was a disguise, too. Because I had black and green camouflage paint on my face and a green hood with frog eyes.

Once we were dressed up, we told Dexter's mum we were going trick or treating. But really, we headed straight for the train station.

Me and Dexter were both nervous waiting for the train. I tried to do my calm breathing, like Miss Hussain is teaching me. But Dexter let us both down, running around the platform, swinging his arms around and barking like a dog.

I was like, 'Dexter! Stop showing us up!' Then the train pulled in, and Dexter freaked out. He said there was a monster under the train, and he'd heard it whispering, 'dead boys'.

'We can't get on that train,' said Dexter. 'The monster will get us.'

I said, 'Mate. You're letting your imagination get the

better of you again. There's no monster. Not under the train. Not down the boys' toilets at school. Not anywhere.'

But Dexter wouldn't stop screaming.

Then the train guard blew his whistle, and I knew it was now or never. So I jumped onto the train and shouted to Dexter, 'Come on, mate! We're on a mission. Don't let a soldier down.'

Talking about soldier missions always works with Dexter. He did a run and jump and got on the train. Except, the train doors closed on his backpack, and he screamed because he thought the monster had got him.

Luckily, a nice, old lady pulled the doors open with her bare hands.

We were both impressed by how strong the lady was, and Dexter asked if she did weight training.

'Yes,' she said. 'I can bench 36kg.'

It took ages to get into town. Seven long, boring minutes.

At the town station, there were loads of people walking around in Halloween costumes, drinking and shouting.

It was a bit scary, to be honest.

I'm used to loud people at the pub, but these ones were different. They weren't nice, happy loud. They were aggro. And I wished I'd dressed as a Ghostbuster, so I had a gun to wave around. Because papier-mâché flippers aren't much use in a rumble.

Dexter went a bit mental when we got off the train. He ran up and down, going, 'We're FREEEEE!' Like that. And he wanted to show his underpants to this gang of teenage boys, but I stopped him. Because that could have got us in big trouble.

Once I got Dexter out of the train station, we walked up the long road towards DeMontford Park. But when we got to the park gates, this red-eyed zombie was there, swigging a big can of Stella Artois and shouting swearwords.

Me and Dexter tried to go through the gates, but the zombie man gave us mad eyes and said, 'Trick or treat!' in this mega scary voice.

So me and Dexter legged it behind the flower troughs and worked out a plan B.

'We should wait until zombie man is scaring someone else,' I said, 'Then run through the gate behind him.'

'That's an alright plan,' said Dexter. 'But I've got a better plan. Let's get some crisps.'

'What is it with you and crisps?' I said. 'How are crisps going to help us?'

'By the time we get crisps,' said Dexter, 'the zombie man might have gone.'

I could see his point. And I did fancy something to eat after the long train journey. So we went to the little Tesco Express, which was right by the park. And that's when our mission ran into BIG trouble with the police.

Cliffhanger!

Because it's break time now ... there goes the bell.

FORTY-THREE

Callum Duffy interview transcript: *Thursday 1st November, 11.01am*

I came in quick from break, Mr Lamb, because you'll want to know what happened next. And I know what it's like, waiting for the next episode of something. It's torture sometimes.

So.

The police.

Me and Dexter got stopped by the fuzz on Halloween, and I blame Dexter for it.

We shouldn't have stopped for those crisps. We were on an army mission. And soldiers don't eat crisps, even on Halloween. They eat energy bars and corned beef from cans.

Anyway, this is what happened.

Me and Dexter headed into the Tesco Express supermarket by DeMontford Park. And Dexter spent ages choosing crisps, like he always does.

I was waving a bag of steak McCoy's at him, saying, 'Get this one. You always get this one.'

But Dexter said he fancied something different, because we were on a special mission.

Then I felt this hard tap on my shoulder.

I admit, I did scream. Because I thought the drunk zombie man had come after us. But it was a lady police officer. She was quite fat, no offence, and had blonde hair pulled back really right in a bun. There was a short, ginger man police officer with her. He had red cheeks like a garden gnome, and was holding two Cadbury's Double Decker bars and a big packet of Cheese Doritos.

The lady police officer said, 'Would you mind telling us what you're doing, gents?'

Dexter said, 'We're thirteen!' In a really high voice.

'I didn't ask your age,' said the lady police officer. 'I asked what you were doing.'

'We're buying crisps,' said Dexter. 'What of it?' Then he pointed to the man police officer's vest, and said, 'Hang on. You're not real police. You're community support. We don't have to tell you nothing.'

Dexter was right. The man had 'Community Support Officer' written on his black vest thing. The lady did too, but she'd hung her police radio over the writing to cover it up. Which was a bit sneaky.

Dexter started jumping up and down, saying, 'You're not the real fuzz. You can't do nothing.'

'Community support officers have special powers,' said the lady police officer. 'And I'll take you down the station if you keep talking back.'

'You can't take us to the station,' said Dexter. 'All you can do is give out fines for dropping litter. And we're not dropping litter. We haven't even bought the crisps yet.'

Not that me or Dexter would litter, Mr Lamb. That's well bad. But Dexter was enjoying himself, winding the officers up.

The lady officer got angry then and asked for our parents' phone numbers.

Dexter said, 'No way.' And ran out of the shop.

I stood there for a minute, like an idiot. Then I thought, actually making a run for it is a good idea. So I legged it after Dexter.

The trouble was, I was wearing flappy frog flippers. And I was still holding the McCoy's Steak crisps, which I hadn't paid for.

When I got near the sliding doors, a security guard pounced on me like a big, fat, bald tiger.

'I'm not shoplifting,' I said. 'I was just catching up with my friend.'

But the police officer lady caught us up and said, 'You're in a lot of trouble, young man.'

'No offence,' said the security officer. 'But you're only community support. I'll take it from here.'

Then the lady police officer started telling the security guard about her special powers. Like she was a superhero or something.

The security guard said he had more special powers because he could sit on people if they tried to run away.

They got into a bit of an argument, after that.

Then Dexter came back and told the security guard to let me go. He can be a good friend sometimes. When he's not stuffing potato croquettes down my pants.

'This is against human rights,' said Dexter. 'My friend needs a lawyer.'

But the security guard wouldn't let me go and told me not to move a muscle.

Dexter got smart then and said it was impossible not to move a muscle. Because your face moves all the time. Which is why weasels bite faces.

After that, the security guard took us both to his office. The community support officers came too. And the lady kept going on about how community support officers have more powers than people think.

'How old are you boys?' the security officer asked.

'We're twelve,' said Dexter.

The community support lady said, 'You said thirteen a minute ago.'

'You look a bit short for twelve,' said the security guard.

'Yes, we are short for our age,' said Dexter. 'We have hormone problems.'

'What, both of you?' said the community support lady.

Dexter said, 'Yes, that's why we're friends.' And he put an arm around my shoulder.

I don't think the adults believed us about the hormone problems, but they couldn't prove how old we were. So they had to let us go.

The community support officers said they'd walk us home, but we said no thank you. Because we didn't want them to know we'd caught the train by ourselves.

'But you could walk us to the park,' I said. 'There's a scary man at the gate. He was drinking a massive can of Stella.'

So the officers walked to the park with us. And they told the zombie man to move on, but the lady officer wasn't very polite about it.

The zombie man wasn't polite either. And there was a bit of a row. Then the lady officer took the man's Stella and poured it down the drain.

After that, the zombie man cried and followed the

community support officers down the street, calling them bullies and telling them they owed him two pounds ninety-seven.

I felt a bit sorry for the zombie man, to be honest. But it was good news for us because he wasn't in front of the park gates anymore. So me and Dexter had a clear route to Angel Rain's house.

FORTY-FOUR

Callum Duffy interview transcript:
Continued ...

I was frightened, Mr Lamb. Any kid my age would be
terrified, walking into a dark park on Halloween. But love
makes you brave. It helps you do impossible things.

Dexter was worried teenagers would try to give us
drugs. Which was stupid. Because people who do drugs are
addicts and want to keep the drugs for themselves.

Anyway, we got through the park and out onto
DeMontford Park Road. And after a little walk up and
down, we found Angel Rain's house.

The Peggs hadn't done anything to their house for
Halloween. No pumpkin. No scary skeleton on the front
door. Not even some Happy Halloween bunting in the
window. It was just the same fancy cars and clean bricks.

I was nervous when we got to Angel Rain's driveway.
And my frog costume didn't seem like such a good idea.

'Tell me the truth, Dex,' I said. 'Does this costume look

stupid?'

Dexter said yes, it did look stupid. And I should have come as a Ghostbuster or a soldier, because girls liked those better than frogs.

'But Angel Rain likes frogs,' I said.

'Well, let's find out,' said Dexter. And he ran up to Angel Rain's house and rang the doorbell.

I wanted to run for it, but I couldn't. Not with papier-mâché flippers on my shoes. So I just stood there like an idiot and watched Gus open the door.

You would have thought Gus would dress as a scary elf or goblin for Halloween, because he looked the part. But he wasn't dressed up at all. He just had on his usual, boring shirt and jeans and looked angry.

'Trick or treat!' said Dexter.

'What have you come as?' asked Gus.

'I'm a Squid Games worker,' said Dexter.

'What's that when it's at home?' said Gus. Then he looked at me and said, 'And why is your friend lurking around back there? What's he come as? A lizard man or something?'

'My froggy friend is very shy,' said Dexter. 'He has hormone problems.'

Gus said, 'I suppose you two are after sweets, are you? Hang on. I've got some flapjack somewhere. I make it especially for my cholesterol.'

And he went back into the house.

Dexter waved me over.

'Look, he's left the door open,' said Dexter. 'Go in and see your girlfriend. It's a dare!' Then he did one of his mad hyena laughs.

'Yeah, all right,' I said. 'Cover for me.'

Dexter looked a bit worried.

'You're not going to do it, are you?' said Dexter. 'That man is getting us flapjack. I don't want my treat bucket mucked up with seeds and stuff. We should make a run for it.'

'No way,' I said. 'This is my chance.'

And I went into the house before Dexter could stop me.

The hallway was dead quiet, but I could hear voices coming from the kitchen. Boring, serious voices, talking about flapjack.

I crept up the stairs as quickly as I could, with my papier-mâché flippers flapping on the carpet.

The twin boys were nowhere to be seen, which was a worry. Because they could be hiding somewhere, ready to jump out and wrap me in loo roll.

On the landing, I looked around for Angel Rain's bedroom. But I didn't know which one it was, and there were so many doors.

Honestly, I nearly bottled it. Especially when I heard Gus downstairs, asking Dexter where his lizard friend had gone.

If I was a Jedi, I would have used the force to open the right bedroom door. But I was just a boy who liked a girl, so I took a lucky guess and tried the first door.

It turned out to be Ferdinand and Felipe's room, and they were inside hitting each other with foam swimming noodles. So I closed their door quick and tried another one.

The next room was Elodie's. I knew that, because the curtains were closed and there were empty coffee cups everywhere.

The third door was the right one.

Angel Rain was sitting at a big desk doing homework. She was concentrating so hard that she didn't even notice the door.

I could hear Gus downstairs, saying to Dexter, 'They're made with low fat spread, too. So it's not just the sunflower seeds that will do you good.'

Dexter was a good wingman. He asked Gus more questions about the flapjacks. Like how come they were so crumbly and dry.

I tried to get Angel Rain's attention, like, 'Pssst! Angel Rain!'

But that wasn't a good idea. Because Angel Rain screamed her head off when she saw me in the doorway.

I tried to calm her down, like, 'It's all right. It's me, Callum.'

But Angel Rain kept screaming, so I took my hood down. Which I shouldn't have done because I was in the enemy camp and no longer in disguise.

Angel Rain calmed down a bit, then. Which was good. And I told her I was dressed up for Halloween. And I'd come as a frog, because she liked frogs.

Then Gus shouted upstairs, 'Angel Rain? Are you alright?'

'I'm fine, Dad,' said Angel Rain. Then she whispered to me, 'You have to hide.'

But I didn't want to hide. I wanted to say the important thing I'd come to say. So I took a deep breath and said, 'Angel Rain, I love you. I'm sorry I didn't say it before at the nature reserve. But we were interrupted. And I really, honestly do love you and I think you're the best girl ever.'

I hoped Angel Rain would say, 'I love you' back, but too late. Gus came crashing into the bedroom.

If I'd been quicker on my feet, I would have pulled my hood up and got back into disguise. But I didn't have good spy skills that day.

Gus did this weird shriek when he saw me. Then he

said, 'Callum.' In a rumbly voice, like a thunderstorm. And he grabbed my arm and pulled me out of the house. Which could have been assault, but maybe not because I'd gone into Gus's house without permission.

When we got to the door, Gus said, 'I am this close to calling the police. This close.' And he pinched his fingers together.

Dexter got lippy then and said we'd already seen the police today. And Gus slammed the door in our faces.

I stared at the door for a bit, feeling upset.

Dexter put his arm around my shoulder and said, 'Come on, mate. Let's make the best of things and hit some of these big houses for Halloween treats.'

But I didn't want to do that. I just wanted to go home. Except we got lost, as you know, because the park was locked. And that's when we found your road and you helped us. Which was brilliant.

So thank you for everything. And you are a hero, Mr Lamb. You really are. You shouldn't keep calling yourself a wimp, because you're not.

We'd better leave it there, Mr Lamb.

I can see the exterminator van outside, so we'll be kicked out of here soon. They found a dead rat under the mindfulness box this week, you see. So they've got to put poison everywhere.

We all think the rat is Mr Rafferty's fault, because he spends so much time in here hiding from his class and eating Hob Nobs without a plate.

We'll talk again after the weekend, alright? I hope you've got a good firework display to go to. Personally, I'm just going to stay at home and be heartbroken. I'm not in the mood for all those whizzes and bangs.

Take care. You're looking well, by the way.

FORTY-FIVE

Michael Lamb

I was due to see Callum again on Tuesday the 6th of November. However, that morning a blizzard came.

Furious snow and wind buried the town, causing school closures, traffic issues and milk shortages. There was no actual deficit in milk, but people stockpile at the first sign of snow. As if milk is some sort of arterial life blood one can't live without. Ridiculous, when the range of long-life milks these days is overwhelming and nutritionally just as adequate.

In some ways, the blizzard came at the right time. My new carpets had been fitted a few days before, so I had much-needed insulation and warmth. On the negative side, I'd spent all of Sunday and Monday mowing, cutting and weeding my front and back gardens. This hard work was now buried under snow and invisible.

Still. The town looked rather beautiful, bathed in

peaceful white. Ifeoma would have called the snow 'angelic'. She had a religious side, but I never held it against her.

I was very disappointed not to see Callum during the week of snow closures, but my time was well spent painting the hallway and upstairs.

My gloomy, cobwebby Victorian mansion has now been totally transformed. It is a warm, welcoming period home. I have gone from one wooden chair in the lounge to a whole furniture suite, carpets, pictures, footstools and a colour-match concept with feature walls and curtains.

As Callum would say, 'the lot'.

A few days into the blizzard, my oven broke. Usually this wouldn't have been a problem. I would have opened a tin of tuna and got on with things. But I'd become used to eating hot, freshly prepared meals now and cold food on a cold day was just intolerable.

All the restaurants and takeaways were closed, except one – my favourite vegetarian restaurant, Curry Lau.

Curry Lau is run by tough Gurkha ex-soldiers who have served food in war zones and halfway up mountainsides. So dangerous weather has never diminished their curry output.

It felt like half the town were at Curry Lau, as I skidded through the entrance way. Presumably, they'd heard Lau on the local radio, as I had, talking about the Gurkha Everest Special he'd invented for the blizzard.

Being around others felt very pleasant. I even chatted a little with an elderly lady, who boasted of ordering a 'shit hot curry', and spoke of the toilet problems she'd have tomorrow morning.

As I was waiting for my Gurkha Everest special, aloo chop and vegetable samosa, a lady came tumbling into the takeaway area, dusting snow from her colourful headscarf.

She wore a faux-fur jacket, training shoes and very familiar elephant-print pantaloon trousers.

My first thought was: 'That clothing is not weather appropriate.

My second thought was: 'Oh good god. It's Ifeoma.'

And it was.

Ifeoma was breathless and shivering, shaking snow from her headscarf and coat.

I was immobilised as she approached the counter and asked for a table for one.

'My heating isn't working,' Ifeoma told Lau. 'Will you warm me up with a wonderful curry and a table in your joyous restaurant?'

But Lau said there were, sadly, no table vacancies until 10pm that evening.

'You can sit in the takeaway area for as long as you like,' said Lau, as a jet of wind rushed under the doorway.

I leapt to my feet.

'Ifeoma,' I said. 'Would you like to eat your takeaway curry at my house? With me.'

Asking that question was, ironically, a lot harder than chasing off the Halloween muggers. Which gave me something to think about.

Ifeoma did a double-take.

'Michael?' said Ifeoma. 'Are you following me? First the hospital and now here.'

'I am not following you,' I said. 'I am ordering a Gurkha Everest Special, aloo chop and a vegetable samosa. This is simply a coincidence. But a happy one.'

Ifeoma laughed then.

'Would you like to accompany me to my house?' I suggested. 'And eat your curry there? I've bought a new sofa. And a footstool.'

A stillness descended over the waiting area, as if everyone were holding their breath.

'It is a wonderful offer, Michael,' said Ifeoma. 'But I'm not sure your house will be any warmer than mine. You never turn the heating on.'

'That's where you're wrong,' I said, with a tinge of pride in my voice. 'The heating is on full blast. And if you're not warm enough, I can light a fire. I have a 'magic fire log' from the Co-op. It starts a cheery fire with just one match.'

Ifeoma stared at me for a moment. A long moment. Then she said, 'If your house is warm, then you have yourself a deal. But let me buy your curry to say thank you.'

I wouldn't hear of it.

'You are a hard-working nurse,' I said. 'You deserve to be treated. I will add your curry to my order. I remember your favourites. Rara with lentils, Nepalese bread, cardamom rice with crisp brown onions and a spiced lentil potato cake.'

Ifeoma looked very happy. 'Thank you, Michael,' she said. 'Thank you very much.'

Our food came quickly. I put the swinging plastic bag of delicacies over one arm and held the other arm out to Ifeoma.

'Let me support you,' I told Ifeoma. 'Your training shoes are inappropriate in this weather.'

Ifeoma looked at me in surprise. 'You're wearing training shoes too,' she said. 'Bright blue ones. Which I like, by the way. And you always said it was patronising for a man to help a woman.'

'I am learning,' I said, 'that sometimes, a person can care for someone else without there being gender politics involved.'

Ifeoma smiled and grasped my arm.

Truthfully, I slipped and slid around more than Ifeoma

in the snow. But it still felt good to make the gesture of care.

We were both laughing by the time we got to my house. But when Ifeoma saw my living room, her laugher stopped.

'What have you done to this place, Michael?' said Ifeoma. 'It looks like a page from a home magazine.'

'Yes,' I said. 'I studied several DIY magazines.'

'It's wonderful,' said Ifeoma. 'Absolutely wonderful. And so warm. Michael, it's like a different house.'

Ifeoma was even more impressed by my dining area.

'This is incredible, Michael,' she said. 'Gold knives and forks! You were always so set in your ways. So practical. But now you have wine glasses and folded napkins. God really does perform miracles.'

When we sat down to eat, Ifeoma asked about my research.

'How is it going with Callum?' she said. 'Are you getting lots of useful data?'

'None whatsoever,' I said. 'My aim was to study toxic masculinity in disadvantaged boys. But I have found Callum to be a very kind, caring person. He doesn't fit my research statement at all.'

'Then maybe your statement is wrong,' said Ifeoma.

'This is why I miss you, Ifeoma,' I said. 'You always help me think outside the box.'

There was a long silence.

'You miss me?' said Ifeoma.

'Of course I do,' I said. 'Every day.'

Ifeoma's beautifully smooth forehead crumpled in confusion. 'That makes no sense, Michael. You never called me. You never made any attempt to win me back. And you said you'd leave me to get mugged. Remember?'

'That's not quite right,' I explained. 'I said I might run away. I didn't know what I would do under pressure. But now, I am sure if you were mugged, I would confront the muggers.'

'But it wasn't just about the mugging thing,' said Ifeoma. 'You didn't want to get married.'

'That was for your benefit,' I explained. 'Marriage is a sexist, capitalist ceremony of ownership where a woman is given to a man. I would not want to diminish you in that way. You deserve better.'

'That all sounds very logical, Michael,' said Ifeoma. 'But sometimes, the heart wants what it wants. And I want to get married.'

'I was always committed to you,' I said.

'But you didn't want children,' said Ifeoma.

'No,' I admitted.

'Have your feelings changed on that matter?' Ifeoma asked.

'I'm not sure,' I answered.

My mind bellowed, 'Ask her! Ask her if she'll have you back!'

But what if she said no, and I ruined the most wonderful night I'd had in a long time?

Cowardliness prevailed.

At the end of the evening, I offered to walk Ifeoma home. Her flat was twenty minutes from my house, and I worried about her walking alone on the treacherous ground.

Ifeoma is a strong, capable adult. Probably stronger and more capable than me. But still, I worried. And Ifeoma was happy to let me walk her.

When we reached Ifeoma's flat, she said, 'Michael, why did you invite me over this evening?'

'Because your heating was broken,' I said.

'Goodbye, Michael,' said Ifeoma.

And she went inside.

FORTY-SIX

Callum Duffy interview transcript: *Thursday 15th Nov, 11.05am*

Mr Laaaaamb! Long time, no see. That snow was fun, wasn't it?

I thought you might not come today, because you weren't here first thing. But then Miss Hussain told me the Calm Corner was used for first aid training this morning. So I hoped I might see you after break time and here you are.

I've got loads to tell you. Something brilliant happened when it snowed, and I'm not heartbroken anymore. I am so, SO happy.

You know about the school being closed, obvs. And that is one reason I've been happy. But it gets much better than that. Just wait until you hear.

There is a bit of bad news first, though.

Let me tell you.

Just before the blizzard, my second to last tadpole, Geronimo, died in his sleep. I found him face down in the pond weed, looking peaceful. And even though he'd been pretty rotten for a while, it was still a shock.

Now there's only one tadpole left: Judge Dredd. And he's quite rotten too, to be honest. There's a black patch on his tummy and he's swimming all slow. Everyone says he's going to die soon, but I am keeping the faith, Mr Lamb. Because if Judge Dredd can survive the snow, he can survive anything. Right? I don't think he'll become a frog this year. That's too unlikely now. But maybe he'll hibernate and become a frog next year, and I can show him to Angel Rain late next spring.

Anyway, after Geronimo died, the snow came.

People always worry when it snows, don't they, Mr Lamb? Usually about milk. Nana bought ten pints of whole milk, five pints of semi-skimmed and a litre of Guernsey double cream on the first day it snowed. And half of it went off.

A few days into the blizzard, I got a letter from Angel Rain.

I couldn't believe it. I thought I'd never hear from her again after the whole mess on Halloween.

I wanted to read the letter by myself, but our house is quite busy. So getting a moment is difficult. It was like that book, Mr Lamb. 'Peace at Last'. You know, when the dad tries to sleep, but his family are always in the way.

Mum was in the bedroom doing her nails. Nana was in the kitchen making her second breakfast and John Boy was in the lounge playing FIFA on the Xbox.

Sambuca the cat was in Aunty Julesy's old bedroom, and he tried to scratch me for sitting on the bed with him. But I explained in my stern voice that the letter was important, and after that, Sambuca settled down and let me read it.

The letter was dated the 8th of November, which was just after the snow started. And this is what it said:

TOP SECRET

Dear Callum,

This is a top-secret letter because my mum and dad do not know that I am writing to you.

Dad is still quite angry, but it is not your fault. He is angry quite a lot.

It is snowing!

Our school has closed and the news says the schools will stay closed all week and some of next week too.

If my school is closed next Tuesday, Elodie will take me to the park. Because on that day, Felipe and Ferdinand have cello lessons, and she likes to be out of the house.

Will you meet me in top-secret, on Tuesday the 13th of November at 9 am at DeMontford Park? Then we can be together and my parents won't know.

It will be very cold so you should bring ski clothes if you have them. I have a nice, blue ski suit, so you will see me very easily.

Remember this is top secret!

I love you.

From Angel Rain Grace Christina Pegg

PS, I love you.

Now, obviously there might be two or three or even ten words wrong there, because I can't remember absolutely exactly word for word. But if you need to see the letter I can bring it in. Because I have it in my special drawer.

Anyway, it was the best letter ever. I read it over and

over again, especially the 'I love you' parts. Then I asked Granddad to read it for me, just to make sure I wasn't reading it wrong. And he said Angel Rain was doing her commas wrong. But other than that, she did love me and wanted to meet me in the park on Tuesday.

I read the letter again, while Granddad was going on about commas. And the bit about ski clothes caught my eye. Angel Rain's wish was to go skiing. But she'd never been before.

My brain started going round, like that old board game, Downfall. Cogs, that's what I mean.

You live quite near DeMontford Park, Mr Lamb, don't you? So you know it has an epic sledging hill. Kids chuck themselves down it whenever it snows.

So I thought – if you can sledge down that hill, I bet you can ski down it too. And maybe, with a bit of planning, I could take Angel Rain skiing on Tuesday and she'd get her wish. Then she'd have two of life wishes out of three, and that's pretty good going at our age.

I'd have to learn to ski myself, of course. So I could teach Angel Rain how to do it. And I'd need skis. They were essential.

'Granddad,' I said. 'Do we have any skis hanging around the place?'

Granddad said that was a ridiculous question. Because this was Great Oakley, not the Swiss Alps.

But then cousin John Boy came downstairs, rolling a cigarette, and said, 'Actually, Uncle Bob, I've got a pair of skis.'

And it turned out John Boy had bought skis on eBay last summer for 99p. Which was a bargain, except John Boy had forgotten he only had one leg. And you need a special, wide ski if you have one leg.

'Can I borrow your skis, cousin John Boy?' I asked. 'I want to learn to ski on the steep road by the pub. And then I can teach Angel Rain to ski at DeMontford Park. And make her wish come true.'

Granddad said that skis or no skis, no one should travel to DeMontford Park.

'The Great Oakley Gazette says no driving unless it's an emergency,' said Granddad.

'But this is an emergency,' I said. 'I'm going to grant a wish for the love of my life.'

'Write back and tell Angel Rain you're sorry, but the roads are treacherous,' said Granddad. 'Our postie will see your letter gets into town. Won't you, postie?'

Later, our postie said yes, he'd get the post into town. But it wouldn't be delivered, because the town posties were a bunch of wimps who wouldn't leave their nice, warm depot in a strong wind, let alone snow.

'Oh well,' said Granddad. 'I'm sure your young lady will understand.' And he went to sweep snow off his vegetables.

'What if Angel Rain doesn't understand?' I asked John Boy. 'And thinks I've stood her up? You should never do that to a girl. She'll be upset.'

'You're right,' said John Boy. 'You can't upset a girl. That's ungentlemanly.'

'Will you do a special mission with me, cousin John Boy?' I asked.

John Boy started doing commando rolls in the snow then, and asked if we were going to take down some drug dealers. But I said no. I needed an elite soldier to drive me to the park early on Tuesday morning.

John Boy said it was no trouble. He'd driven to the All Days shop and back in the snow for his Mirror newspaper and Mega XL Pot Noodle that morning. Because Land

Rovers were made for ploughing through thick snow and frozen mud. Even really old Land Rovers.

So that was my transport sorted.

Now, I just needed to learn how to ski. I decided to start simple, with a couple of beer trays strapped to my trainers.

It was quite hard, making holes in the beer trays for the string. John Boy caught me with his jungle knife and gave me a big telling-off. Then he tried to make holes himself and cut his thumb open. So we asked Granddad to help, and Granddad got his hand drill and measuring tape out and did a really neat job.

Granddad was happy with the beer tray skis. He called them 'budget-saving fun' and said kids these days were too quick to go out and buy plastic rubbish when they had perfectly good things at home.

Granddad said that when he was a lad, they sledged on sheets of metal stolen from the Volvo factory. But they'd had to stop that when one boy dangerously sliced his leg on a raw metal edge.

Once the beer trays had strings on them, I went to the steep road by our pub to try them out.

Loads of kids were sledging there. And Dexter was trying his luck on a pile of bin bags, which went faster than you would think. But the quickest way to go down the hill was my beer trays.

I'll be honest – skiing was scary at first. The trays went in all directions and my legs went with them. And even though my ankle was better, it still hurt a bit. And doing the splits on a cold road is never fun if you're a boy.

But as the morning went on, I got the hang of things. Part of the trick was avoiding Dexter. Once I'd worked that out, I could go all the way down the hill without falling over.

At lunchtime, I went home for a quick tomato soup and

a sit on the radiator. Then I was out again, practising all afternoon.

By Monday, I thought it was about time I tried the real skis. So I stuffed John Boy's ski boots with four pairs of Granddad's woolly socks and carried them out to the road.

Let me tell you, Mr Lamb. Standing at the top of a steep slope with skis on is scary. I very nearly bottled it. But I thought of Angel Rain, closed my eyes and got Dexter to give me a push.

I won't lie. I did scream. Skis are a lot faster than beer trays. But they do go dead straight, which was good. So they were easier than the beer trays, in a way.

I did have a few problems stopping and I knocked some kids off their sledges at the bottom. But then I learned a good trick, which was falling over on purpose. And that worked well.

By the end of Monday, I had bruises all over me, but I could go down the hill without screaming, as long as no one else was in the way.

I felt dead proud of myself, and I could not wait to see Angel Rain and make her wish come true.

I will tell you more after lunch.

What have you got for your lunch, Mr Lamb? It looks like cold curry from the Gurkha restaurant. Are you going to eat in the staff room again? If you do, look out for me. I'll be waving at the window.

FORTY-SEVEN

Callum Duffy interview transcript: *Thursday 15th November, 1.05pm*

Did you have a nice lunch, Mr Lamb? I saw you chatting away in the staff room. Miss Hussain is well nice, isn't she? And did Mr Rafferty shout about politics and blame the government for everything? That's what he usually does. It's not very grown up, but that's teachers sometimes.

Anyway.

Learning to ski was frightening, Mr Lamb. But love lifts us up where we belong. And although I was very scared, I knew I had to do it for Angel Rain.

The night before the park date, I was nervous. There were so many things to worry about. What if I broke my neck skiing? What if Angel Rain didn't turn up? What if the snow melted?

It was such a relief to wake up on the Tuesday morning and find the snow deep and crisp and even, like the Good King Wesley song.

Nana made a really good breakfast that morning – banana pancakes with Nutella. Fuel for the cold weather, you know? The pancakes were dead sweet, but nothing is sweet enough for John Boy. He added golden syrup and hundreds and thousands to the pancakes, then washed them down with his usual six-sugar mug of tea.

After breakfast, John Boy said, 'Ready for our secret mission, soldier? The Land Rover will handle this snow, no trouble.'

But as it turned out, John Boy's rusty old Land Rover didn't like the snow very much that day. Because it cut out three times before we even made it out of the village.

Luckily, John Boy had a special trick for getting the car going again. He put Hotties hand warmers on the car battery and revved the engine until it started.

Once we were out of the village, the main roads were a lot better. And we made it into town without the engine cutting out.

The big sledging hill at DeMontford Park was empty at 8am. Because no one else was mad enough to go sledging that early. But it was good news for me, because it meant I could do a bit of ski practice without anyone hearing me screaming.

I won't lie. The hill was dead scary. It was loads bigger and steeper than I remembered and I was terrified to ski down it. But love helps you do amazing things, Mr Lamb. And I was a superhero that day, bombing down that massive slope swearing my head off.

I went so fast. At least 100mph, I reckon. I did a lot of swearing at first. But pretty soon I could ski silently with my eyes wide open.

The park-keeper was well impressed. He came out of

his little cottage to tell me I was going to break my neck. So I must have been going like a rocket.

John Boy did a ski lift for me, pushing me up the hill. So that saved some time.

After a bit of ski practice, the cafe opened.

John Boy said he'd head up and grab us some bacon sandwiches. But then I saw Angel Rain coming through the south gate with Elodie. She was early too.

I was so happy. I waved and waved and shouted, 'Angel Rain! Angel Rain!'

Angel Rain looked like a snow princess in her blue ski suit and matching bobble hat. She was excited to see me too, and she went proper mental when she saw the skis. She jumped up and down, shouting, 'Oh my goodness! Oh my goodness! You're skiing!'

'Sort of,' I shouted back. 'I'm getting there.'

I tried to run towards Angel Rain, but I'd forgotten about the skis and fell over. It took me a while to get up, and when I did, Angel Rain was standing over me giggling away.

'You silly billy,' she said.

I got up and said, 'Fancy doing some skiing?'

Angel Rain's eyes got really big and serious, and she said, 'What really? I can have a go on these skis?'

And I said, 'Yeah, of course. It's okay for your heart, isn't they?'

Angel Rain said yes. She could do everything a normal child could do. Except sky diving, but she didn't want to do that anyway.

'Let me just show you how to stop,' I said. 'And then you can have a go.'

And I showed her how to fall over on the skis.

Elodie crossed her arms in her big coat and said, 'That is not how to stop. I will show you the way.' Then she unstrapped the skis and boots from my feet, marched up the hill and came whizzing down on the skis, doing this slalom thing, left and right. She was a really good skier.

At the bottom of the hill, Elodie threw herself around, so the skis went sideways. Which was a better way of stopping, actually. And you didn't get soaking wet that way.

Angel Rain really wanted a go at skiing then.

'John Boy will take you to the top,' I said. 'He's our ski lift.'

'No,' said Elodie. 'You must start halfway down the hill, Angel Rain. And when you get better, then you go from the top.'

Which was a good idea. I wish I'd thought of that when I'd been practising on the tea trays.

I helped Angel Rain get the skis and socks on, and she was nervous and held on to me really tight.

'This is harder than I thought,' she said. 'I don't think I can do this, Callum.'

'Just give it a try,' I said.

So Angel Rain held on to me and did a little ski from halfway down the hill. When she got to the bottom, she was all emotional.

'I ... never ... thought ... I'd ever ski,' she said. 'I am ... so happy ... Callum.'

And she gave me the biggest hug and cried. But in a good way.

I was dead pleased for her.

'Come on,' I said. 'Let's try again. But without you holding on to me this time.'

So John Boy helped Angel Rain up the hill, and she skied on her own, screaming the whole time.

Angel Rain got loads braver as the morning went on. And by 1oam, she was skiing from the top of the hill, screaming her head off. There were quite a few sledges on the hill by then, so the screaming was good. Because it got everyone out of her way.

I knew it was true love that day, Mr Lamb. Because I wanted a go on those skis, but seeing Angel Rain get her wish was much more important.

Angel Rain must have gone down that hill at least twenty times. She loved it. But at snack time, I said we should take a break.

'Don't overdo it,' I said. 'You're not long out of hospital. Let's warm up in the cafe.'

While Angel Rain was taking all Granddad's socks off, she felt around her legs like they were sore.

'Are you alright?' I asked her.

'I'm alright, Callum,' said Angel Rain. 'I am very happy. The happiest I have ever been. I have two of my life wishes now. What could be better?'

'Three of them,' I said. 'But don't you worry. I'm going to make it happen with my last tadpole. Just give him until next year.'

Angel Rain looked sad for a moment. Then she nodded and said, 'Let's go warm up.'

FORTY-EIGHT

Callum Duffy interview transcript:
Continued ...

Have you ever been to the DeMontford Park cafe, Mr
Lamb? It's really nice. They don't do ice cream in winter,
but it's warm inside and they do bacon sandwiches and
baked potatoes and all sorts.

Angel Rain fancied a hot chocolate, so we could pretend
we were in a ski lodge. So that's what we had. And it was
really good, because the cafe did these extra-thick Italian hot
chocolates, with whipped cream and brown sugar and a
cinnamon stick. And you also got this little bit of mega-dry
Italian cake on the saucer called biscotti that you could dip
in the hot chocolate.

When the hot chocolates came, Angel Rain couldn't
stop laughing.

'What's funny?' I asked.

'It looks like a pudding,' said Angel Rain.

And the hot chocolates were a bit like that, because they were so thick you needed a spoon.

Then Angel Rain got all serious and ate the hot chocolate really carefully. She took a long time, sort of thinking about every spoonful.

'What do you reckon?' I asked.

'It is very chocolatey and a bit strong,' said Angel Rain. 'I might not finish it all. But it is a good experience.'

'What about the skiing?' I asked. 'Did you have fun doing that?'

'It was different to how I imagined,' said Angel Rain. 'I thought it would be like flying. But it only felt like that sometimes. Mostly, it was quite scary.'

'Are you disappointed, then?' I asked. 'That it wasn't how you imagined?'

'I'm not disappointed, Callum,' said Angel Rain. 'Life often isn't how you imagine. But I have been skiing and I am very happy. You made my wish come true.'

Then Angel Rain gave me her big, gappy smile and I smiled back.

While we were finishing our hot chocolates, John Boy said he needed to go outside for a smoke. And Elodie went with him, so me and Angel Rain got some quality time.

'I'm really glad you sent that letter,' I told Angel Rain. 'I was having the worst week. My second-to-last tadpole died. There's only Judge Dredd left now. And he looks a bit ropey, truth be told. He's got the same manky skin Geronimo had. But I still hope he'll become a frog next year.'

'I don't think he will become a frog, Callum,' said Angel Rain. 'Because if he was going to hibernate, he would have hibernated by now. I think he will always be a tadpole. And maybe he'll die soon. But that doesn't mean his life hasn't been full of wonderful moments.'

Then she looked out in the snow, like, really thoughtful.

'I shouldn't have gotten so attached to those tadpoles,' I said. 'Everyone said they never stood a chance.'

'You should never regret loving something,' said Angel Rain. Then she held my hand and said, 'I really have had the best day.'

The snow started falling and it looked so nice, floating around outside the window. Me and Angel Rain watched it for a while without saying anything.

Then Angel Rain said, 'Callum, I might have to go back into hospital again soon. But you mustn't worry about me. Okay?'

I had a big, sad feeling in my chest.

'What's happening?' I asked.

'I'm not sure,' said Angel Rain. 'But I feel like something's not right. My legs felt a bit swollen earlier. And that's a sign of my heart being under pressure.'

To be honest, I wanted to start thumping things, the way I sometimes do when I feel upset. But I couldn't do that around Angel Rain. Because she needed me to be grown up and look after her. So I just said:

'Are you feeling all right? Do you need a lift home?'

Angel Rain said she was feeling very good and could walk just fine.

I felt really bad then. Like maybe the skiing hadn't been good for Angel Rain. But Angel Rain said, no, her ankles were swollen before she came out. And she'd hoped they'd go down in the cold, but they hadn't.

'You should see a doctor, then,' I said. 'Promise me you'll see a doctor.'

'I will,' said Angel Rain. 'I'll have to.' Then she gave me her big, serious eyes and said, 'Callum, how would you feel if I went somewhere really far away? And you couldn't see me or phone or even send letters? But it was a nice place and I could ski every day and my body felt better. Would you be happy or sad?'

'I'd be sad,' I said. 'Because I would miss you so much. But I would try to be happy that you were in a nice place.'

Then Elodie came back into the cafe and said, 'We are going home now, Angel Rain. Because this cold is hell on earth, it really is. And I am standing in the snow smoking cigarettes without filters, and I don't know what I am doing with my life.'

Angel Rain held both my hands then and said, 'Today has been one of my biggest wishes. But every day is a wish come true.'

'We'll have loads more days like this,' I said. 'More wishes all the time.'

Angel Rain gave me a big hug that lasted ages. Then she went home.

It was the best day, Mr Lamb. The very best day.

I hope Angel Rain isn't back in hospital again, because she hates it there. I really do love her, Mr Lamb. I really do.

What's up, Mr Lamb? Why are you getting your things together? We've got ages left.

FORTY-NINE

Michael Lamb

As I left the Calm Corner, I felt overwhelmed. Angel Rain clearly wasn't well. And she was hiding her illness from Callum.

People often do hide serious illnesses. My mother did, when she was ill.

I needed to speak to a qualified medical professional, for Callum's sake. He needed a clear picture of what was going on. We both did. So I called Ifeoma.

Ifeoma's phone rang and rang, but this was normal. Her phone was probably hidden among the mints, inexplicable paperclip and empty Galaxy Caramel wrappers in her compartment-less bag.

After nine rings, I hung up and tried again. And again. But Ifeoma didn't answer.

It was disheartening, but I didn't let despair get the better of me. Instead, I cycled over to Ifeoma's flat.

Ifeoma didn't answer the buzzer at first. So I rang quite a few times, in case she hadn't heard.

Eventually, an elderly lady came onto the balcony and shouted at me for wasting electricity.

'We all have to pay for the buzzer system,' she shouted. 'It comes out of our management fees.'

'I need to speak to Ifeoma,' I shouted.

'Is Ifeoma the black lady?' the woman asked.

'She's the human being living in this building,' I said. 'The colour of her skin is quite incidental.'

'Alright,' said the lady. 'I'm not being racist. My grandson is mixed race.'

'Madam,' I said. 'We are all mixed race.'

'The nurse?' the woman said. 'Ifeoma's the nurse, isn't she?'

'Yes,' I replied.

'She'll be sleeping now,' said the lady. 'She just got back from a night shift. I wouldn't disturb her if I were you.'

At that moment, Ifeoma's fiery voice came over the speaker.

'Who is this?' she demanded.

I cleared my throat and said it was me, Michael.

'Michael?' said Ifeoma. 'What do you want? I was sleeping.'

'It's an urgent medical matter,' I said.

A long, crackling sigh came through the intercom.

'Hang on,' said Ifeoma. 'Let me buzz you in.'

Ifeoma's flat was as small and damp as I remembered it, but she had done her best to make it cheerful, with colourful scarfs draped over inexpensive furniture.

The living room / kitchen area smelt like coconut and

lavender, but there was an underlying smell of mould. The smell reminded me of my house, before I'd started putting the heating on.

There was a plastic Christmas tree in the corner, sparsely decorated. One of the decorations was a chunky, wooden heart. The same heart Ifeoma hung on my front door when we lived together. I felt my own heart flutter at the sight of it.

'I'm sorry about the cold,' said Ifeoma, pulling her dressing gown tight. 'The new storage heaters are lukewarm at night and cold all day.' She gave me an embarrassed sideways glance. 'But I still try and make this place feel like a home, you know?'

'You've done a wonderful job,' I said. 'And a Christmas tree. Already.'

'I know November is a little early,' said Ifeoma. 'But I'll be working until five o'clock on Christmas Eve. And then from 7am on Christmas morning. So I thought, if I'm working over Christmas, I'll start earlier at home.'

'You still have our wooden heart,' I said, pointing to the tree.

'Our heart?' said Ifeoma. 'Don't you mean *my* heart? You always hated it.'

'I found it impractical,' I admitted. 'But I never hated it. Quite the opposite. Anyway, I am not here to talk about the past. I am here to talk about Callum's friend, Angel Rain. She could have a serious medical problem. I am very worried. I think someone should check on her –'

'Michael,' said Ifeoma, sounding very sad and tired. 'I shouldn't talk about patients. Their details are confidential. But if you're asking what I think you're asking – yes, Angel Rain is in hospital. And this time, she may not come out.'

I felt like I'd been hit around the face with a stack of bricks.

May not come out.

It was all too much. The horror and the worry and the pain of it all.

Oh, it was unbearable.

All of a sudden, I had to get away from Ifeoma. And people everywhere. The humanness of it was agony.

'Thank you for your time, Ifeoma,' I said. 'I won't ask you any more questions. In fact, I have decided to terminate my research. I won't be seeing Callum anymore. I'm supposed to be studying toxic masculinity. Not pain, despair and awfulness.'

'This is life, Michael,' said Ifeoma. 'You are learning about people with this research. So learn.'

'I don't want to learn, Ifeoma,' I said. 'I want to go back to my office with the heating off and study mathematics. And not talk to anyone or see anything or feel like this ever again. This is awful, Ifeoma. It's just awful.'

'Michael,' said Ifeoma, in a gentle voice. 'This is the business of being a human being.'

'I would like to be alone,' I said.

And I left.

FIFTY

Callum Duffy interview transcript: *Tuesday November 20th, 9.37am*

I don't know why you're not here today, Mr Lamb. And I need to talk to someone, I really do. Because something really, really bad has happened.

Miss Hussain said I could come and talk into the iPad, because I'm not doing well in class. Or out of class. Or anywhere, to be honest.

This is like a bad dream. I still can't believe it.

And now you've gone too. At the worst time.

If only you knew what was happening, you would be here. Because we are friends now, aren't we? And friends look after each other, like you did on Halloween. And I know you wouldn't let me down.

Miss Hussain says you're probably sick and have forgotten to phone the school. I hope that's the reason and that nothing has happened to you. Because if you've had an accident on your bike, I don't think I could cope right now. So I really hope you're okay.

I hope you don't mind me doing this interview without you, Mr Lamb. But I am very distressed, and I think you should know my feelings. And it's making me feel better to talk, even if you're not here to listen.

I will pick up with the story where we left off. Just like always. Which was after me and Angel Rain went skiing. But if my voice goes funny and the words come out wrong, you will have to bear with me.

Alright. Here we go.

After me and Angel Rain went skiing, the snow went all slushy and manky and you couldn't slide on it anymore. You probably remember the slush. It was still there the day you came to interview me.

Slush is really miserable isn't it? Because it's all grey and you can't do anything with it. Dexter still gave sledging a go on his bin bags, but he just got tarmac burns and soaking wet.

So I was watching the slush melt, and waiting and waiting on another top-secret letter from Angel Rain. But I knew post could be quite slow, especially with the snow. So I was trying to be patient.

Then you came to interview me. That was on the Thursday. When you left in a hurry. Friday was quiet. And then Saturday, that's when it all kicked off. Because Angel Rain's mum phoned.

It was the weirdest thing. Luciana had never called my mum before. And even weirder, she asked to speak to me.

I was in the garden at the time, picking slugs off the cabbages. And throwing them over next door's fence, because the neighbours had been rude to Nana about our Christmas lights. Saying Nana had put them up too early, which was stupid, because all the shops are selling mince pies already.

Mum came running outside in her flamingo pyjamas, holding her phone and looking worried.

'Callum,' she said. 'It's Angel Rain's mum for you. You might want to come inside.'

On the way upstairs, I thought Angel Rain's mum must have found out about the skiing trip. So maybe she was phoning to tell me off. But that didn't really make sense, because Gus was the one who did the telling off. Luciana was quite nice really. So it was very weird and confusing.

Me and Mum went up to the lounge, and John Boy turned the Xbox off and left us to it.

Then Mum gave me her phone.

'It's about Angel Rain,' said Mum. 'I think something's happened.'

I felt like those garden slugs were in my stomach then, Mr Lamb. Because I knew 'something's happened' can never be a good thing.

I took the phone and said, 'Hello Mrs Pegg. Everything all right?'

I thought Luciana was somewhere windy at first. There was all this rustling. But then I heard, like, sobbing noises.

That squirmy feeling went everywhere then and I felt sick. Because I knew something really bad was going on.

'Mrs Pegg,' I said again. 'Is everything okay?'

'No, Callum,' said Luciana. 'Everything is not okay. Angel Rain had a cardiac arrest last night.'

Then Luciana made a weird noise, like an owl hooting. And I realised she was crying.

For a second or two, I was numb, Mr Lamb. Because I didn't know what a cardiac arrest was, but I knew it must be something bad.

'Is Angel Rain back in hospital, then?' I asked.

'Yes,' said Luciana. 'She is in intensive care. Callum. We are losing her.'

If I hadn't been sitting down, I would have fallen over. Because I'd watched enough episodes of Coronation Street to know what 'losing her' means. But I couldn't believe it. Luciana must have got it wrong.

Then Luciana said, 'You should come and see her today, Callum. To say your goodbyes.'

I had the biggest lump in my throat. But I told myself, this is all one big mistake. Adults get things wrong sometimes. Luciana's just panicking. I'll go to the hospital and Angel Rain will be all right. So I said:

'Will Gus be okay with me coming in?'

'Today is not about Gus,' said Luciana. 'It is about Angel Rain. You were Angel Rain's good friend.' There was more shaky breathing. Then Luciana said, 'Angel Rain told me about the park and the skiing and the hot chocolate. Thank you for doing that for her before ... before ...' Then she started crying again.

'Don't you worry, Luciana,' I said. 'I'm on my way.'

Luciana sniffed a bit, blew her nose and said, 'You should know, Callum. Angel Rain does not look the same. She has a mask on her face. There are machines. But I think you should see her. Otherwise, you will have regrets.'

'I don't care about machines,' I said. 'Angel Rain always looks beautiful to me. She's my girl.'

Luciana made a noise then. Like, a really loud sob. Then she said, 'See you soon.' And hung up.

I didn't exactly fall over, but I sat on the floor. After a few seconds, I shouted, 'Mum! Mum!'

Mum came running into the room.

'What's going on?' she said.

'Angel Rain is in intensive care,' I said. 'It sounds really bad. I have to go see her.'

'I'll drive you,' said Mum. 'Come on. Let's go.'

'You can't,' I said. 'You've got an exam today.'

'Don't be stupid,' said Mum. 'This is more important than any exam.'

'No way,' I said. 'You can't miss another one. You'll fail your course. There are three other adults in the house who can drive me.'

Except there wasn't. Because Nana was doing a deal with a brewery in Sudbury and John Boy said he was possibly still drunk from the night before and an unfit road user. So that left Granddad.

'All right,' said Mum. 'Your granddad can drive you. As long as you take your phone.'

'I'm not going to call you in the middle of your exam,' I said.

'Yes you will, Callum Duffy,' said Mum. 'You'll call me if you need me.'

But I knew I wouldn't.

We found Granddad outside the pub, clearing ice off the pavements with his favourite shovel. He said he'd drive me to hospital as soon as he'd finished doing the pavements. Because they were slippery for the elderly.

But Mum said, no Dad. Callum has to go now. Angel Rain is in intensive care.

So Granddad got his coat. But he still spent ages scraping ice off the front and back windscreens.

I kept saying, Granddad can we please go now. I'm so worried.

But Granddad said safety first, and checked the tyre pressure and moved all the mirrors around. Finally, he got his driving gloves and we were off.

I don't remember the drive, but I do remember getting lost in the hospital looking for children's intensive care. Which was stressful, because I'd told Luciana I'd be there ASAP.

We kept bumping into doctors and nurses who were like, turn left by the blah blah cardigan-ology and then you'll be on broccoli-ology by the uncle-logy.

When we finally got to intensive care, a nurse took us to a waiting area. It wasn't a very nice waiting area. There were those big chairs that old people like, with high backs. The wipe-clean ones. And wipe clean always makes you think of what's being wiped clean.

Luciana and Gus were in the waiting area, sitting on those chairs.

They looked so different.

Luciana's hair was all wild like a lioness. And she didn't have any makeup or jewellery on. She just looked plain and tired and sad.

Gus had on an England rugby shirt and his eyes were red. He looked really, really old.

'How are you two doing?' I asked. Which was a stupid question, because they obviously weren't doing well.

Luciana tried to say something, but then all these tears came and she couldn't speak.

Gus just stared at the wall.

After a minute or two, Luciana got it together and said, 'I'm sorry, Callum. They say you're not allowed on the ward. Because of infection. But there is a special window you can look through.' Then she started crying again, really crying.

You know when it hurts to swallow? That's what it was like. But I was sort of numb, too. Like I couldn't take it all in.

I said, 'How long do you think Angel Rain has left, then?' And it sounded like someone else's voice.

'We don't know,' said Luciana.

'Not long,' said Gus. He looked at me, then. And I've never seen pain like it, Mr Lamb. Not ever. Behind his elf mask, Gus was suffering so much.

I know I haven't said much today, but it's getting to an upsetting part. I have to pace myself if you know what I mean. So I'm going to sit in the cosy corner of the Calm Corner and finish reading Tom Gates. Which is a funny book, and I could do with cheering up.

I hope you'll be back on Thursday, Mr Lamb. Because I really need you around.

FIFTY-ONE

Callum Duffy interview transcript: *Thursday 22nd
November, 11.03am*

I wish you were here, Mr Lamb. When will you come back?
If you're sick, you must be really sick. And I hope, with all
my heart, you get better. Because there's too much sickness
in the world. There really is.

Mrs Bullard said I couldn't talk into the iPad this
morning. She said I was making excuses to waste school
time. But Miss Hussain was my hero again. She said I was
suffering emotional difficulties and needed some alone time.
So that's why I'm here again, but I can't stay all that long.

Mrs Bullard says I have to come back for maths, which is
stupid, because there's no way I can concentrate. And I
wasn't good at maths to begin with.

I'm trying to remember what I talked about last time, Mr
Lamb. Like, where I was up to. Because I feel confused
today, let me tell you. I hardly even know what day it is. Do
you ever feel like that?

I told you about seeing Gus and Luciana, didn't I? In the hospital. Outside intensive care. And I stopped there, because a bad thing happened after that.

Luciana asked one of the nurses if I could see Angel Rain. But the nurse said no, because kids aren't allowed on the intensive care ward. She wasn't being mean. She said I looked like a very nice, clean boy, but children often carry infections. And she couldn't change the rules. Even for someone who supported Arsenal.

So we all felt quite upset.

Luciana got this really high, wobbly voice and said, 'My sons are allowed to see her. What is the difference?'

The nurse said family was okay, but I wasn't family.

Granddad said we should go home and leave Angel Rain's parents in peace. But on the way out of the waiting area, I saw Nurse Kolawole at the vending machine, buying a Galaxy Caramel chocolate bar. It was so good to see her, Mr Lamb. I hugged her and cried and told her about Angel Rain.

Nurse Kolawole knew about Angel Rain already, and said, 'It's times like this I question my faith in god. But also when I need him more than ever.'

I started talking really, really fast, about intensive care and how I couldn't see my girl. It was like the words were climbing over each other.

'You must see Angel Rain,' Nurse Kolawole said. 'I can't let you into intensive care, but there is another way. Come with me.'

Then Nurse Kolawole used her plastic lanyard to let me and Granddad into a special nurse's bit. It had lots of old, soft chairs and tea mugs and a big window that looked into the intensive care ward.

'This is an observation room,' said Nurse Kolawole.

'People think nurses have breaks, but even on our breaks we are working.'

'Like guardian angels,' I said. And Nurse Kolawole smiled.

I went to the big window then, and looked into intensive care. It was a bit like looking into a fish tank. There were all these grey-faced kids hooked up to machines. And one of those grey-faced kids was Angel Rain.

Luciana was right. Angel Rain did look different. It wasn't just all the machines around her or the breathing thing on her face. She was all empty and soft and flat like there was nothing much of her left inside. It was a shock to see her like that.

I wanted to say something, but I couldn't. My throat was really sore and tight. And anyway, I knew Angel Rain couldn't hear me through the window. So I decided to send my thoughts instead. Like I do with my tadpoles.

I didn't want to say goodbye or anything. Because I didn't want to give Angel Rain ideas about going anywhere. So I told her about Judge Dredd and how he was enjoying his new bridge. And that he was a bit mouldy looking and tired, but still with us. And maybe he'd try extra hard to become a frog now, to make her wish come true. Because ... because ...

It was hard to concentrate with those grey faces and white bed sheets and machines everywhere. But I did my best.

Then Nurse Kolawole said, 'I'd better take you out now, Callum.'

So we left the big window and all those sick, sleeping kids.

Nurse Kolawole took us a roundabout way, and we ended up back in the intensive care waiting room with

Luciana and Gus. Mum was there too, which was so weird. Because she wasn't supposed to be at the hospital, and I was starting to think this was all a dream.

Mum took one look at my face and said, 'Come on, Callum. Let's go and get some fresh air.'

'What are you doing here, Mum?' I asked. 'You've got an exam. You'll fail your course.'

Mum told me not to worry about that.

'You needed me here,' said Mum. 'I'll work out my course another day.'

And truthfully, I was really glad to see my mum.

'Thank you,' I told Nurse Kolawole. 'For helping me see Angel Rain.' Then I turned to Luciana and Gus and said, 'And thank you too. For telling me to come into hospital. What you must be going through ...'

Mum said, 'Let's leave everyone in peace now, Callum.' Then she told Luciana, 'If you need anything. Child care for the twins. Anything. You just call me, all right?'

Luciana gave Mum a sad nod, but Gus was still staring at the wall.

On the way out of the hospital, Granddad offered to buy me a 'Ronald McDonald's'. So I must have been in a right state because Granddad thinks McDonald's makes cardboard food and ruins the planet. But I had to pass up his offer of a 'happy burger' because I was too upset to eat.

I held it together until we were outside the hospital, and then I cried and cried. Like, really badly. I almost couldn't breathe.

Mum helped me hug it out. Then she said, 'Let's go home and have a nice cup of tea.'

'I don't want to go home yet,' I said. 'I've got some more thoughts to send Angel Rain. Can I go and sit by the duck pond? It's right outside the intensive care ward.'

Mum said yes, and I should take as long as I needed. But Granddad checked his watch and said, 'Send your thoughts quickly, Callum. If we go past the hour, it's another three pounds for parking.'

While Mum was going mental at Granddad, I walked around to the duck pond by myself. Even though it's winter now, the duck pond was sunny and sparkly and nice. The willow tree was bare, but its swingy, swishy branches hung into the water and the ducks swam around them. They were quacking away, those ducks, thinking I had food. But I said, 'Sorry, ladies and gents. Not today. Maybe next time.'

I did have a thought – maybe I'd see a frog and could bring it in to Angel Rain and grant her last wish. But there wasn't much chance of finding a frog in that pond. And I knew the doctors and nurses wouldn't let me bring frogs into the hospital, anyway.

So I just sat on the bench and cried again. Then I pulled myself together so I could send my thoughts to send Angel Rain.

I made my head all clear and looked at the intensive care window and thought:

'I love you, Angel Rain. You are the most special friend I ever met. And if you want to go to that nice place where you can ski all the time and your body feels all right, you should go. My tadpoles will say hello to you there. They might even be frogs by now, so your last wish will come true. And it is okay for you to go because I want you to be happy. And that's what real love is. Wanting you to be happy even if it makes me sad.'

When I'd finished sending my thoughts, I saw this old, white-haired lady near the willow tree, smiling at me. She was wearing her nightie but she didn't look cold.

'Sometimes, love means letting go,' she said. And her

voice was all croaky, in a nice way. 'But you'll grow around the loss. You'll see.'

'Do I know you?' I asked. Because it felt like I did.

The lady said, 'I should think so. My middle name is Grace. Maybe you can sing me a song next time.' Then she looked up at the sky.

I looked up too, because you do when someone else looks up. And I saw this white flash. Like lightning. But it couldn't have been lightning, because there was no rain or anything. And you can't have lightning without rain, because it needs water.

People say weird things happen when someone dies. Like, granddad saw five robins at his dad's funeral, and robins were his dad's favourite bird.

Well, I saw a shooting star that morning. All right, I could have imagined it. I was in a bit of a state. But I do think I saw Angel Rain going up into the clouds. And when I looked back down again, the old lady was gone.

I hope you're back next week, Mr Lamb. I am keeping all my fingers and toes crossed.

I really want to know you're okay.

FREE ROMANTIC COMEDY STARTER LIBRARY

Join my free insider club for your starter novella, plus one complimentary kindle book every year at:

suzykquinn.com/suzynews

Scan the QR code for your free romantic comedy download

FIFTY-TWO

Michael Lamb

I am in what my father would have called a 'pit of despair'. I have not ventured out of my house. I have not turned on the heating or lit a fire. I am only eating canned and packet goods, because there is no fresh food. I have no wish to visit the Co-op and have conversations about plastic bags costing twenty pence or anything else. And the delicatessen is right out.

I am wracked with shame and guilt, but I see no way forward, other than to hide away.

I should never have undertaken qualitative research. Why would I want to understand others? Human beings are unfathomable and painful.

Christmas lights are springing up everywhere. I have seen them on my brief trips to the All Days convenience store, whilst stocking up on canned goods and packet noodles. Their incessant twinkle gives me a headache. I have had no desire to engage with Christmas, or anything it signifies.

I want to be alone.

FIFTY-THREE

Callum Duffy interview transcript: *Tuesday 27th November, 9.01am*

I'm really sad that you didn't come in today, Mr Lamb. And I am quite angry with you, to be honest. Because Miss Hussain called your university, and they said you might not be doing your research anymore.

If you've run out on me without saying goodbye, then it is so bad it is unbelievable. I am going through enough right now without having my heart broken again.

Miss Hussain says you must have something serious going on with your life, so we should send you love. But I think, whatever you have going on, you still should have phoned or texted.

But anyway. You wanted to hear a story about boys and girls being friends. So I am going to finish my story, Mr Lamb. Because I have done a beginning and a middle. And now there is an end.

On Saturday the 24th of November, Angel Rain left her body that was hurting her and floated up to the clouds.

We were all back at the pub when we heard the news. Luciana messaged to tell us, which was kind of her. Because she must have been going through so much.

You see what I mean, Mr Lamb? It's not hard to send a message. If Luciana could do it, I'm sure you can too.

The text message said there would be a funeral soon, but Luciana didn't know the date yet. She said Angel Rain had died peacefully in her sleep and would be an organ donor for other children.

It's brilliant that Angel Rain is helping other people, even though she's died. And I'd like to be an organ donor too. Because organ donors are heroes. Without the donor heart, Angel Rain would never have got two of her life wishes. And I wouldn't have got moved off the purple table. Because, did I tell you, Mr Lamb? I'm on the blue table now, as an improved reader. I am getting better all the time, thanks to Angel Rain.

Luciana's message came while we were having our Saturday night takeaway, which could have been bad timing. Because if I'd had my usual crispy beef in chilli sauce, it would have come right back up. But luckily, I wasn't hungry that evening and had only eaten a few prawn crackers.

We all cried when Mum read the message. Even Granddad. But then Granddad went straight into Granddad mode and told Mum she shouldn't have her phone at the dinner table, and the message could have waited until after our meal. So that ended up in a bit of a row.

That's all I have to say today. You're probably not going to read any of this anyway. But I hope you do. Because you should know how much Angel Rain means to me and what good friends we are.

Were.

Bye Mr Lamb. I'm going now.

FIFTY-FOUR

Michael Lamb

Today, I received two phone calls.

One from Bethany Balls.

The other from Ifeoma.

Bethany Balls called to shout at me for quitting my course.

'Why didn't you talk to me first?' Bethany demanded. 'You know Gary is competing with me over retention rates.'

I told Bethany I had already emailed the student admissions department and saw no need for further discussion.

'Of course there's a need,' Bethany barked. 'You've got a good rapport going with your research candidate. You're really getting somewhere.'

'That's exactly why I can't continue,' I told Bethany. 'My emotions have been compromised and I am at risk of severe researcher bias. The research was a terrible mistake. I had no idea of the emotional consequences. I do not have the skills for qualitative research.'

'At least wait until the New Year to make your decision,' said Bethany. 'You'll miss the university Christmas party if you quit now. I've bought five litres of tequila.'

'I don't want tequila,' I said. 'I don't want parties. I don't want any of this.'

And I hung up.

A few hours later, Ifeoma called.

I shouldn't have picked up, but there's something about a ringing phone that makes me compelled to answer. I have to return calls too. It is some kind of extreme OCD, probably to do with when my mother was ill.

So I picked up the phone.

'How are you, Michael?' said Ifeoma, in a brisk voice.

'Not good,' I told her.

'Have you spoken to Callum recently?' Ifeoma asked.

'I have not,' I said.

'He needs you right now,' said Ifeoma. 'A child can never have too much love and support at a time like this.'

'A time like what?' I asked.

'Just go and see Callum,' said Ifeoma. 'Okay?'

'There is no reason to see him,' I said. 'I am just a researcher. A peripheral person in his life. And now the research has ended.'

'Don't be ridiculous,' said Ifeoma. 'That little boy needs you. Grow a pair of balls, Michael.'

Which made me think of Bethany Balls. I wondered if she'd drink my share of tequila at the mature student Christmas do.

'I am not designed for all these feelings,' I said. 'They are too much.'

'We all feel pain, Michael,' said Ifeoma. 'You're not the

only one. But right now, you are causing pain to others by running away, and that is unforgivable. You are being a coward.'

Then she hung up.

Ifeoma's words shouldn't have hurt me. Cowardliness is nothing more than a construct of masculinity, after all. A story told to send soldiers into battle. I have no need for courage. So why did I feel so wretched?

I am not part of Callum's life. He has no need for me. And watching him struggle whilst Angel Rain endures a difficult illness is simply too painful.

I steered clear of relationships until my forties. And I was right to do so. Sharing one's life with others brings an unbearable onslaught of feelings. True – some of those feelings are magical and wonderful. But there is also disappointment, fear and heartbreak.

Callum's story has taught me, in the cruellest way, that letting love in brings pain. And as much as I am enjoying my warm house and soft furnishings, these are external things.

My internals remain unchanged.

FIFTY-FIVE

Callum Duffy interview transcript: *Thursday 29th November, 9.47am*

I'm starting to think you've run away forever, Mr Lamb. Like my dad did. Only you're worse than him. Because you went to university so you should know better.

Miss Hussain says you haven't had an accident, because she spoke to your university. And she thinks you'll come back, because you left your iPad here.

If you do come back, you've got a lot of explaining to do. Because I have abandonment issues and you have hurt me a lot.

Anyway.

I'm going to tell the last bit of my story. And it is good, getting out of class right now. School has been a challenge this week. I can't get my head straight.

Mum said I could take some time off, but there's no way I want to be stuck at home with my brain going round and round. So I haven't missed a single day this week. And it's been alright. Except, this morning we made lolly stick hearts for Christmas trees. And I got upset because I wanted to give my heart to Angel Rain.

I started proper hyperventilating when the saucers of glitter and glue came round. Which is breathing too quickly and making yourself dizzy. And Miss Hussain had to take me to the medical bay. Which is this room, by the way. See that red cooking bowl on the shelf over there? That's what they give you to be sick in.

You feel all sorts of things when you lose someone, Mr Lamb. You feel angry sometimes. Because you think, how can the world do things like this? And then other times you feel really sad and tired, like, what's the point of anything? And you want to go to bed, but bed is boring. So you try to read a book or watch TV, but you can't concentrate.

Yesterday, Angel Rain's mum sent us another message. This time it was about the funeral. Luciana said it would be on the Saturday, at the crematorium, and there would be a wake at the house.

Well, there's no way I'm going to a funeral, Mr Lamb. I don't want to see Angel Rain stuck in a box. To me, she's everywhere. In the clouds and the trees and the sky. I don't want to think of her dead body. It just isn't right.

Mum was like, 'It will give you a chance to say goodbye, Callum. That's what funerals are for. Just ask Granddad. He's been to hundreds of them.'

And Granddad said he was fed up with everyone making jokes about him going to funerals. And he had known the man in the chemist quite well, no matter what Nana said about it.

'I don't need to say goodbye,' I said. 'Angel Rain isn't in that place for dead people. She's here with me and Judge

Dredd. Anyway, Gus hates me. I don't want to ruin his day. So best I stay away.'

'Well, me and your Aunty Julesy are going,' said Mum. 'I can't carry that condolence hamper by myself.'

And Mum wasn't joking about the condolence hamper.

After Luciana's message, Granddad put together a hamper for the Pegg family. Like, homemade jam. Cheese. Crackers. A bottle of wine. Stuff like that.

But then Nana got involved and filled the basket with four-litres of caramel vodka, a giant lemon traybake and hundreds of teatime biscuits from the cash and carry. Then the basket broke. So Nana bought one of those massive treasure-island trunk things. And she's spent this week filling the whole thing.

Granddad said two-hundred bourbon biscuits were too many, but Nana just keeps on filling that trunk. Because for Nana, more biscuits means more love. And Nana wants to show Angel Rain's family as much love as possible.

People keep going on and on at me about the funeral, Mr Lamb. Telling me I should go.

Nana came into my bedroom last night and asked me how I was doing. And I said I wasn't doing well. Which was obvious, because I was just sitting there, staring at the wall.

Nana said she wasn't doing well either. And she was surprised I wasn't going to the funeral, because she thought I'd want to say goodbye.

'I've already said goodbye,' I told Nana. 'And Angel Rain is in the sky now. Floating around the clouds. Swimming with my tadpoles. It won't make me feel happy to see her dead body in a box.'

Nana gave me one of her nice smiles. The ones that make her eyes go all crinkly like screwed-up paper.

'Do you know something, Callum?' she said. 'You're a

very wise little boy. But I don't think funerals are supposed to make you feel happier. They're about giving love and support to others. Angel Rain's parents might need that tomorrow.'

'I'm sorry Nana,' I said. 'But I don't have it in me. I'm just hanging on as it is.'

Nana left me to it after that.

But then Mum came in and said she'd bought me a smart black suit from Sainsbury's, just in case.

I said no, thank you. I would stay at home with Judge Dredd. Because Judge Dredd isn't doing too well, to be honest. He's looking quite rotten and spending most of his time at the bottom of the tank.

I said to Mum, 'Judge Dredd needs all the love I can give him. He's on his way out too.'

Because I've stopped believing that Judge Dredd might be a frog now.

The funeral is in two days, Mr Lamb. On Saturday morning at 11am. I am dreading that time, to be honest. Because I know when Mum and Aunty Julesy drag that big hamper into the car and drive off, I'm going to feel really sad and empty inside. And I'll be thinking, maybe I should have gone. And I know why I'm not going, and it's not a good reason.

I'm scared Mr Lamb. I'm scared of feeling worse than I already do, because I think it might break me, to be honest. And I know you should do things you're scared of. But right now I'm giving myself a break because I really have been through a lot.

I know what will happen when Mum and Aunty Julesy leave. I will go up to my bedroom and stare at the wall and watch my transformers clock until the hands go past 11am. And then I will think about Angel Rain and cry.

It's probably not the right thing, hiding away. But sometimes, life just hurts too much and it's okay.

You were the one who taught me that.

FIFTY-SIX

Michael Lamb

This morning, as I poured UHT milk on Weetabix cereal, there was a knock at the door.

I have a Victorian gremlin-faced door knocker, and sometimes people hammer with unnecessary vigour. But this was a distinctively gentle knock.

I stayed rigid in my kitchen, willing the person to go away.

The knocking continued. Then I heard the letter box creak open and a soft voice call, 'Mr Lamb. It's Miss Hussain from the school.'

I remained stiff and unmoving.

'Mr Lamb,' said Miss Hussain. 'I know you're in there. I can see your sandals.'

I looked down at my feet and realised I'd gone back to old habits of wearing Velcro trekking shoes with socks.

'You left your iPad at school,' Miss Hussain continued.

'Callum has been telling his story this week. I thought you might want to hear it, Mr Lamb.'

It was all slightly humiliating, hiding away in the kitchen with Miss Hussain watching my shoes. So I bit the bullet, went to the front door and opened it.

'Thank you,' I said, taking the iPad and placing it on my new hallway table. 'I appreciate your time. Have a good weekend.'

I would have closed the door, but Miss Hussain was still standing there, smiling away.

'There's a delivery for you too, Mr Lamb,' said Miss Hussain. 'Did you know?'

She pointed to a small, cellophane-wrapped basket in the corner of my porch. I'm not sure how long it had been there. Perhaps days. I had been too caught up in my own misery to notice.

'It's from Abi's deli,' said Miss Hussain. 'I always get my Christmas bits from her. Are you stocking up for the festive season?'

'No,' I said picking up the basket. Cellophane crinkled and pink streamers fluttered in the winter wind. 'It's probably for a neighbour.'

'Callum has been sad without you,' said Miss Hussain. 'He's having a hard time. Did you hear about what happened? With Angel Rain?'

'She's back into hospital,' I said.

'No, Mr Lamb,' said Miss Hussain. 'She died.'

My stomach clenched. Spots swam before my eyes. There was a buzzing noise coming from somewhere. The cellophane, I think. It was making startled, electric noises under my clenched hands.

'It's just awful, isn't it?' said Miss Hussain, and her kind face crumpled. 'For the family. And for Callum. He won't even go to the funeral. He's too devastated. But we'll do what we can to support him, won't we, Mr Lamb? Will you read what he's written while you've been away? I do think it would help if you shared his journey.'

'I'm ending my research,' I said.

'Yes, your university told me,' said Miss Hussain. 'But you should still read what Callum's written. He so rarely gets any attention for his stories. And he's a wonderful storyteller. Please Mr Lamb. Do something kind for him, won't you? He deserves kindness right now.'

Miss Hussain was so hopeful. So trusting.

'Angel Rain's funeral is this morning,' said Miss Hussain. 'Maybe you could read Callum's notes before then. Your house is lovely, by the way. I like your sofa.'

'It's a good place to hide away,' I said.

'We all have to face the real world some time, Mr Lamb,' said Miss Hussain. 'With all its ups and downs. But there are more ups than downs, aren't there? When all is said and done.'

Then she gave me a cheery wave and off she went.

I closed the front door and put the basket on the hallway table, beside the iPad. There was a note on the basket. It said:

Michael, have you turned hermit again? I haven't seen you. Whatever's going on, hot chocolate makes everything better. Make yourself a cup of this stuff immediately. It's Italian.
Abi.

Under the cellophane, I observed cocoa powder, cinnamon sticks bound in red ribbon, brown sugar rocks in a clear bag and a tin of condensed milk.

I don't often have sweet things early in the day. But I found myself whisking up a hot chocolate with the condensed milk, cocoa powder and brown sugar. Then I poured it into Callum's 'Hug in a Mug' and floated a cinnamon stick on top.

Hot chocolate in hand, I took the iPad into the lounge and sat on my new sofa.

I stared at the iPad for a long time. I thought of Callum and Angel Rain and how courageous they were. Then I found my own courage and started to read.

Callum's last interviews were awful. Beyond awful. I felt a rollercoaster of guilt, fear and crippling loss and sadness. By the time I'd finished reading, I was weeping with shame and despair.

One thing was very clear. I had let Callum down in his hour of need. Worse, I had provided him with a template for adult cowardliness. Yes cowardliness. It was real. And now, Callum might not go to Angel Rain's funeral.

I couldn't let that happen. I knew that with certainty. I must go to Callum. Immediately. And tell him that hiding away is no kind of life. He must go to the funeral. He must.

It was 10.30am.

Angel Rain's funeral was at 11am.

For once in my life, I wished I could drive a car, even though cars are dangerous and an environmental menace. But all I had was my bike and the desire to get somewhere very quickly. So that would have to do.

The Great Oakley Arms was a twenty-minute cycle ride, but I clicked my bike into high gear and made it in ten minutes. Once there, I stumbled into the pub garden on jelly legs, red and sweating, shouting, 'Callum! Callum!'

Like a mad man.

Callum's grandmother, Shirley, came to the back door.

'Mr Lamb?' she said. 'I thought you were a drunk wanting me to open early. I was about to get the sledgehammer out.'

It took a while to catch my breath. But I managed to stammer, 'Did Callum go to the funeral?'

'Unfortunately not,' said Shirley. 'The others have left. He's still upstairs.'

'He must go,' I said. 'I'm here to tell him. He'll regret it if he doesn't.'

'Well, I agree with you,' said Shirley. 'But I don't think you'll persuade him.' She inclined her head towards the staircase and roared, 'CALLUM! CALLUM! There's someone here to see you.'

A sad, tired looking Callum appeared at the top of the stairs. He looked surprised to see me. Perhaps even horrified.

'What are you doing here, Mr Lamb?' Callum demanded. 'You left. Miss Hussain said you left.'

'You must go to Angel Rain's funeral, Callum,' I spluttered. 'You mustn't hide away. Or you'll have guilt and regrets for the rest of your life.'

'How do you know about Angel Rain's funeral?' Callum asked.

'I read the iPad,' I gasped. 'Miss Hussain brought it to my house. I'm sorry, Callum. I have been cowardly and pathetic. I didn't want to share your pain, so I ran away. My behaviour was inexcusable. Please don't follow my terrible example. Go to the funeral, Callum. You must go.'

'It's too late,' said Callum. 'It's ten-forty-five. I've been watching the time on my Transformers clock.'

'Callum,' said Shirley. 'If you want to go to that funeral, I can get you there. You've seen the way I drive.'

'But I don't want to go,' said Callum. 'It's too hard.'

'It will be hard,' I said. 'But if you don't face difficult emotions, you'll end up like me. Living alone. Hiding from life. Go now, Callum. Quickly. You won't get a second chance.'

'He's right, Callum,' said Shirley.

Callum gave the tiniest little nod. 'Yeah, I know.'

'So you'll go?' I said.

'Alright,' said Callum.

'Hop on upstairs and get that suit on, Callum,' said Shirley. 'And I will drive like greased lightning.'

'I am still upset with you, Mr Lamb,' said Callum. 'For running out on me and not phoning to say why. But I will go to the funeral because it is the right thing to do.'

Then Callum vanished into the flat and I cycled home.

I have done many cowardly things in my life. But I have done some brave things too. And today was a brave thing.

There is something infectious about courage.

I have decided to finish my research. Callum and Angel Rain deserve an ending to their story, even if it's not a happy one.

FIFTY-SEVEN

Callum Duffy interview transcript: *Tuesday 4th December, 9.01am*

I don't want to talk to you today, Mr Lamb. It has been a difficult weekend and I am still quite upset with you. I would like to go back to class if that is okay.

FIFTY-EIGHT

Callum Duffy interview transcript: *Thursday 6th December, 1.30pm*

It is brave of you to come in again, Mr Lamb. After I told you to get lost last time. And I'm glad you came, to be honest. I want to be angry at you, but I don't have it in me. Nana says when you lose someone you get bigger. Like, more grown up. So you leaving me at my hardest moment and not saying a word about it and not phoning the school to say why seems quite small right now.

And I do appreciate you coming to the pub, all sweaty and red-faced like a lunatic and saying sorry. You were right about me going to the funeral. So all in all, I am very glad you came.

I will talk to you. But I am not quite ready to look at you when I'm talking, so I will just look at the iPad if it's all the same with you.

This is what happened after you left the pub.

We got to the funeral on time. Well, sort of. We were a

little bit late, but Nana did her best. Our old Toyota made proper screeching noises on the corners and the crematorium gravel flew everywhere.

There were loads of cars outside the crematorium, but no people. So we knew we were late.

'This is bad news, Nana,' I said. 'I reckon the funeral has already started. Look – the doors are closed.'

'It's all right,' said Nana. 'We'll go in the side entrance. No one will see us.'

So we went around the side of the crematorium, and there were some more doors there. Big, wooden ones. They were closed too, and you could hear church music playing.

'Are you sure these are side doors, Nana?' I asked. 'They look quite big.'

'I am 85% certain,' said Nana. She tried to open the doors all carefully and quietly. But when the doors wouldn't open, she gave them a big, noisy shove.

Well, you can guess what happened next.

We hadn't gone in the side way at all. We'd come in the vicar's entrance, right at the front of the crematorium. And everyone was staring at us. Including the vicar, who looked quite angry.

I was wearing my orange trainers too, which are real showstoppers. Don't me wrong – I was respectful, and wearing the black suit Mum bought me from Sainsbury's. But if Angel Rain was looking down from above, I wanted her to know it was me.

I could see Mum and Aunty Julesy sitting on a pew in the middle of the crematorium. Aunty Julesy looked embarrassed. But Mum was mouthing, 'There's a seat here, Callum.'

We couldn't sit with Mum, though, because it meant climbing over people.

You could hear people complaining about us in whispering voices. So me and Nana bowed our heads and took an empty bench at the front. Sort of trying to look invisible.

Then the main doors opened, and Gus, Luciana and the twins walked through the crematorium carrying flowers. They put the flowers on the stage at the front and stood there for a minute.

It got very silent. I couldn't see a coffin anywhere, which was good. Because I really didn't want to see that.

Then Nana whispered, 'I wonder where Angel Rain's family are going to sit? All the seats have gone.'

I had a bad feeling then.

'Nana,' I said. 'I think we've taken their seats.'

Nana shifted around and pulled a card from under her bottom.

The card said, 'Pegg Family'.

'Uh oh,' said Nana. 'Quick. Leg it before they notice.'

But it was too late. Gus, Luciana and the twins turned around and saw us on the front bench.

Nana stood up and said, 'Sorry. We're in the wrong seats. Story of my life.'

Which is true, because once Nana took the wrong seat at Wimbledon, and it belonged to a man who looked like Russell Crowe. And the Russell Crowe man was quite rude, so Nana was rude back and ended up threatening the Russell Crowe man with violence. And the Russell Crowe man got scared and gave Nana his seat and his strawberries and cream. So it was a right result, because it was a good seat and strawberries and cream at Wimbledon are expensive.

We still don't know if it was Russell Crowe, or just someone who looked like him.

Anyway.

I did worry that Gus might kick off when he saw we'd taken his seat. But he didn't. He just gave me this tired smile and said, 'Hello Callum.'

So I said, 'Hello, Sir Gus.'

'There's no need for sir today,' said Gus. 'Just Gus is fine.'

Angel Rain's dad looked different. It was like all the rage had been sucked out of him and left behind this tired, sad old man.

'Here,' I said. 'Have your seats back.'

'No, stay where you are, Callum,' said Gus. 'Angel Rain would have wanted you at the front.'

That was a surprise, let me tell you.

So we all squashed on the bench together, which was a bit tight because Nana is a large lady. But we managed it.

The vicar started the service, and we all sang a hymn, 'Nearer My God to Thee.' Which would have been all right, except the vicar was one of those vicars who fancied himself as a singer when he wasn't. And he sang really loud and sounded like a dolphin on the high notes.

After the hymn, the vicar made a speech. He talked about Angel Rain and how she'd been born with a broken heart and had loads of operations and was really brave. And how she was good at school and worked hard, even though she was ill. And how she loved frogs and her favourite book was *Heidi*.

Which all sounded right, but it didn't feel right. Because you could tell the vicar had never met Angel Rain. So it felt a bit flat.

Angel Rain was clever and good at school. But she was also funny and silly and mad, in a good way. And he didn't know that stuff about her.

While the vicar was talking, Nana took my hand and squeezed it.

Nana must have known what I was thinking, because she whispered, 'Vicars are like doctors, Callum. You get good ones and bad ones.'

Then the vicar said, 'Now we will play Angel Rain's favourite hymn, Amazing Grace. Performed by the Celtic Woman.'

That made me smile. Because I knew Angel Rain did love that song.

The vicar pulled a silver screen down and messed around with a projector for a bit. Then a video came up of these three women wearing massive Cinderella dresses. But no sound came out.

The vicar was like, 'Technology always ruins best-laid plans, ha, ha, ha.'

And he kept trying to get the sound to work. But he couldn't.

I was going to jump up to help. Because I'm quite good with technology, and my guess was it was a speaker issue. But before I could, the vicar said, 'Well, not to worry. Rather than keep you all waiting, we'll go to plan B.' Then he cleared his throat and said, 'I hope you'll permit me to sing this beautiful song. I may not be a Celtic Woman, but I have done plenty of singing in my time, ha ha ha.'

Well, I was not happy about that, Mr Lamb. Not happy at all. That vicar who'd never met Angel Rain, singing in his thin, horrible voice? No way.

I looked at Gus and Luciana. And I could tell Luciana wanted to say something but she was too embarrassed.

So I stood up and said, 'I'll sing that song for Angel Rain, Mr Vicar.'

And the crematorium went quiet.

The vicar gave this annoying laugh, you know how adults do. And he said, 'Singing in a room this size isn't easy, young man. Best leave it to the professionals.'

'I am a professional,' I said. 'I was lead in our church choir, and I did solo at Norwich Cathedral, which is loads bigger than this. And all right, that was a while ago, because I'm too cool for church now, no offence Mr Vicar. But I can still sing really well. And Angel Rain asked me to sing 'Amazing Grace' for her loads of times, but I never did. So I want to sing it for her now. She should hear that song from someone who loved her, don't you think? Because she's up in the sky listening to all of this.'

There was a long silence.

Then Gus stood up and said, 'Sing away, Callum. Sing away.'

And Luciana nodded and looked all tearful.

So I got up on the stage in front of the whole crematorium. And I moved the vicar's microphone down and tested it a bit and gave my voice a little warm-up. Like la la la la la la laaaaa. Because you should do that before you sing to a big crowd.

Then I looked right at the back of the room and took a big breath.

I thought it best not to do any beatboxing. Because it wasn't the right crowd. But I sang from my heart and this is what I sang:

Amazing Grace, how sweet the sound
That saved a wretch like me.
I once was lost, but now am found.
Was blind, but now I see.

I sang that same verse four times, because I didn't know any of the other verses. And I did it without crying. And when I finished everyone was staring at me with their mouths open. Which can be a good or bad thing. But that day it was a good thing, because then everyone started clapping.

Gus beat his hands together really loudly.

And although I'm not religious, I understood 'Amazing Grace' that day. Because I was lost. And Angel Rain found me and helped me see. And even though she'd gone, she had done good in the world, and I was some of that good.

When I sat down, Luciana said, 'Thank you. Thank you.'

Gus grabbed my hand and squeezed it really hard. A bit too hard, to be honest. You know how men are sometimes, Mr Lamb. They find it hard to show their feelings. But I knew he was trying to say thank you too.

Everyone wanted to talk to me after the service. To tell me I was brave and all of that. But I wasn't brave. Because you choose to be brave. And I had no choice about singing for Angel Rain that day. I wasn't going to let her down.

When we got outside, a bit of sun came through the clouds and the day looked better. Not as grey. And I thought I saw that old woman again. The one in the nightdress from the hospital. She was waving and smiling and looked happy. But then I had to get into Nana's car, and when I looked back the lady had gone.

I'm going to have a little break now, Mr Lamb. I am getting a bit tired. We'll start again in five minutes, alright? I just want to stare out of the window for a bit.

FIFTY-NINE

Callum Duffy interview transcript: *Thursday 6th December, 2.13pm*

I'm ready to carry on now, Mr Lamb. Thank you for waiting.

Have you ever been to a wake?

It's basically cups of tea and biscuits after a funeral. We've done loads of wakes at our pub, because people feel at home there. Some people feel a bit too at home, like Yorkie, who never leaves. But you know what I'm saying. Our pub is a friendly place.

Even though the Great Oakley Arms is a pub, Nana and Granddad never do alcohol at a wake. Because Nana says alcohol makes sad people sadder. So you should stick to tea and hugs from friends. And maybe Coca-Cola, if it's sunny.

Angel Rain's wake was at her Mum and Dad's house by DeMontford Park. Nobody told us to take our shoes off when we came inside. In fact, Luciana told us not to worry about shoes. And would we like a biscuit? She had hundreds of them.

We didn't stay for very long. Just one cup of tea and a few bourbons. Because we weren't family or anything and didn't want to get in the way. But as we were leaving, Gus came over with a book in his hand.

'Callum,' he said. 'We want you to have this. To remember Angel Rain by.'

And the book was *Heidi*.

'I can't take this,' I said. 'This is Angel Rain's special book. The family should have it.'

'No,' said Gus. 'Angel Rain wanted you to read it. And that's what we want too.'

And he shoved the book into my hand. Then he squeezed his eyes really tight and looked like he wanted to cry.

I felt bad, then. Like I'd upset him.

'Thank you so much,' I said. 'I'll take really good care of it. And if you ever want it back, just let me know.'

Gus got himself together and said in his policeman's voice, 'Don't just look after this book, young man. Read it. That's what Angel Rain would have wanted.'

I gave him a nod and said yes, Sir Gus. I mean Gus. Of course. I will read it. And I will keep up with my reading for Angel Rain, because she wanted me to pass exams and be a vet. And thank you very much.

I tried to shake Gus's hand, but he hugged me instead. Which was a real surprise. And I appreciated it. Then Gus stuffed five bourbon biscuits in my hand and told me I was a good lad. Which was nice to hear.

I was so glad I went to the funeral, because Nana was right – even though it was sad, there was a lot of love that day.

When we got home, Mum hugged me so tight I thought she might break me in half. She said she loved me so much and was sorry for telling me off about Lego all the time. But FYI – Mum still tells me off about my Lego, Mr Lamb. Just in case you're wondering. So that apology was quite short-lived.

I'm glad I went to the funeral, but I did feel quite empty and sad afterwards. When we got back to the pub, I was in a bit of a daze, just drinking sugary tea and watching Christmas stuff on Disney Plus with my family.

Then I had a panic because I realised I hadn't checked up on Judge Dredd. And I went running down to his tank and couldn't find him anywhere.

For a bad moment, I thought Judge Dredd had disappeared, like Juggernaut. But he was the only tadpole left, so he couldn't have eaten himself. That made no sense.

Then I saw Judge Dredd moving all slow and tired at the bottom of the tank. He didn't swim up to see me like he usually did, and he didn't look well at all. And the dark stuff was all over his body.

'You look how I feel, mate,' I said. 'I wish there was something I could do for you. Here – have a bit of biscuit.'

But Judge Dredd didn't take any of the bourbon biscuit crumbs I gave him. He just watched them float past.

While I watched Judge Dredd looking all sad and tired, Granddad came and put his arm around me.

'He looks in a bad way, doesn't he?' said Granddad. 'I think it's time to say goodbye to another friend today. If I were him, I wouldn't want to spend my last few days in a tank. I'd want to be in the nature pond under the sky. You've learned a hard lesson today, Callum. Love is a wonderful thing. But sometimes, it changes to something else.'

I know Granddad is right. It's time to let go. And Judge Dredd should swim in the fresh air before he dies. But it's still totally brutal, Mr Lamb. Because I've just lost my best friend. And now I have to let go of my last tadpole. So it's sad all round. But I suppose you know that already, Mr Lamb. It was never going to be a good story today, was it? After a funeral.

So there you go, Mr Lamb. You wanted a story about a boy and a girl and this is the ending. She dies, he doesn't, the ship sinks. Which is John Boy's joke about the Titanic movie, except he says, 'he dies, she doesn't.' And I hope that's not a spoiler for you.

Life has endings, doesn't it? But endings come with beginnings too. Like when the football season ends. You know there'll be another beginning soon. And I think being friends with you is a new beginning. And my reading is a beginning too, because I'm on the blue table now.

So I do forgive you, Mr Lamb. It's the time of year for it, and I can see you're trying to make things better. That counts for a lot.

I know we won't see each other at school anymore, because my story really is finished now. And also, it's the Christmas holidays soon and all of that. But come by the pub on Christmas Eve, won't you? Come around first thing, and Nana will do you breakfast sherry and a mince pie.

Don't be a stranger, yeah?

SIXTY

Michael Lamb

I have formed an emotional attachment to Callum. A boy who wears hooded tops and kicks tables. Who knows about football leagues and uses the word 'well' as an intensifier.

Much is made of researchers influencing subjects. But few studies consider how subjects influence researchers. My study will be one of those few. And I am very happy to have been influenced by my subject. In fact, as Callum would say, I am well blessed.

I am sad for Callum. Devastated is a better word. But Bethany Balls is right – it is better to have loved and lost. Even though Callum can't be with Angel Rain anymore, she is still part of him. Just like Ifeoma is part of me.

My home was warm and inviting when I returned from the school, but I didn't stop to enjoy it. I popped on my Arsenal slippers and went straight up to my office.

My computer sat there, watching me. A black, unblinking eye.

I hadn't looked at my research paper for a long time. Not since I'd heard about Angel Rain's return to hospital.

I sat at my desk and read my research statement:

Boys from disadvantaged backgrounds are exposed to a culture of toxic masculinity. This negatively affects their relationships with females.

I looked long and hard at the statement. Then I deleted it and wrote:

Boys from disadvantaged backgrounds are capable of overwhelming courage, love and compassion. They are a misunderstood group, and we should work harder to understand them.

Then I began to write.

I wrote until my hands ached and my head hurt. As midnight approached, I began to misspell common words. For example, 'and' became 'nads' far too frequently. But I kept going.

By 7am, the first draft of my new research paper was finished.

This was the last paragraph:

Much has been written about researchers influencing subjects. But less is said about subjects influencing researchers. Through Callum, I am learning to be a more courageous human being.

I wish I could have written 'I *have* learned to be a more courageous human being'. But I don't think I'm there just yet.

However.

I will try to call Ifeoma a little later today.

SIXTY-ONE

Michael Lamb

Ifeoma hasn't returned my calls. Or my text messages. So I have decided to open my heart to Christmas instead. It's a step in the right direction.

People often talk about Christmas creeping up on them. As if it were some sort of clandestine burglar moving closer in the dead of night. What a ridiculous analogy, I used to think. But this year, Christmas really did creep up on me. Because I actually participated.

When you take part in Christmas, there is a lot to do. My ethically sourced Christmas tree was simple enough to order. But it needed correct potting and placement in the lounge. Then there were the hanging ornaments, which took considerable shopping. Additionally, the fresh holly and ivy bouquets took forever to make, as did the colourful wreath for my front door.

In terms of outdoor festive lighting, I admit I went a little over the top. For years, mine has been the only house on the street without Christmas lights, save for one abandoned property on the corner with boarded-up windows. So I felt I had some making up to do. And making up I did.

It took several days, a long ladder and some industrial hoop nails to hang my festive lights, but it was well worth the effort. When I'd finished, my house looked like a fairground attraction. Lights sparkled from every window, wall, roof tile and gutter. I know my electricity bill will be astronomical, but it's worth it to bring so much festive cheer.

Children, it turns out, are mesmerised by sparkling houses. My tube-light Santa climbing the chimney, flashing north stars, racing sleigh and herd of nodding reindeer have been the talk of the town.

The lights now bring quite the crowd of an evening. I have taken to handing out refreshments, and suggesting an optional donation to the local community centre. So far, I have raised £407.85, which is a new record.

Along with hanging Christmas lights, I have been busy with festive community activities.

Then there are the fairs with and without 'y's to attend. Wreathes to make for elderly neighbours. Biscuits to bake for the hordes of people coming to see my Christmas lights. I also hosted the 'Green Cocktails at Christmas' event for the Green Party this year, and enjoyed an evening drinking toilet-cleaner coloured drinks with friends old and new.

So the December days are speeding by and I am enjoying every moment.

I used to see Christmas as an overblown, garish event for people who enjoy fripperies like wrapping paper and bath products. But this year, it is an opportunity to let the world in again. So I am revelling in all the bright colours and inventive coffee flavours and human being ness of it all.

Obviously, the person I would most like to let in is Ifeoma. But I understand why she hasn't returned my calls or messages. She made it very clear what she thought of me the last time we spoke. And if Callum, who is a hero in my eyes, doesn't get a happy ending, then I certainly don't deserve one.

It is time I moved on from my loss, just as Callum is moving on.

Ifeoma and I are over, but that doesn't mean I have to be alone for the rest of my life. I have a community around me and many ways to connect with others.

Callum and I did indeed remain strangers after our last interview, but I did receive two cryptic text messages from him.

The first one was in early December and read: 'Do you believe in Christmas miracles?'

It was a hard question to answer by text, because there was a lot to unpack, ideally with graph paper.

I replied, 'I really would need more data.'

Then a few weeks later, I received another message:

'Dear Mr Lamb, you will not believe what's happening. It is the best surprise. Bring the iPad when you come on Christmas Eve. I need to finish our story.'

This was a little confusing, since we had already finished Callum's story. But I was too tactful to say so. I had already returned the iPad to the university, but decided to buy Callum his own tablet as a Christmas present – thus killing two birds with one stone.

On Christmas Eve morning, I cycled to the Great Oakley Arms. There was quite a bit of noise and commotion as I reached the back gate, with Duffy family members coming and going through the beer garden with suitcases and boxes of food.

Shirley, with a suitcase on either shoulder, indicated I should go straight upstairs. Which I did, side-stepping Brandi on the way. Brandi carried a bin-liner of presents and didn't express any surprise to see me in her house.

'Alright, Mr Lamb?' she said. 'Callum's in the kitchen. He's just having a second breakfast. In case he doesn't like the food where we're staying.'

'You're going away?' I asked.

'We're off to the Dalton Estate after lunch,' said Brandi. 'It's going to be pukka. With cocktails.'

Then she descended the staircase with her bin liner.

Tentatively, I poked my head into the kitchen.

Callum was there, sitting at a tinsel wrapped table with a fried breakfast, two thick cut slices of bread and butter and a mug of tea.

The radio was playing 'All I want for Christmas is You.' As it always does this time of year.

'Hello Callum,' I said.

Callum didn't look surprised to see me either. I suppose the Duffys are used to comings and goings at Christmas time.

'Alright, Mr Lamb?' he said. 'You took your time. I told you to be here first thing.'

'I had to make a quick stop in town,' I said, presenting Callum with a new iPad. 'Happy Christmas, Callum. This is for you.'

Callum made lots of exclamations, some of them using rather adult language. But the gist of it was, he was happy with the iPad.

'This is amazing, Mr Lamb,' said Callum, clutching the tablet tight to his chest. 'The most amazing present ever.'

'I've already downloaded the dictation app,' I said. 'So you can do as much story telling as you like.'

'EPIC!' said Callum. 'Can I offer you a mince pie, Mr Lamb? We've got puff pastry or ones with sherry cream inside. Or I could do you a Scottish shortbread finger or a festive Cadbury's Mini Roll with a chocolate snowflake on top?'

'Or a slice of Christmas pudding,' announced Shirley Duffy, staggering into the kitchen with a Christmas pudding the size of a football. 'I over-shopped again. This one is going spare. Do you want a slice, Mr Lamb? I'm going to cut it up for the pub regulars, so it's no trouble.'

I gratefully accepted a slice of currant-filled Christmas pudding and a large, strong cup of tea.

'I know the research is finished now,' I told Callum. 'But it would be my honour and privilege to be in your life, perhaps as a sort of nerdy uncle who helps you with mathematics. And I am happy to hear your stories whenever you want to tell them.'

'I'd like that, Mr Lamb,' said Callum. 'And I do have more to tell you about Angel Rain. Just one last little bit. For your research.'

'Is there much else to say about Angel Rain?' I asked tentatively.

'Yeah,' said Callum, taking a big swig of tea. 'A miracle. Are you sitting comfortably? Then I will begin.'

SIXTY-TWO

Callum Duffy interview transcript: *Monday 24th December, 10.13am*

The last thing I told you about was the funeral, Mr Lamb. And the wake. And then Judge Dredd was in a bad way. That was right at the beginning of December and it was such a sad time.

After the funeral, we started getting the house ready for Christmas. Which felt bad at first. To be celebrating, you know? When we were all so sad about Angel Rain. But then Nana got the singing reindeer head out, and break-dancing Santa Claus and twerking Mrs Claus and everything felt a bit more normal. Not like other years, but all right.

By the time we got the second tree up in the pub, and Nana had filled the fridge with white chocolate roulades and Heston Blumenthal puff-pastry mince pies, I felt a bit more like myself.

Judge Dredd wasn't doing well, though. For days, he'd

been sitting under his bridge like a big raisin. Not moving at all.

So as December went on, I made a brave decision. I would set Judge Dredd free. Because if I hung on much longer, he would never get to see the sunset before he died.

It was quite an emotional moment, telling Judge Dredd how much I loved him and all of that.

'I'll never forget you, mate,' I said. 'And I'll miss you so much. But good parents do what's best for their kids. And you should see the clouds and the sun before you go. And then you'll fly up to the big pond in the sky and become a real frog. And my friend will be there and she'll look after you.'

That night, I cried myself to sleep. But the next day, I woke up early, ready to set Judge Dredd free.

It was cold in the pub that morning, because the heating hadn't come on yet. And dark, too. And it smelt like lemon cleaning stuff. John Boy always gives the bar a good scrub down at closing time.

I climbed up on a bar stool and asked Judge Dredd if he'd had a good sleep. Then I said: 'I'm setting you free today, mate. You'll get a good bit of food to keep you going too. But then it'll be proper nature. You won't forget me, will you?'

The tank was still. Too still really, and I had a bad feeling.

I turned on the light, and Judge Dredd was at the bottom on the colourful gravel, not moving.

My heart sunk. Because I thought I was too late and Judge Dredd had become Judge Dead. But then I tapped on the tank, and Judge Dredd started swimming around really fast. Like his old self.

And guess what, Mr Lamb? You will never guess what. Not in a million years.

Judge Dredd had legs.

Well, sort of. There were two feathery protrusions near his tail, clear as anything.

For a minute, I thought – maybe I'm dreaming. Honestly, Mr Lamb. I even splashed a bit of fish tank water on my face, just to make sure.

But I was wide awake, because that water was really cold.

I couldn't believe it.

Then I got excited. I stood on the bar stool and did my happy dance and hugged the fish tank.

'I knew you could do it!' I said. 'I knew you had it in you. You're doing it, mate. You're turning into a frog in winter. It's a froggy miracle!'

Then I shouted, 'Everyone! Wake up. Come quick! It's important'

There was all this bumping about upstairs, and then Nana, Granddad and Mum came running into the pub.

Nana had on her Santa onesie, and she was waving this big casserole dish, ready to whack someone with it. Granddad had his fists up, and Mum had her Keratin-smooth Big Curls Hot Brush. Also ready to whack someone.

Then the back door crashed open, and John Boy hopped in from the caravan holding his false leg like a weapon. Well, you know what I'm going to say. He was ready to whack someone.

This makes my family sound violent, but they're all very big-hearted, Mr Lamb. They're just protective, that's all.

I felt a bit bad, then. Because I'd panicked everyone.

'It's all right,' I said. 'There's no burglar. It's just my tadpole.'

Mum was not happy, because it was only 5am. So she shouted at me and said she was going back to bed. But Nana said that since we were all up, she may as well do a fry-up. And did we all want home fries? Because it was home fries weather. And John Boy said, yes please Aunty Shirley, and a slice of black pudding if you have it.

'Forget about the home fries and black pudding,' I said. 'A miracle has happened. Judge Dredd is turning into a frog.'

I thought everyone would be as excited as me. But Granddad just gave me a sad pat on the shoulder and said, 'Tadpoles don't become frogs in winter, Callum. They either hibernate or they die. And that little scrap of a thing is on his way out.'

'No, he isn't,' I said. 'Angel Rain has made a miracle happen.'

Granddad said it was a nice thought, but there was a fine line between faith and lunacy. And I mustn't become one of those people who saw Jesus's face in slices of watermelon.

'See for yourself,' I said. 'Judge Dredd has feathery protrusions. Clear as anything.'

Granddad came to look at the tank. He shook his head and said, 'Good lord.' Then he went upstairs to get his magnifying glass. Which he keeps in the kitchen because he says food labels are getting smaller. And he looked again and said, 'This is unbelievable. He really is growing legs.'

'It's Angel Rain,' I said. 'She's turning him into a frog. Because it was her life wish to see one. So she's up there in the clouds doing magic.'

'Well, that's good news,' said Nana. 'How about a fried breakfast to celebrate?'

'You're not taking this seriously, Shirley,' said Granddad. 'This really is a scientific miracle.'

And Granddad went on about important messages for medical science all the way to the kitchen. Where we had a big breakfast and I talked about Angel Rain, while Granddad asked about the water cleaner I'd used.

'Perhaps a drunk person put something in the tank,' said Granddad. 'I shall have to do an investigation. And buy some more graph paper.'

While Granddad was going on, I whispered, 'Thank you, Angel Rain.'

It was the best Christmas present ever.

That's when I messaged you, Mr Lamb. Do you remember? To tell you about the miracle.

And for all of December, Judge Dredd kept growing and growing. After he got his back legs, he turned into a froglet. That's like a tadpole with four legs, and it looks a bit weird, to be honest. But when you're a parent, you love your kids through all their awkward stages.

Granddad was well excited. He contacted the National Trust and the World Wildlife Federation and the Natural History Museum to tell them about our miracle of nature.

None of those big organisations were interested, though, because they said weird stuff happens in nature all the time.

'You'd be surprised,' said the man at the Natural History Museum. 'Spiders with nine legs. Daffodils in December. If we put them all in the museum, we'd have no space for the dinosaur skeletons.'

Which seemed fair enough to me.

As December went on, Judge Dredd got more frog-like. And he wasn't happy in the tank, you could tell. He kept coming up for air and sort of wriggling about up there. Like he wanted to get out. So I knew it was time to set him free.

I won't lie. I did feel a bit sad. Because me and Judge Dredd had been through so much together. But then Granddad said we could dig a pond in the pub garden, and that cheered me up loads.

'It'll be like John Boy in the caravan,' I said. 'Judge Dredd will be right outside. I'll get to see him all the time.'

Granddad looked at it more scientifically.

'Judge Dredd is a natural wonder,' he said. 'We should keep him where we can find him. The scientific community may yet change their minds and want him studied.'

So a few weeks ago, me and my family dug a pond for Judge Dredd in the pub garden.

Nana was the foreman, which meant she drank tea and bossed everyone else around. Cousin John Boy did most of the hard work because he gets stuck into jobs like that. And me and Granddad dug quite a lot too. I wanted Judge Dredd to have a massive gangster mansion pond, not a little old lady bungalow.

Once we'd dug the hole, we lined it with this thick plastic stuff called Pauline. Otherwise, the water would have gone through the soil and soaked away.

We made a nice border around the Pauline with stones. Then we filled the pond with water. Good stuff that Granddad got from the nature pond. With the right bacteria, because tadpoles don't like clean water.

When the pond was ready, I fished Judge Dredd out of his tank and held the net in his new watery home.

You could tell Judge Dredd was nervous, because he wouldn't swim out of the net at first. But I gave him encouraging words.

'I know this pond looks big,' I told him. 'But you're going to be big too. You'll be a mean, gangster frog mate. The biggest in the village.'

Then I thought about Angel Rain and said, 'But you'll
be a nice gangster. One who tells the truth and reads books.
And if your girlfriend gets ill, you'll look after her. You know
about my friend, don't you? She's looking down on you right
now.'

That's when I realised my family were all listening, and
they'd gone quiet.

Granddad cleared his throat, and I thought he was going
to tell me that I'd got the science wrong and a dead human
can't look after a tadpole. But instead, he said, 'Angel Rain is
still with you, Callum. Of that there is no doubt.'

Let's take a quick break there, Mr Lamb, and have
another cup of tea. Would you like any more Christmas
pudding?

SIXTY-THREE

Callum Duffy interview transcript:
Continued ...

Don't worry, Mr Lamb, I'm not offended. That Christmas pudding is quite filling. I couldn't manage two slices either.

By the way, did you notice the new pond when you came through the back garden? It's epic, isn't it? A proper gangsta pad.

I hadn't seen much of Judge Dredd since we put him in the pond. But this morning, I sat out there for half an hour and guess what?

I saw two little black eyes at the edge of the pond. I couldn't believe it. Judge Dredd had turned full frog, Mr Lamb. With arms, legs, greeny brown frog skin – the lot.

I had the biggest smile on my face when I saw him.

'Hello mate,' I said. 'Happy Christmas.'

Judge Dredd didn't say anything back. Because he's an aquatic creature and he doesn't really know what Christmas is. But I could see him looking at me and sort of taking me in.

We had a little chat about the weather, and I told him that more cold weather was on the way.

'I reckon you're like Granddad,' I said. 'You won't notice the cold all that much.'

Then I looked at the sky and said, 'I don't suppose you'd pass on a few messages to Angel Rain, would you?'

I had a lot to tell Angel Rain this morning, Mr Lamb, because I'm reading *Heidi*. The proper version, which is well difficult. But I've got the audiobook as well, so that helps.

'Tell Angel Rain she was right,' I said. 'The proper *Heidi* book is better than the easy one. There's loads more in it. Like, Heidi getting rid of her heavy, smart clothes so she can be free like the goats. And sledging down the hill with her granddad.'

Then Mum shouted that I had to come inside. So I asked for three more minutes. Because when you say that, adults always forget and give you ten.

I put the plastic lily pad in the pond and the bit of mince pie. And I thought about all the fun me and Judge Dredd would have together now he's a frog.

'Probably, you'll have kids next year,' I said. 'And then I can be a grandparent. Nana says being a grandparent is epic. Because you do all the fun stuff, like reading stories and giving unhealthy treats. But you don't have to worry about being responsible.'

So I've got a new ending for this story now, Mr Lamb. And it is a bitter sweet ending, because I have lost my friend. But Angel Rain is telling us she's still here and love lasts forever.

I've talked a lot about heroes in this story. Mr Holland

was the first hero. And Miss Hussain was the second. And then there was whoever donated their heart to help Angel Rain live longer.

But Angel Rain is the real hero of this story, Mr Lamb. She is the bravest person I ever met because facing death is scary at any age, but it's hardest of all for a child. And she saved me and made me better and made a miracle happen with Judge Dredd. And now I am an improved child and doing well at school and will pass exams and be a vet when I'm older.

And maybe you'll give things one last try with Nurse Kolawole after hearing this. Because if my story teaches you anything, it's that anything is possible.

SIXTY-FOUR

Michael Lamb

It took a while to leave the Great Oakley Arms. Shirley wanted to give me several weighty slices of Christmas pudding wrapped in tin foil, but as I explained several times – they were simply too heavy for my bike panniers. And Callum berated me for spending Christmas Day alone.

'It's not right to be lonely this Christmas,' Callum said. 'Don't listen to that Elvis song. Santa doesn't like it. Not at all.'

'I won't be alone for the whole day,' I explained. 'I've befriended some neighbours. Professor Zhu and her husband have kindly invited me over for roast pork, dumplings and spring rolls in the morning. And the Hofers are having me for braided bread and cherry liquor in the afternoon.'

'But you'll wake up alone on Christmas morning,' said Callum. 'It's just not right. You should ask Nurse Kolawole for a sleepover, Mr Lamb. Then you'll have someone to open your presents with.'

'Ifeoma won't want to spend Christmas with me,' I said. 'She hasn't returned any of my calls or messages. And she left me on Boxing Day, so I imagine this time of year holds bad memories.'

'Uh oh,' said Shirley. 'What did you do?'

'I told her I didn't want to marry her,' I said. 'And that I didn't want children. And that I might run away if I saw her get mugged.'

Shirley took a sharp intake of breath.

'We all make mistakes, Nana,' said Callum. 'Mr Lamb is learning. Like we all are.' Then he turned to me and said, 'Give Nurse Kolawole one more try, Mr Lamb. It's Christmas Eve. Magical things happen at this time of year.'

'Not to me,' I said. 'Last Christmas, Ifeoma took my heart. Literally and metaphorically. She ended our relationship and removed a meaningful wooden heart from my front door handle. I'm only just starting to live again. Small steps.'

Callum wasn't happy, but eventually the Duffys let me leave. I was seen off with lots of hugs and season's greetings. But as I mounted my bicycle, Callum tore across the garden shouting, 'WAIT! Wait, Mr Lamb. I never gave you a Christmas present.'

'You don't need to give me a present,' I said. 'Your friendship is more than enough.'

'You said your girlfriend took your heart,' said Callum.

'Yes,' I said. 'She did.'

'Then you should have this one,' said Callum, holding out a collection of glittery, red lolly sticks. 'I made it at school.'

Callum handed me the lolly sticks, which were glued

into a wonky heart shape and coloured with scruffy, red felt tip strokes. There was an overly generous amount of glitter on the sticks, clinging to gummy lumps of solidified glue. A gnarled piece of green garden twine formed a hanging loop at the top.

It was a spectacularly ugly object. But at the same time, it was the most beautiful thing I'd ever seen.

The emotions were quite overwhelming.

'Thank you, Callum,' I said. 'I will hang this in pride of place on my front door. I have a porch, so it won't be affected by the weather.'

I cycled home feeling happier than I had all year. And the moment I got to my front door, I hung Callum's decoration on the handle. Then I got to work, baking biscuits for the evening's Christmas lights visitors.

I'd been warned that Christmas light spectators come out en-mass on Christmas Eve, so I baked 40 spiced Christmas trees and 20 gingerbread ringing bells. But when dusk fell, I feared I hadn't baked enough. There were already well over 60 people outside my front garden. More, if you included toddlers. And toddlers like biscuits – it's well known.

When I turned the lights on outside, a cheer went up. I felt like some sort of celebrity. It seemed a shame to ruin my Santa-like status by saying, 'Only one biscuit per person please. No second helpings.' But the crowd was understanding and extremely friendly. I felt greatly cheered by their excitement.

One little girl said, 'These lights are better than the Frozen musical I saw in the West End.' The girl's mother looked quite annoyed, and said the Frozen tickets had cost 'an arm and a leg'. But secretly, I was pleased.

For an optimistic moment, I wondered if Ifeoma might

be somewhere in the crowd. She always loved Christmas lights. But then I reminded myself that Ifeoma was working. And she thought me a coward. So the odds were slim.

As I passed through the crowd handing out biscuits, a memory flashed.

'Children are messy, confusing and inconvenient.'

That's what I told Ifeoma last Boxing Day.

What an awful thing to say.

As shame stung my cheeks, a white-haired lady tugged at my coat sleeve.

I offered her the biscuit tin.

'I don't eat biscuits anymore,' said the lady. 'I wanted to tell you that I like your heart. The big, sparkly one.' She pointed at my front door, where Callum's lollypop heart twirled and sparkled.

'A friend gave it to me,' I said. 'It's the best gift I've ever been given.'

'It's very nice,' said the lady. 'Hearts can be fragile. You need to take care of them.'

Callum's lolly stick heart twinkled at me. It felt brighter, somehow, than all the sparkling, flashing lights outside.

I thought of the heart Ifeoma brought to my house. Oh so messy, confusing and inconvenient, but I wanted it back so very badly.

It was 4.55pm. Ifeoma said she finished work at 5pm on Christmas Eve.

I glanced up at the stars. There were no clouds, which made the biting cold all the more biting. Terrible weather for cycling. Yet, I found myself placing the biscuit tin on the front wall and heading towards my bike shed.

'Help yourselves to biscuits,' I called, as I wheeled my bike back through the crowd. 'I have a Christmas emergency.'

Bicycle clips and woolly gloves be damned – there was just no time.

'Where are you going, Michael?' asked Professor Zhu, as I cycled onto the icy road.

'I left my heart at the hospital,' I called back. 'And I am going to get it. Because magical things happen at Christmas.'

There was a ripple of applause among those who understood romantic symbolism. But Professor Zhu took my comment semi-literally and asked if I was having medical issues.

I didn't have time to explain. Instead, I cycled into town, swerving two fool-hardy, tinsel-covered teenagers sharing an electric scooter. I narrowly missed a pothole as I whizzed down the steep hill outside town, and had a stuck gear disaster going up the small hill before the hospital.

I made it to the hospital by 5.10pm, sending fervent prayers to a god I didn't believe in. But deep down, I knew it was too late. Ifeoma always jumped on the bus the moment her shift ended.

Day staff filed out of the main hospital doors, but there was no Ifeoma. I'd missed her. Maybe I could catch her at home instead, if she would answer the door to me.

As I turned to go, there was a curious flash in the sky. Like lightning. It came and went in an instant, but as I was wondering what it was, I noticed a queue of people boarding a bus.

I stared.

There, helping an elderly lady onto the bus, was Ifeoma.

Ifeoma wore a faux fur coat over her nurse's uniform and the Australian sheepskin boots that seem eternally popular with women of all ages.

'Ifeoma!' I shouted. 'Wait!'

But Ifeoma boarded the bus, and the electric doors whooshed closed. Then the bus pulled away.

I remounted my bicycle and gave chase. The downhill stint outside the hospital was okay. But as I ascended the steep hill into town (commonly referred to as the 'hill of broken chains'), I feared a heart attack. I didn't think I'd ever make it to the top. I did, though. And as I turned onto the high street with shaking knees, the bus was waiting, rocking slightly as passengers descended from its strobe-lit innards.

I pedalled the last few metres, threw my bike down and leapt aboard the bus – much to the shock of an elderly lady in reindeer antlers, who was touching her OAP pass on the sensor.

'Ifeoma!' I shouted. 'Ifeoma!'

'You have to buy a ticket, mate,' said the bus driver. 'I might be fat and old, but I'm not Santa Claus.'

The bus was a microcosm of society. Young people. Old people. Tired people. Jolly people. Tinsel. Santa hats. All of life was there. And from that crowd, Ifeoma rose, tall and dignified, like a goddess of the NHS.

'Honestly, Michael,' she said. 'What is wrong with you?'

I was so happy.

'I have come to win you back, Ifeoma,' I said. 'I want to see your heart hanging on my front door again.'

'Have you been drinking sherry, Michael?' Ifeoma asked. 'You look very red in the face. You should go home.'

'It was only a home when you lived there,' I said. 'Right now, it's a house. A very comfortable, warm and inviting house. But still a house.'

Ifeoma stared at me.

'Ifeoma,' I said. 'If you were mugged, I would stay and chase off the muggers. This has now been conclusively proved.'

'What are you *talking* about?' said Ifeoma, glancing awkwardly at her fellow passengers.

'I have changed, Ifeoma,' I said. 'I am not the same man you walked out on. I want to marry you and have children.'

'You don't want to get married, Michael,' said Ifeoma. 'You made that very clear last Christmas.'

'I've changed my mind,' I said.

'You don't mean that,' said Ifeoma. 'You are saying these things because you are lonely and it is Christmas. But words and actions are very different.'

'You are quite correct,' I said, falling to one knee. 'It is time for action. Ifeoma Kolawole. Will you marry me?'

There was a collective gasp from the bus passengers.

Ifeoma stared.

The elderly lady in reindeer antlers said, 'This is why I like the bus. You never see anything like this on the train.'

'You are asking me to marry you, Michael?' said Ifeoma.

'Yes,' I said. 'And then I would like us to have children. Messy, chaotic, inconvenient children.'

The bus driver turned off the engine and the bus grew very silent.

Ifeoma was still staring at me like I was a mad man. But then she said, 'Okay, Michael. Yes.'

I was momentarily stunned.

'Did you say yes?' I clarified.

'Yes, Michael.' Ifeoma was smiling. 'Yes, I would like that very much.'

The lady in reindeer antlers gave a short, 'Woo hoo!' and the bus driver gave a few friendly hoots of his horn. Soon, everyone on the bus was clapping and cheering.

Ifeoma came towards me, and I threw my arms around her.

'Thank you,' I said, 'for giving me the best Christmas

present I could possibly wish for. May I return the favour and buy you an engagement ring?'

'Okay Michael,' said Ifeoma. 'That would be very nice.'

As Ifeoma and I descended the bus, arm in arm, our fellow passengers clapped and cheered and patted us on the back.

The bus driver, seemingly overcome with emotion, stood up and shouted, 'It's CHRISTMAAAAAAS!' emulating the popular Slade song.

Out on the high street, we were swept up in a tide of Christmas cheer. People of all ages were smiling and laughing and singing Christmas songs. It felt like they knew our good news and were celebrating with us.

The bus driver gave us another toot as he drove off, and I put my arm around Ifeoma. She put her arm around me too and we smiled at each other.

It was magical.

'Please let me know your life wishes,' I said. 'And I will do my best to make them come true.'

'You have already taken care of two of them,' said Ifeoma. 'I would like to get married and have children. And I would also like to visit Salzburg and see where they filmed the 'Sound of Music'.'

'I will make all these wishes come true,' I said. 'Ifeoma, I love you to the moon and back. And I promise that you and I will be a love story. A great love story. The second greatest love story ever told.'

DEAR BIG HEARTED READERS ...

Big hearts come in all shapes and sizes. Sometimes, they wear football shirts and bright-orange trainers. And sometimes, they look just like you.

If you loved this book, please share that love with a big-hearted Amazon review. I read all my reviews (and yes, the bad ones do make me cry) and they make me happier than you could ever know.

Big love,

Suzy xx

Click to write your review on Amazon

Suzy K Quinn xx

WHAT TO READ NEXT?

The Bad Mother's Diary

Read more about Callum's laugh-out-loud family in the Bad Mother's Diary series, perfect for Bridget Jones, Sophie Kinsella and Jill Mansell fans

January 1st - Juliette Duffy's Diary

When I became a single mother, it felt like my world had ended. Dreams of rose-covered cottages, rolling pins and two parents living with their own biological child were well and truly shattered.

But life goes on. And I am determined not to be broken by an irresponsible man who can't step up to fatherhood.

Nick has left me holding the baby. But I WILL find love again. Time to get up, show up, never give up.

'Suzy K Quinn is the literary equivalent of hot chocolate ...' – Liza Foreman, New York Times

Amazon:
£2.99
$3.99
Free on Kindle Unlimited

Scan the QR code above to find the Bad Mother's Diary on Amazon

MORE BOOKS BY SUZY K QUINN

**Use your camera to scan this QR code and find
Suzy's books direct on Amazon:**

The Bad Mother Series
1. The Bad Mother's Diary
2. The Bad Mother's Detox
3. The Bad Mother's Holiday
4. The Bad Mother's Christmas

5. The Bad Mother's Virus
6. The Bad Mother's Wedding
Novella: The Bad Mother Begins

Coming soon:
Love or Your Money Back

Printed in Great Britain
by Amazon

31044958R00211